STELLA SH

The Baby Train

30 YEARS
ACORNPRESS
Celebrating thirty years of
Island stories and voices.

Disclaimer:
Any resemblance to actual persons living or dead or actual events
is purely coincidental.

....

Cover: Tracy Belsher
Design: Rudi Tusek
Editor: Penelope Jackson

Library and Archives Canada Cataloguing in Publication

Title: The baby train / Stella Shepard.
Names: Shepard, Stella, 1954- author.
Description: Sequel to: Ashes of my dreams.
Identifiers: Canadiana (print) 20240456211 | Canadiana (ebook)
2024045622X | ISBN 9781773661681
   (softcover) | ISBN 9781773661698 (EPUB)
Subjects: LCGFT: Novels.
Classification: LCC PS8637.H474 B33 2024 | DDC C813/.6—dc23

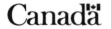 

Canada Council   Conseil des arts
for the Arts   du Canada

The publisher acknowledges the support of the Government of Canada,
the Canada Council for the Arts and the Province of Prince Edward Island
for our publishing program.

ACORNPRESS

P.O. Box 22024
Charlottetown, Prince Edward Island
C1A 9J2
acornpresscanada.com

The Baby Train is dedicated to the unwed mothers who were given no choice but to put their infants up for adoption. They are the inspiration for this novel. One mother's joy is another mother's sorrow.

" *The Baby Train* is a gripping story of the trials and tribulations of unwed mothers on Prince Edward Island in the 1970's. I started reading and couldn't put it down until I finished the whole book. It takes the reader through a wide range of emotions as "Apple", the main character takes you on a whirlwind story of her life. This book is a tribute to all the women and children affected by the "Baby Train" which was run by Catholic Family Services, Charlottetown. "

Scott Parsons is a singer-songwriter from PEI. He has many Music PEI and East Coast Music awards. He has received The Father Adrian Arsenault Senior Arts Award from the Province, The Queen Elizabeth Diamond Jubilee Medal and was recently (2023) Inducted into The Order of PEI for his contributions to Island society.

" I was completely engrossed in 'The Baby Train' from beginning to end. Stella's perfected her craft of weaving words into a story told so well you feel like you are there in it. Each scene was so full. There were harsh moments of visceral pain from Apple's unpredictable and often sad life, but they were balanced by the most beautiful heartfelt moments, often coming from the simplest things. This is one of the most mesmerizing books I've ever read and one of the most important stories to tell. I feel like I know these characters. It was an all-too real experience for many young women in the Maritimes and beyond. Thank you Stella for writing this story that needed to be told. I'd recommend this book to everyone. "

Kinley Dowling is a songwriter and multi-instrumentalist from PEI. She toured the world with indie rock band Hey Rosetta! for 10 years. As a session musician, she has performed on over 500 songs, including: Hey Rosetta!, Matt Mays, Jenn Grant, Two Hours Traffic, Buck 65, Classified, Rita McNeil and many more. She has earned multiple ECMA and Music PEI Awards and uses her growing popularity and platform to draw awareness to causes close to her heart – particularly women's rights and prosperity. She's proud to have her music video for 'Microphone' in grade nine health curriculums across PEI to teach about consent.

AUTHOR'S NOTE

Birth Alert is a practice in Canada that allows hospital staff to alert child welfare workers if they have concerns for the safety of newborns. The concerns could range from newborns being born into poverty, a history of domestic violence in the home, drug use, or a history with child welfare. The newborn is apprehended without informing expectant parents and placed in foster care.

Birth Alert is part of a system that gave control to people of privilege who assumed certain kinds of mothers were incapable of caring for their children, and these children needed being rescued. However, there are no clear rules for when a Birth Alert should be issued.

In June of 2019, the final report of the National Inquiry into Missing and Murdered Indigenous Women and Girls recommended the abolishment of the practice of Birth Alerts from Indigenous mothers after birth because it was racist, discriminatory, and a gross violation of the rights of the child, mother, and community. As well, the Birth Alert practices disproportionally affected hundreds of Indigenous and other racialized peoples.

Prince Edward Island ended the use of Birth Alerts in February 2021.

In the postwar period, about 350,000 women throughout Canada were forced into giving up their "illegitimate children" for adoptions by churches, social workers, government agencies, and sometimes their own families.

In 2016, Origins Canada called for the federal government to hold an inquiry into the forced adoptions so mothers would have a chance to tell their stories.

The Standing Senate Committee on Social Affairs, Science, and Technology met in 2018 to hear testimonies of mothers who were forced by families and institutions into surrendering their children.

A Senate Committee heard testimonies from several mothers who were not married and stayed at maternity homes across Canada, where thousands of forced adoptions occurred between 1945 and the 1970s. The maternity homes were operated by religious denominations. The testimonies of women who stayed at the homes brought to light the rampant, systematic abuses by nurses, priests, nuns, social workers, and other authority figures towards unwed mothers who were shamed and humiliated into giving up their children.

One of the Senate recommendations is for the Government of Canada to issue a formal apology on behalf of all Canadians to the mothers and their children who were subjected to forced adoption practices in the years following the Second World War.

In 1965, St. Gerard's Home for Unwed Mothers opened on the top floor of the Catholic Family Services in Charlottetown, PEI. Over a period of twenty-two years, 1,700 island women resided at St. Gerard's Home.

More than 95 percent of the babies born to the unwed mothers staying at St. Gerard's Home were adopted. It is estimated over nine hundred babies were moved to New York and New Jersey. One might speculate the reason international adoptions were preferred was because of the large sums of money received in "donations" from wealthy families who adopted the babies.

Birth Alert was used in apprehension of newborns born to unwed mothers.

Climb aboard *The Baby Train* for the untold stories of unwed mothers and their infants snatched at birth.

CHAPTER 1

Apple fled the hospital in fear, defeated and without her infant boy. The nuns in their long black robes with their beak-like heads were crows that had shadowed Apple since childhood.

Sister Henrietta, a crow, had snatched her infant and sold him to strangers. The teenager wiped away the tears and snot streaming down her face.

The crow had robbed even memories of holding her newborn. A nurse had whisked the infant out of the delivery room immediately after birth, and a prick of a needle had lulled Apple into a state of drowsiness. Hours ticked away before she had awakened and become aware of what happened.

Rushing down the street, Apple passed the maternity home for unwed mothers where she had been staying. She could not go back to pack the few possessions she owned. The crows would be waiting for her.

An earlier attack on Sister Henrietta at the hospital could earn time in a youth detention centre. The crow had mocked her. It laughed and said the baby had been adopted by a good Catholic family and would never know the sin of his mother. Apple lashed out, hitting the nun like a madwoman. The old nun was no match for the released anger as she slumped to the floor. Apple kicked the nun in the gut several times before running blindly out of the building, not caring where she was going.

*

She had feared and hated the crows since childhood. They had taken her from Nana. And now, they had stolen her infant boy. The teenager had little money and no place to hide. Apple crumpled to her knees in hopelessness and drained of the willpower that fuelled her survival at the home for unwed mothers. Her infant boy had been adopted. She had failed to protect him.

She would have stayed on the sidewalk until dragged away by the crows and dumped in a home for troubled girls. But in a final act of desperation, she cried out for divine intervention. The outburst surprised her. She must have hit rock bottom to seek service from a god that had abandoned her years earlier. A god that never protected her from the evil crows. A god that allowed the crows to take her baby. A guilt Apple would live with until her dying day.

"Apple!" a voice hollered a short distance away. She recognized the voice of a friend, Sneakers. He helped Apple to her feet. She clung to him and cried. Perhaps divine intervention didn't come nicely wrapped. A streetwise thug, Sneakers was the answer to a desperate prayer for help.

"Stan and Hilda are in the city. They came for you and the baby."

Her body jerked with a convulsion of sobs. "They came too late. Sister Henrietta took my baby and gave him to strangers."

Sneakers cursed. The nuns had no mercy. With wrapped arms around Apple, he guided the distraught teenager down the street, away from the home for unwed mothers.

"I will find my baby if it takes the rest of my life. Sister Henrietta will pay for this," Apple swore with vengeance.

CHAPTER 2

H er birth name was Gladys, but most people called her Apple—
except for the foster parents who drifted in and out of her life,
including the nuns she hated and feared. When she was a child,
her nana told her the nuns were brides of the Catholic Church.
The brides of the Catholic Church said Nana was too old to take
care of a mischievous little girl. They seized Apple and placed her
in foster care.

Apple was born in the western part of Prince Edward Island;
with fewer than 110,000 residents it was Canada's smallest province. The Island resembled a spot of land floating in the Atlantic
Ocean on a map of Canada. A person could travel the Island tip-
to-tip by train within a day, with whistle stops along the way.

A ferry to the mainland and an airport were the only way for
travellers coming to or leaving from the Island. Trains crisscrossed
the Island transporting dry goods, mail-ordered items, livestock,
and passengers. People seldom travelled outside of the region
unless there was a good reason to. There were communities of
people who were born, lived, and died on the Island without
crossing the strait to other parts of Canada.

Apple had been born in a farmhouse with the assistance of
a woman experienced in delivering babies, six months after a
hasty wedding of teenaged parents, Elmer and Mary-Jane. Apple
entered the world in 1950, at a time when electricity and indoor

plumbing were years away from being introduced in rural Prince Edward Island, unlike the larger towns that dotted the province. The rural people marvelled at the luxury when they visited homes in more populated towns, homes where a dark room changed to brightness with a flick of a switch. The country folks didn't give it much thought that they didn't have indoor plumbing; there were more pressing matters to deal with, such as feeding hungry bellies and keeping the fires burning during the isolated winter months. Money was scarce, but people never thought they were poor. Their bellies were filled with an abundance of food harvested from the land and the sea. A collection of whitewashed homes scattered along the coastline connecting families, friends, and foes. Fishing dories rested on the shoreline and screeching seagulls circled an endless summer sky. Washed-up seaweed and Irish moss plugged the air with a strong salty odour. On hot summer days, the young and the old swam at the wharf and dove deep into the belly of the ocean. A cannery at the end of the wharf processed seafood, providing the community with much-needed jobs. Farmhouses dotted the land that stretched across ploughed fields on the outskirts of villages.

Generations of people in rural communities lived and died without venturing far from home unless it was necessary.

Community members were connected through blood or marriage. A last name could identify a person's religion and the political party the person supported. Family feuds were often born out of political and religious differences. The next generations inherited the feud. The police were seldom alerted to any shenanigans. The people had their own law of conduct.

It was no secret that Big John and Rita blamed Mary-Jane for tricking their son into getting married. They would tell anyone who listened that Mary-Jane got pregnant to trap their son. "You don't have to marry her," Big John argued with Elmer. "How do you know for certain you are the father? You are going to throw away your life getting tangled up with a hussy. Her daddy was a good man who drowned while out fishing. Her daddy was not around to keep her in line, keep her decent. But she's not our problem."

Elmer was the runt of eight siblings. He'd shadowed Big John around the farm since he could toddle like a miniature little man. Big John picked the best plot of farmland where Elmer and a wife would someday build a home and raise a household of children.

"I love her, Pa. She is good to me. I'm going to marry her." He begged Big John to come to the wedding. Rita finally broke her silence.

"They best get hitched soon. She is going to start showing. People are going to start talking. It does not matter if it is his or not; people will say it is. Our names will be dragged through the mud if he doesn't make an honest woman of her."

Big John shot a hateful look at Rita. "Keep your mouth shut, woman." The burly farmer stomped out of the farmhouse in a rage. No one escaped being gossiped about on the Island. Neighbours would talk, just as Rita predicted. Gossip could get nasty and ruin a hard-earned reputation.

"Elmer can have his bride, but he will pay the price for going against my wishes," he later told Rita. "He's never to cross the doorframe of this house with that woman. If he wants to visit, he comes alone."

The plot of land designated for Elmer and a future family would be given to an older brother.

Big John and Rita showed up at the church wearing dark clothing, as if they were attending a funeral and not a wedding. Mary-Jane and Elmer exchanged wedding vows in front of a dozen people, mostly curious neighbours. Rita and Big John did their duty by attending the wedding to avoid gossip. They walked out of the church after the wedding Mass without congratulating the bride and groom.

The newly wedded couple moved in with Mary-Jane's mother, the Widow Sadie. Their baby entered the world six months later.

Elmer and Mary-Jane bickered about names for the baby. Elmer picked the names, Rita-Marie after his mother, Rita, and parental grandmother, Marie. He said it would please Pa to name the baby Rita-Marie, which could open a door of invitation to visit with Mary-Jane and the baby.

Mary-Jane favoured Gladys, after her paternal grandmother. The Widow Sadie suggested putting the names in a brown paper bag. She would pick a name to end the argument. Mary-Jane and Elmer reluctantly agreed. The Widow Sadie closed her eyes, picked a slip of paper, and announced the name, "Gladys." She put the piece of paper back in the brown paper bag and fed it to the flames of the wood-burning stove.

Widow Sadie said the rosary twice before going to bed. "Lord Jesus, I just could not stand to have my precious granddaughter named after Big John's kin." She confessed to God and prayed for forgiveness.

Gladys grew to be a plump toddler with a moon-shaped face. A ball of reddish hair on the top of her head earned her the nickname Apple.

Widow Sadie cared for Apple while Elmer and Mary-Jane worked at a nearby fish plant. Elmer helped with chopping the firewood and taking care of the few livestock that contributed to the family food supply.

The church was an extension of the family home. The church pews were filled with the faithful Sunday morning. People in the community were either Catholic or Protestant. The two religions seldom mixed; Catholics married Catholics and Protestants married Protestants. A mixed marriage divided families, often for a lifetime.

Big John and Rita sat at the front of the church and ignored Elmer and Mary-Jane. Rita turned in the seat when she heard a baby cry. Big John poked her with an elbow in the ribs. He guided Rita out of the church after Mass and ignored Mary-Jane cradling the baby.

Rita hinted about meeting their granddaughter over a Sunday dinner of roasted chicken, mashed potatoes, and fresh greens. "I couldn't help but notice how proud our Elmer looked holding his baby girl at church today." Big John flashed an angry glare in her direction. Rita lashed out in desperation to reunite the family.

"At least she's a Catholic girl. He could have gotten tangled up with a Protestant like that boy from the Bay. The scandal it caused for the poor parents. The heartache drove the poor mother mad with grief."

Big John ignored Rita.

"She is our grandbaby." Rita begged Big John to be reasonable.

"Elmer is welcome in the house as long as he comes alone." And that was the final word from Big John. A stubborn Elmer refused to visit unless Mary-Jane and Apple were also welcomed.

Apple was six months old and had not been baptised. It was a known fact in the Catholic religion that if their baby died before baptism, her little soul would remain in Limbo, unable to enter heaven.

Elmer agonized over not having family members at the baptism. The couple had been praying Big John would come around and welcome Mary-Jane and the baby into their home.

"Our baby should have been baptised at six weeks like me and my siblings were," he blubbered to Mary-Jane. "I am going to mention the baptism to Pa after mass. Pa is stubborn as a mule, but he will not dare say no in the house of the Lord."

Elmer cornered Big John and Rita after Sunday Mass and begged them to come to the baptism. Big John grabbed a tearful Rita by the arm and ushered her out of the church without answering Elmer.

"Pa refuses to come to the baptism. I know Ma would come, but he will not allow it. None of my brothers or sisters will be there. They're too scared of Pa to come."

Mary-Jane cuddled the infant. She was so perfect, thought Mary-Jane. "Why does he hold such a grudge?"

Elmer did not have an answer that satisfied her. "Pa is stubborn and not one for changing his mind. We don't need godparents, my family, or Pa. We will get the priest to baptise the baby after Mass. Father Preston will not deny the baby the right to be baptised."

Mary-Jane dressed the infant in a white knitted gown with a matching bonnet and booties. She wrapped Apple in a snow-white blanket and rocked the fussy infant in her arms. They waited at the back of the church after Sunday Mass. Elmer did the talking. "Father Preston, we need to have our baby baptised. She is six months old. We don't have godparents. No one in the family is willing to stand for fear of upsetting Pa. What if something happens to our baby and she is not baptised?"

Mary-Jane wept with agony at the thought of her precious daughter doomed in the afterlife.

Elmer begged the priest to protect the soul of his infant daughter. "We'll take her to Mass every Sunday and make sure she's raised as a good Catholic."

The priest motioned the couple and the Widow Sadie inside the rectory. Within minutes, holy water splashed on the infant's head saved the little soul from the jaws of Limbo. Elmer carried the baby home. Mary-Jane prayed in silence that no harm would ever cross their precious daughter's path.

Mary-Jane and Widow Sadie prepared a special Sunday meal to celebrate the baptism, sacrificing one of the six hens. Mashed potatoes were drenched in hot gravy and a pot of carrots and turnips bubbled in hot water on the wood-burning stove. An apple pie cooled on a rack. The infant, with a belly full of breast milk, dozed through the celebration.

CHAPTER 3

Monday was washday for Widow Sadie and Mary-Jane. A row of white cotton diapers flapped on the clothesline on a breezy fall day. Work at the cannery slowed as the fishing season came to an end. An unemployed Mary-Jane stayed at home, but Elmer still worked at the cannery. The mother and daughter were busy heating water on the stove, lugging buckets of hot water to the tub on the porch, and scrubbing the clothes clean on washboards. It was labour-intensive work that demanded attention.

Apple fussed in a nearby playpen with another tooth coming in. Mary-Jane gave Apple chunks of hard cookies to gum on to relieve the teething pain. It was early afternoon when she finally settled.

"Two more loads and we are finished for the day," commented Widow Sadie. The two women carried the final baskets filled with wet clothing to the line. "The baby is sleeping. She will be fine in the playpen till we finish putting out the clothes." Widow Sadie reassured an overly protective Mary-Jane, who feared leaving the child alone.

A few crows circled the sky and spied the hardened chunks of molasses cookies in the playpen. The black-feathered moochers took advantage of there being no humans in sight. They swooped down and landed in the crib. Apple dozed without moving as the crows feasted on the crumbs. One of the crows pecked the top of Apple's head as it attempted to steal a big chunk of a cookie that got tangled in her hair. A startled Apple woke up, saw the crows, and screamed with pain. The crows were as startled as Apple. Their sharp cawing terrified the toddler as the moochers took to the air with flapping wings. The crows disappeared in the quick moment it took for Mary-Jane and Sadie to race around the side of the house to the front porch. Mary-Jane swooped up Apple. She noticed a tiny bubble of blood oozing from a prick mark on Apple's head.

"It must be a bee sting or a bug bite," Mary-Jane surmised as she cuddled her traumatized child. It was a mystery to Elmer and Mary-Jane in the days that followed why Apple screamed in terror anytime she spied a crow in the yard.

A band of missionary sisters were visiting Catholic parishioners. They came with gifts of crucifixes with Jesus Christ nailed to the cross. The Catholic parishioners regarded the visits and the gift a high honour. They would donate money to the foreign missionaries in exchange for the crucifix.

Mary-Jane and Widow Sadie washed the kitchen walls and scrubbed the worn linoleum flooring. They baked a rare treat of sugar cookies, along with a pan of bread that would be served with fresh churned butter and strawberry preserves. The priest told Widow Sadie after Sunday Mass that the missionary sisters would be visiting Friday afternoon. It would be one of the last scheduled visits in the community.

Widow Sadie matched the two dollars' worth of coins Mary-Jane and Elmer collected for the missionary sisters. The money would have paid for a bag of flour, teabags, and canned milk. But the financial sacrifice was for a good cause. Widow Sadie, Elmer, and Mary-Jane had never been off-island, but they delighted in believing their contribution would bring the good word of the Lord to heathen savages living in a strange part of the world across the vast ocean.

The family washed up, dressed their best, and waited. Mary-Jane had bathed Apple and dressed the toddler in a white cotton outfit with a matching bonnet. She heard the missionary sisters were giving children gifts of a tiny cross on a silver chain. She desperately wanted Apple to receive one. The cross would be a treasured gift she and Elmer could never afford.

A toddling Apple became tired and cranky. Mary-Jane put her down for a nap. "She will be in better humour to meet the missionary sisters," she reassured Elmer.

The sisters arrived with Father Preston late Friday evening. He blessed a wooden crucifix the missionary sisters gifted the family. Elmer, Mary-Jane, and Widow Sadie were speechless, and admired the crucifix as if it were pure gold. It was Elmer's duty, being head of the household, to shake the priest's hand and to thank him and the missionary sisters.

"It's an honour and a pleasure to meet you," Elmer stammered, not really knowing what to say to such distinguished company. "Welcome to our humble home."

He motioned the priest and the missionary sisters to sit down at the kitchen table constructed of timber. Elmer sat on a chair at the head of the table. Widow Sadie and Mary-Jane sat on the two remaining chairs across from the priest and the missionary sisters.

It was time for tea and a bite to eat, the custom when company came calling. The Widow Sadie and Mary-Jane hustled about setting the table with bread, jam, butter, and sugar cookies.

The priest blessed the lunch with a prayer of gratitude. The missionary sisters explained the work they were doing in parts of Africa, which they referred to as the Dark Continent.

Elmer and Mary-Jane sat around the table and listened with fascination and nibbled food. Widow Sadie bustled about the kitchen with offers of more tea and bread.

Mary-Jane desperately wanted the gift for Apple she had heard about. "I hear our baby crying in the back room," she mumbled, an excuse to get Apple. "Gladys must be waking up from her nap."

Mary-Jane picked up the sleepy toddler. "Wake up, darling. The sisters have a gift for you. Do you want a cookie? Mama will give you a cookie if you smile for the sisters out in the kitchen. Let me fix you up to look pretty." Mary-Jane brushed the tousled hair.

"What a dear little pet," exclaimed one of the missionary sisters. "Bring her over to the table."

The missionary sisters, dressed in a long black robe and a black head covering, a sign of their consecration to God and the Catholic Church, stood and circled Mary-Jane holding the sleepy toddler. The missionary sisters dressed in black resembled the crows in the playpen. The child screamed in terror and began choking with fright. Her rounded face turned cherry red. The missionary sisters moved away, but the toddler screamed louder.

Elmer jumped up from the chair he sat in. He grabbed Apple out of Mary-Jane's arms. He feared his daughter would choke to death.

The priest and missionary sisters watched in horror. The priest speculated the child might be possessed by demons to be so frightened by the missionary sisters. He had heard stories of demons entering the souls of sleeping children. If it could happen in other parts of the world, he reckoned, it could likely happen on the Island.

"We better take her outside for air. Get a cup and fill it with water," Elmer instructed a shocked Mary-Jane. Widow Sadie had no words to explain the sudden outburst.

"We need to be going," the priest told Widow Sadie. The missionary sisters agreed.

A frantic Elmer and Mary-Jane were still trying to calm Apple outside.

One of the missionary sisters approached Mary-Jane before leaving. She pressed a cross on a silver chain into Mary-Jane's outstretched hand and quickly hurried to the waiting car.

Apple eventually stopped screaming but sobbed until she was exhausted.

Elmer and Mary-Jane hauled a wagon two miles down a dusty road to a grocery store, the following day. They loaded the wagon with brown bags filled with groceries with the four dollars in dimes, nickels, and pennies they had collected for the missionary sisters.

CHAPTER 4

On a breezy day, red, gold, and yellow autumn leaves fluttered in the air and littered the ground. Elmer pushed a laughing Apple in a wheelbarrow through the maze of fall colours. The days were getting shorter. In a few months, the land would be covered with ice and snow. Mary-Jane and Widow Sadie were pickling harvested garden food they would feast on during the winter months. The jars would be later stacked in the clay cellar next to dried salted cod, turnips, and burlap sacks of potatoes.

"Elmer is like a big kid playing with her. I think he's having more fun than Apple," Mary-Jane said.

Widow Sadie agreed.

❀

Elmer and Mary-Jane snuggled on a swing on the veranda. Glowing stars brightened the night sky. "Let's give Apple a little brother," Elmer whispered in Mary-Jane's ear. She responded with a hug. "It would be good for her to grow up with a playmate."

But fall and winter passed without a brother for Apple. Then one day, out of the blue, Mary-Jane announced she would be knitting baby booties.

Elmer jumped in the air with excitement. "If we are blessed with a son, we will name him John, after Pa. I talked to Pa at the general store last week. The talk was brief, but he was friendly enough and asked how I was doing. Pa would be right proud if we were to name a son after him. It would make things right with him."

Mary-Jane suspected Widow Sadie had cheated Elmer out of naming the baby Rita-Marie. "John would be a fine name for our baby."

Elmer smothered her face with kisses. "Thank you, my love."

❊

Elmer and Mary-Jane knew their dancing days would be over with a baby on the way. "Come on, Mary-Jane, let us go dancing while we can. One more dance before we call it quits till after Little John is born and starts toddling around."

Mary-Jane enjoyed the dances as much as Elmer but was uneasy about going. She was almost three months pregnant. Next month, the pregnancy would be more noticeable. She figured the dance would not hurt if they were careful. "No fast dancing, waltzes only." Elmer agreed.

Barn dances were popular in Island communities. It was not uncommon for young people, both married and single, to walk two or three miles along country roads to barn dances. Apple fussed about being put to bed after supper. It was late when the couple hoofed down a red clay road on a moonlit night with a trillion blinking stars.

Elmer patted Mary-Jane's pregnant belly. "I just know it's going to be a boy. He'll be our strong Little John. Pa will be so pleased."

Elmer and Mary-Jane hooted with gladness when they heard the racket of a truck barrelling down the road. "It must be Jimmy Fraser. He's late for the dance, too."

Jimmy Fraser was a young fellow who worked at the sawmill, one of about a dozen people in the community who owned a vehicle. Jimmy was sweet on a pretty girl from a neighbouring farm. The eighteen-year-old craved a steady girlfriend who could eventually become a wife. He had been too shy to ask the farm girl out on a date. But tonight, he would be bolder with the few shots of shine whizzing through his bloodstream. Damn boss kept him late. He worried another fellow at the dance might notice the farm girl and ask her out.

Attempting to hail down Jimmy, Elmer and Mary-Jane moved closer to the ditch and out of the way. They waved their arms in the air, but he never saw the couple until it was too late. Jimmy heard the thud, stopped, and jumped out of the truck. The stench of fear swallowed the air when he saw the lifeless bodies tossed into a ditch like ragdolls thrown across a room. He stiffened with panic, unable to move. In a split-second decision, he jumped back into the cab, turned the beat-up Ford truck around, and headed for the hills to hide out. He later parked the dented Ford in the yard. He snuck into the house without being heard, climbed into bed, and waited for the news to hit the community.

Widow Sadie got up early, as she had for years, to start the morning fire. She could hear Apple crying in the crib tucked in a corner of her parents' bedroom.

Why on earth can't they get out of bed and take care of the child? It was not like Mary-Jane to let Apple cry for so long. Sadie knocked on the bedroom door. There was no answer. She opened the door and gasped. The bed had not been slept in. Fear stabbed Widow Sadie in the gut. Something was not right. The Palmer family never missed a dance. They lived a good twenty-minute walk away. They might know what had happened to Mary-Jane and Elmer. Perhaps Elmer and Mary-Jane had stayed the night with the Palmer family instead of walking home late at night. The thought gave the old woman hope that everything would be fine. She dressed Apple and rushed out the door only to be greeted by a couple of distressed neighbours. They had discovered the bloodied bodies of Elmer and Mary-Jane while walking to Sunday Mass. Three-year-old Apple had become an orphan.

❀

Big John told Widow Sadie without a hint of sympathy to go bury her dead and he would take care of his own when she approached him about the funeral arrangements. The old woman wandered home in despair, crippled with grief. She put Apple in the crib for a nap. She dropped to her knees and prayed for strength. She would visit the parish priest and request a funeral Mass and the sooner the better.

❀

Community members were questioned by the law including Jimmy Fraser. He told a police officer the truck broke down on the way to the dance. The dance was almost over by the time he got it running. The old beat-up Ford had so many dents from accidents from reckless driving it was uncertain if the vehicle could be responsible for the accident or not.

"He is a good son. We never had a lick of trouble with him since the day he was born," Jimmy Fraser's parents told the police. "That old truck has been around the farm since our boy was in diapers. It hardly works, always breaking down."

The parents swore their son was in bed sleeping the night Elmer and a pregnant Mary-Jane had been run down.

No one had seen Jimmy at the dance. And people in the community thought it strange, because he seldom missed a dance. He was well liked, mostly because he had a truck. At the end of the night, a group of people would pack the back of the pick-up truck for a ride home.

With no witnesses, there were no charges of a hit-and-run that snuffed out the lives of Elmer and Mary-Jane.

❀

"My boy didn't deserve to die and be left in the ditch like a dog," Big John snarled. "He was my flesh and blood, even if he disobeyed me and married that wild girl. He was still my son." Rita rocked in a chair, dressed in black. "He's gone forever," she sobbed. "He can never come home now. He is gone forever." She shot a hateful look at Big John. "It's your fault he never visited." Her body shook with convulsions of sobs.

Big John did not respond to the accusation. He quietly walked away. In the comfort of the barn with the welcoming smell of hay and animals, he plunked down on a bail of straw and bawled his guts out.

Widow Sadie buried her pregnant daughter at the bottom of the cemetery. Big John purposely laid his son to rest at the back of the cemetery, as far away from Mary-Jane as possible.

❀

Jimmy Fraser blessed himself with the sign of the cross when questioned by his parents what happened the night of the dance. Jimmy, frightened to death of going to prison, swore on his grandmother's grave the truck broke down a mile down the road. The dance was almost over by the time he got it running.

It was easier for the parents to believe a lie than entertain the truth. His father closely monitored the drinking jug of moonshine stashed in the shed. Without a doubt, someone had a few good swigs. He questioned the son.

"I swear to God, I didn't touch your stash, Pa. You got to believe me, Pa. You believe me, don't you, Ma?" With a bowed head and drooped eyes, she bit her lower lip and mumbled, "I believe you, son."

People in the community speculated and gossiped it had to be Jimmy Fraser because he didn't show up at the dance. The truck breaking down didn't make any sense to the gossipers; they all knew Jimmy Fraser was a wizard at fixing machinery. He'd have it running in no time if the truck broke down. But without evidence or a witness, no charges were laid.

❀

On a moonlit night, a gunshot ripped through the air and killed Jimmy Fraser as he crossed the yard on his way to the outhouse.

Rita swore on a Bible that Big John never left the house of the night of the killing when she was questioned by the police. Big John's sons were also questioned, but no charges were laid.

Jimmy Fraser was buried in the Catholic cemetery a few feet from Elmer's mangled body.

❀

It was easy for the grandmother to take care of Apple when she toddled about and took afternoon naps. But with each passing year, Apple became more difficult to care for.

Widow Sadie had not crossed the doorway of Big John and Rita's whitewashed farmhouse since the funeral. Big John was built like a bulldog, with short, stocky legs, a barrel chest, and a scrunched face that spouted unshaved whiskers. He strutted bow-legged around the farm like a bulldog on guard. No one messed with Big John. It was well known that he could be as a mean as a rattlesnake or as kind as a Good Samaritan whenever it suited him.

A German shepherd viciously greeted Widow Sadie and Apple as they approached the farmhouse. The dog growled and sniffed the back of their heels. Big John came out of the house and stood on the veranda. He yelled for the dog to "GET." Apple and Widow Sadie walked faster. The screen door slammed shut behind them. Big John pulled out chairs from the kitchen table and ordered them to sit.

"Keep that child still," Big John commanded. "Don't need her running about the place."

The kitchen smelled of pipe tobacco, fresh baking, and brewing tea.

Apple spied hot cookies cooling on a rack. "Can I have a cookie, Nana?"

Big John answered before Widow Sadie could tell her to hush up: "Did you not teach her any manners? In my day, children were seen and not heard."

He studied the old woman and the child. Sadie had dressed the child in a second-hand pink dress with matching hair ribbons. There was little money for store-bought clothing for a growing child. Widow Sadie scrubbed clean a pair of white knee socks Apple wore only to church on Sundays, and oiled, buckled black shoes that were too small for the child.

An old brown dress framed Widow Sadie's equally worn out, skeleton-frail body. He figured the old woman had a reason for calling.

Rita came into the kitchen with a basket of garden greens. She'd caught glimpses of the child with Widow Sadie in the country store and sometimes at church, but never dared speak with her out of fear of disobeying Big John.

"Would you like a cookie?" Rita offered and pressed it into Apple's outreached hand.

"Don't go fussing, because they're not staying long. State your business, Sadie," Big John ordered. "Why did you come?"

Apple snatched the cookie and popped it in her mouth but did not say thank you.

"She has no manners." Big John was quick to point it out. "The child is wild-looking like her momma. Marrying her momma was the death of our boy. He would have been toiling next to me on the land instead of working like a mule on a rundown farm."

Widow Sadie had not come for a lecture. She kept her mouth shut instead of telling Big John he worked his sons like oxen in a field. Elmer had a lucky escape when he married Mary-Jane.

Rita searched Apple's greenish-tinted eyes and studied her chubby face for clues of a dead son. Big John spoke up and answered the question Rita was searching for.

"She doesn't look anything like our boy," he grunted. "None of our tribe has reddish hair. Some of them boys from the Harbour are redheads."

Widow Sadie realized the trip was a waste of time. She would not beg nor ask Big John and Rita if they or any of their grown children would give Apple a home. She would not be thought a fool. She knew Big John and Rita had figured out why she was visiting. There was no need to tell them about her crippling arthritis and Apple becoming a handful.

She was too ashamed to tell Big John and Rita about the letters from three sons and a daughter now living in Boston. They'd written back, saying they were too busy with back-breaking jobs and were just getting by raising their own kids without having another mouth to feed.

"The damn dogs would probably eat the child if I left her with the pair of you." Widow Sadie yanked Apple by the hand and marched out of the house before Big John could have the last word.

"Who was that man? He was not very nice, but I like the lady."

Widow Sadie only half-listened to the endless childish chatter. She had to come up with another plan. Who would be willing to take care of her granddaughter? Who could she trust to give her a good Christian home?

"Can we stop at the store, Nana? Can I get a treat? My feet hurt. I want to take my shoes off." She sat down and pulled off the shoes and the socks without waiting for an answer.

Widow Sadie spotted Father Preston getting out of his car as they walked pass the church rectory. Of course, why hadn't she thought of it earlier? She stopped to speak to the parish priest and invited him to visit in the evening after Apple had gone to bed. The blond priest eyed Apple with suspicion. He figured the child was the reason for the invitation as he watched Widow Sadie limp home.

The hard years of scratching out a living on a rundown farm and bringing up kids had caught up to her. Time was not on her side. In a couple of years, she would be too frail to care for an overactive child. She could trust Father Preston to find a Christian home where Apple would be loved and cared for.

❋

Apple soaked in a big washtub of soapy water early Saturday morning. Widow Sadie scrubbed the nine-year-old until the water was murky brown with dirt from creating mud pies.

Apple enjoyed making mud pies. It was a harmless game—until she got the notion to bake the pies. She had watched Nana light the wood-burning stove for years. All she needed were the matches Nana kept in a tin can in the kitchen, a few sticks, and shreds of old newspapers. Nana had turned the corner of the house with a basket of laundry at the same time Apple struck the second match.

Nana talked as she poured warm water over the child's head and scrubbed it clean. "I want you to be a good girl and behave yourself. I want you to promise you won't be any trouble where you're going."

Apple sat upright squeezed into the wash tub with her knees buckled up. She looked up at the grandmother with a puzzled face. "Are we going to church today, Nana? Is that why I am getting a bath?"

Why was Nana crying? Nana never cried. "Is it hurting you, washing all the mud out of me, Nana?"

Instead of answering, the grandmother mumbled, "Stand up, child, and I will dry you off."

Apple stepped out of the washtub. Nana wrapped the child in a hand-sewn towel that was once a white flour sack, now dyed red. She dressed Apple in a yellow print dress bought with precious egg money she had been saving.

"I am going to give you my Saint Anne's medal," she said, taking it off and looping it around Apple's neck. "Don't lose it. Saint Anne will keep you safe."

Apple did not want to dress up on a Saturday morning in new churchgoing clothes. She wanted to run wild and chase the chickens and bake mud cakes in the ditch behind the old farmhouse. Nana gave Apple a colouring book and broken crayons with strict commands to stay at the table and not to get dirty. Apple scribbled through the colouring book with stubbed crayons, but it could not keep her attention. Apple sneaked from the kitchen table, but her grandmother saw her.

She smacked Apple across the buttocks with her hand. "Gawd, child, why can't you listen and do what you are told?" Apple stiffened, waiting for another smack on the bum. Instead, the grandmother wrapped her arms around a confused Apple and sobbed. "I just wish, child, I were younger so I could look after you proper. My old bones ache godawful with rheumatism most days." She squeezed a squirming Apple. "Doing this more for you than for me," she stammered between bouts of sobs.

"I'll be good, Nana. I will be a good girl," Apple repeated as she struggled to break free of the hold. The grandmother released Apple. She scurried back to the kitchen table and started colouring.

The grandmother pulled back the curtains, looked out of the window, and waited. A sleek black car drove up the rutted driveway to the whitewashed farmhouse. A nun stepped out of the car, her face framed by wired eyeglasses. Apple hid under the kitchen table when the grandmother opened the door and invited the nun inside.

Her grandmother told Apple the nuns were brides of Christ. But Apple feared the nuns dressed in long black gowns. The nuns looked like crows to Apple. She was convinced the nuns spread their arms and flew to homes of sleeping children at night. If the bedroom windows were opened, the crows could get inside and steal children. They would never be seen again. Apple was sure of it. She would make sure Nana shut the bedroom window tight before going to bed.

"This is Sister Henrietta. She has come all the way out to the country for a visit. Come out from under the table, Apple. We are going to go for a drive with the nice nun. Come out, now. We will go for a drive in a big fancy car. Won't that be fun?"

Apple refused to budge. The nun would snatch her and take her away, never to be seen again. Apple whimpered like a frightened puppy under the kitchen table.

"You dear little pet, come out from under there. I have a bag of candy, but you must come out from under the table," coaxed Sister Henrietta. She teased Apple with a brown bag stuffed with candies. Nana never bought candies, even when Apple kicked up a fuss at the general store. She always told Apple there was no money to waste on candies that would rot her teeth and give her worms. Apple came out from under the table and grabbed the bag from the outreached hand.

The grandmother picked up a paper bag crammed with clothing. She took Apple by the hand and led her outdoors to the sleek black car. The grandmother kept repeating, "Be a good girl and behave." Apple never paid attention. She was busy popping the sweets in her mouth in case Nana decided to take the candies from her.

Nana opened the door of the back seat. The crow got behind the wheel and started the car. "Hurry let's get in the car," Nana said. "Quick."

Apple had never been in a car. There was no need for one in her small world. She walked to the nearby church with Nana and down a long red clay road to a one-room schoolhouse.

Apple jumped in the backseat and waited for Nana to get in. Nana placed the bag of clothing on the seat, pushed the door lock down, slammed the back door shut, and stepped away from the car.

The car wheeled down the mud-filled laneway. Horrified, Apple realized Nana had tricked her. Apple spied the door handle, but it would not open. She was locked inside with the human crow. She pounded the car window with rounded fists and screamed, "NANA!" as the car motored away from the farmhouse.

A year would pass before the spirit of death released Widow Sadie from the heartache and guilt of tricking Apple into the car.

Apple ignored the candy bag ditched on the floor of the car. She curled up on the back seat like a fetus in the womb and whimpered like a kicked puppy. The pretty yellow dress became soaked with urine. It was dark by the time they reached the foster home.

The crow reached out to grab the sleepy child. Apple screamed in terror and sank teeth into the nun's hand.

"You little snot," the nun sneered. Apple yelped with the pain of a slap across her face. She kicked and squirmed and yelled for Nana. The crow yanked Apple by the arm and dragged her out of the car.

The foster mother was quick to notice the bloodied teeth marks and the smell of urine. "She better not gives us trouble," the foster mother told the nun. A confused Apple stood in the doorway with the human crow. Where was she? Is this where the crow took stolen children at night? Would there be other stolen children inside the house? Why did Nana allow the crow to take her away?

"This is where you are going to live," Sister Henrietta explained. "You better behave. I don't want to make another trip out to the country because of you."

The foster father, a tall, scrawny man with a pinched face and pointed nose, studied the child before speaking. "She's chubby enough. She looks like trouble from that bite on your hand. I will not stand for any nonsense. If there is, I'll be expecting more money."

The nun shot back, "Don't be so greedy. You will get paid the monthly fifty-dollar fee for fostering and not a penny more. If she is too wild to handle, I know a family that would be willing to discipline her. They would be more than grateful for the generosity of the church."

The foster father, Horace, shut his mouth. This was their first foster child. He had no patience for children. They were to be seen and not heard. He had to figure a way to feed his children with a failed crop and hard times. His wife, Lena, would be responsible for the care of the foster child.

How hard could fostering be? A neighbour down the road was getting paid good money for housing foster kids. The neighbour said harsh discipline and hard work were required in fostering and there was no lack of either under Horace's roof.

A girl a few years older than Apple stuck her head in the doorway. Apple looked at her in fear and backed up into a corner. The foster mother shouted, "Margaret, come out to the kitchen. This is the foster girl who is going to be staying with us. She is sleeping with you tonight. It's too late to put her in the room with the younger ones."

Margaret came out from behind the door. "She smells funny. I don't want her in my bed."

The foster father slammed a fist on the kitchen table. "Do what your mother tells you. Take that one to bed before I take the switch down."

Margaret grabbed Apple by the hand and dragged her out of the room. Lamplight guided them to a darkened bedroom at the end of a hallway. Apple climbed in the bed without getting undressed. "You stay on your side of the bed," Margaret warned Apple.

CHAPTER 5

The farmhouse came alive Sunday morning with crying toddlers. The foster mother decided to stay home with the three younger children. "She can stay home too," growled Lena, pointing at Apple. Margaret and two teenage boys walked to the church with their father. They would be expecting a hot breakfast when they returned home.

"You get changed out of that pissed dress and help me get the kids dressed," ordered Lena. "You're going to earn your keep if you're going to stay with us. I got no time for laziness. If you are not going to listen, I will take the switch down."

Nana had slapped Apple across the bum, but never used a switch to beat her. "I want my nana. I want to go home," Apple begged and cried.

The clock on the wall struck nine. Mass would soon be over. The family would be coming through the door. Horace would not be pleased if there was no food on the table. Lena would be the one tasting the lash of the switch and not Apple. It had been Horace's idea to foster a child as a way of getting more money coming into the house. Lena figured she had enough work taking care of a houseful of kids and did not welcome the idea.

"There's no home to go back to. You do as you are told, or I will take the switch down. Watch the kids and keep them busy while I start breakfast."

Margaret and the older brothers ignored Apple in the following days.

Apple tried to stay out of their way. The younger children were sulky, cried for attention, and picked on each other.

"Get out of my way snotface," one of the teen boys shouted at Apple. She ducked under the safety of a bed and trembled with fear. It had always been just her and Nana. The older boys at school ignored little kids like Apple. Living with half-grown men terrified her. But she feared Horace the most.

Two weeks passed, and Nana did not come to rescue her. The teen boys did not go to school. Horace figured a grade eight education was enough. He worked the boys in the woods like men.

Margaret and Apple walked to and from school without saying a word. Apple slumped in a seat in silence. She hid behind the school during recess till the school bell rang.

The teacher ignored Apple and focused on the other students. She suspected Apple would be a slow learner being a foster child. What would be the point in trying to educate her?

Apple entertained the thought of running away but had no idea how to get back home.

Nana had to be searching for her. But perhaps she was too far away for Nana to find her. Apple hatched up a plan to get home that nearly killed her. She grabbed stick matches used to light the stove when Lena was not looking. She stuffed a water bucket with papers and hid it behind a chair in the bedroom.

Apple snuck out of the bedroom without making a noise after everyone had gone to bed. She struck a match by the light of the moon pouring through a window. The fire would not escape the bucket, she reasoned. She would scream, the foster father would come running and put out the fire. The foster family would send her back to Nana for sure. But the plan backfired. Flames spilled out of the bucket and licked the floor. Apple yelled,

"FIRE!" Horace jumped out of bed and smothered the flames with a blanket.

Horace pulled Apple from where she was hiding under the bed and dragged her into the kitchen. He reached for the switch over the doorway. Apple screamed with pain and begged him to stop. An exhausted Horace finally dropped the switch. Had he gone too far? The bloodied body twitched. The child was still breathing. He shouted to Lena. "Clean her up and put her back to bed."

Lena picked up the limp body.

"We could have been burned in our beds," Horace said, justifying the beating.

"You almost killed her," Lena replied.

Apple drifted in and out of consciousness. Lena sponged her with a wet cloth to bring down the fever. At first Apple thought Nana was giving her a bath. But she realized it was the foster mother. She cried out for Nana in a raspy, strained voice and slipped into a disturbing sleep. The foster mother brushed away tears, observing the suffering child crying for her grandmother. The child had to go before Horace could hurt her again. He might kill the child in a fit of rage the next time. And what would happen to the family if he did?

The foster mother softly sang to Apple as she cleaned the wounds and administered ointment to avoid an infection. But Horace had no empathy.

❊

"You tell the teacher Gladys is too sick to go to school," Margaret was told. "We do not need to give people a reason to come snooping around. Do you hear me?"

Margaret kept her mouth shut about the beating. She would be trading places with the foster girl if she were to start blabbing. The two teen boys figured the foster girl got the beating she deserved. They would be glad to see her leave.

Lena walked to the country store and used the telephone without telling Horace. Sister Henrietta listened to the frantic woman. Gladys deliberately set the house on fire. Horace managed to put the fire out before it could spread. "My precious children could have been burned to death in their sleep," Lena sniffled. "Come get her."

There was no bag of sweets or coaxing into the car when Sister Henrietta arrived at the foster home. The nine-year-old had been labelled mentally disturbed by the nun and Horace agreed. Lena remained silent. She had nothing more to say. But she would not have another foster child enter the home.

"They teach bad girls like you to behave where you are going," snapped Sister Henrietta, the crow. She pushed Apple in the back seat of the car. The vehicle sped through the country for miles before coming to a stop at a blackened brick building in the middle of nowhere with dozens of fenced windows.

Apple feared the gruesome building had to be a home for ghosts and monsters. She refused to get out of the car. "Be stubborn. Stay in the car." Sister Henrietta returned with a man wearing a starched white uniform. He grabbed Apple and carried her towards the door of the Brick Monster. Her yells echoed through the trees as the Brick Monster gobbled her up. Sister Henrietta returned to collect Apple a month later.

Apple rushed ahead of the nun towards the familiar long black car. She leaped in the back seat and curled up on the floor. The crow drove to what would become one of many foster homes for Apple.

❊

The car journeyed through dirt roads before it came to a stop at a log cabin nestled in a clearing in the woods. A young woman, Agnes, greeted the nun with a smile.

"Is this the girl you were talking about? I was expecting an older girl to help after the baby comes." Agnes rubbed a rounded belly. "Since she is here now, we'll keep her. Jasper will be out in the fields until dark."

Sister Henrietta had packed donated clothing in a small suitcase for Apple. The child held the suitcase as if she were attached to it.

Apple stood not daring to say a word wearing a mended mud-brown dress that was a size too big for her. Wool socks made her legs itchy and worn-out shoes with frayed edges pinched her toes. She desperately wanted to scratch her legs and remove the shoes, but she dared not move.

Lena had washed the new dress Nana had purchased for Apple and put it away for a daughter who would eventually grow into it.

"You behave and do as you are told," Sister Henrietta snapped at Apple.

Agnes guided Apple inside the home. A wide-eyed Apple watched Agnes with mistrust, waiting for instructions, and noticed there was no switch over the doorway.

"Where are the kids?" Apple asked Agnes.

"He is still inside my belly." Agnes laughed. "It will be another four months before he is born. He is going to be a big one by the size of my belly."

❄

A stew simmered in a pot when a six-foot burly man in his twenties came in from the fields. "Is this the girl? She looks awfully young to help with the baby. Can we send her back and get an older girl?"

Agnes set the table and explained she was in desperate need of help with the cooking and the cleaning with the baby on the way. But most of all Agnes craved someone to talk with during the long days alone in the house. She missed the city, and the quietness of the country spooked her. Living without an indoor toilet in the middle of nowhere without nearby neighbours was not the adventure she had been seeking when Jasper proposed marriage.

Jasper had been working in Toronto when they met at a pub. A girlfriend talked Agnes into going to a bar. Jasper and a group of guys were sitting around a table drinking beer. She was smitten by Jasper's handsome rugged appearance. Agnes and the girlfriend were sitting at his table before the end of the night.

Jasper told Agnes stories of living in paradise on a small island on the east coast, where he owned property. The stories intrigued her. They dated and married. Jasper hated city living and convinced Agnes to move with him.

The Island was the land of paradise for Jasper, but eighteen-year-old Agnes, a Torontonian, could not get used to country living.

"This is Gladys. She is here now. Let her stay." Jasper agreed on the condition that Agnes was not to be left alone while he was toiling in the fields or in the woods cutting lumber.

"No need for her to go to school. You can teach her at home," Jasper grumbled. Apple smiled; she'd rather be at home with Agnes than go to school.

Apple had frightening nightmares of crows pecking the bedroom window. The crows were without mercy as they tormented Apple in her sleep. Her crying out in the dark annoyed Jasper.

Agnes crawled out of the warmth of the bed and comforted her.

"I want Nana. Please take me home." Apple begged Agnes in the darkness of the bedroom.

"Oh honey, there is no home to go back to. The nun tells me your nana is too old and not well enough to take proper care of a little girl. You are living with us now. But you must behave to be able to stay. If you misbehave and don't listen, Jasper will send you away."

Apple trembled with fear of horrid memories of the Brick Monster swallowing her up, being locked in a tiny room without windows and a lumpy mattress on the floor to sleep on. "I will be good, I promise. Please don't send me away."

Apple watched Agnes rub the growing belly. She tried to imagine a baby inside. "How did the baby get inside your tummy?" Apple probed with a puzzled expression. "You'll find out when you are older," Agnes replied with a chuckle. "But don't grow up too fast. Stay young for as long as you can. Don't be in a rush to marry and have babies." It was advice she wished someone had shared with her. It would have spared her becoming a pregnant teenage wife living in the country miles from nowhere and with no one to talk with except for Jasper.

Agnes read a romance novel and stories from a Bible for reading lessons; those were the only books in the log cabin. She taught Apple to multiply and divide arithmetic sums. "You are smart and catch on to numbers quickly. I will talk to Jasper about sending you to school next year so you can learn the proper way."

The inappropriate romance novel about a young couple in love brought Elmer and Mary-Jane back to life. Nana used to talk about Mary-Jane and Elmer. Nana said Mary-Jane would sing songs as she rocked Apple to sleep, and Elmer played games with her. Apple had no photographs of her parents and little memory of who they were. The romance novel fuelled Apple's daydreams that her parents were still alive. They would find her and take her home to Nana. And they would all live in the same farmhouse with no switch over the door. She would never be sad or frightened ever again. And the nightmares about crows pecking the window would end.

The pretending gave comfort that blocked out the memories of being almost whipped to death by an angry foster parent.

Jasper only spoke to Apple if he had to. Agnes trained her to peel vegetables, cook meat, and sweep and dust, which seemed to please Jasper, who expected a clean house and hot meals.

"You remind me of my little sister. My heart aches to see her. But she is too young to travel so far on her own. Mama writes they plan to visit next year. They're excited about the baby."

A startled Apple stopped peeling turnips. It was not easy being good all the time. She behaved and did what she was told and never gave Jasper any trouble. Was it all for nothing?

"Will you be keeping me?" Apple asked with a hint of worry. There was a funny feeling in the pit of her stomach waiting for an answer.

"Of course we will." Agnes chuckled. "We are not going to send you away when Mama and Sissy come to visit. You and Sissy could be playmates. And Mama will be pleased to know you've been good company while Jasper is busy working."

Apple smiled for the first time in a long time. She could stay. No more foster homes. No more Brick Monster.

Agnes explained Jasper would take her to the hospital where she would push the baby out of her belly. And Apple and Jasper would be staying at the farm while she was at the hospital. Jasper would come fetch her a week later and take her and the baby home. The plan sounded simple to Apple except the part about pushing a baby out of a belly.

"You must be good while I am at the hospital. Don't give Jasper any reason to get mad at you. Have his meals ready on time. And keep the place clean and tidy while I am in the hospital with the new baby."

❄

Life has a way of creating pain and heartache without warning. It had been an ordinary day like any other day. Agnes and Apple worked on the school lessons. They took a packed lunch to the field for Jasper. Agnes took an afternoon nap while Apple practiced reading and arithmetic assignments. She glowed with the compliments for being a quick learner.

Agnes and Apple peeled potatoes and vegetables for supper. A pain in the gut stabbed Agnes as she lifted the pot to drain the boiling water. The baby was not due for another two months.

"Finish putting supper on the table for Jasper," she instructed Apple. "He will soon be home. I am going to the outhouse."

Apple had mashed the potatoes and placed dinner plates on the table by the time Agnes returned from the toilet with a face as white as snow. She stumbled across the kitchen for the bedroom. "You feed Jasper while I rest."

Apple focussed on preparing supper because Jasper determined if she stayed or not.

"Where's Agnes?" Jasper inquired.

"She's resting in the bedroom," Apple answered.

Agnes squirmed about in the bed and sweat poured down her face. Jasper gasped. "Why didn't you send the girl to fetch me?"

"It's too early for the baby to come. I just need to rest." A contraction caused her to screech like a scalded pig. Jasper failed to get her out of the bed to take her to the hospital, a forty-five-minute drive. "I can't move, Jasper. The contractions are coming too fast." Agnes rolled about in the bed delirious with pain unaware the baby was breeched; it was coming down the birth canal feet first.

"Stay with Agnes," Jasper roared at Apple and slammed the front door.

He jumped in the cab of the truck, stomped the gas pedal to the floor, and drove like a madman to a country store a mile away to telephone the hospital.

Apple watched in horror as Agnes screamed as if she were being tortured. "What can I get you, Agnes?" The poor woman could not answer. Apple repeated the question. Agnes squirmed and moaned which triggered a memory of a foster mother wiping her face to bring down a fever after a whipping that left scars on her body. She soaked a facecloth in a basin of warm water and dappled the face of the moaning woman in labour. The moaning became weaker and weaker.

It was almost nighttime by the time the doctor arrived. Apple quietly exited the bedroom as not to disturb a resting Agnes. She slumped into bed, exhausted. She imagined waking up to a smiling Agnes cradling a baby the next day.

Agnes had stopped breathing before midnight. Blood soaked the bedsheet. The doctor reached inside of the deceased woman and pulled out the lifeless infant.

The silence of the house in the early morning warned Apple something bad had happened in the night. She tiptoed out of the bedroom to be greeted by a tearstained Jasper at the kitchen table. "Get your things packed. And do not go near the bedroom. There is nothing in there for you to see." She knew it was his way of communicating that Agnes and the baby had died.

A tearful Apple packed a hairbrush, a toothbrush, a few items of clothing, and the romance novels Agnes had read to her while trying not to look at the closed bedroom door.

She sat on the front doorstep and waited. It was midafternoon when Sister Henrietta arrived. Jasper stayed indoors without saying goodbye or offering a word of thanks, not that Apple was expecting him to.

The bereaved husband buried Agnes and a stillborn son in a nearby cemetery.

CHAPTER 6

The next foster home was near a seaside village close to Tignish. Apple arrived with a brown suitcase and the romance novel that had belonged to Agnes. She stepped inside the house, glanced up at the doorway, and noticed a switch.

Apple grabbed Sister Henrietta by the hand and begged the nun not to leave her. A household of curious children watched Sister Henrietta pull Apple by the hand into the room.

"Let go of my hand," Sister Henrietta demanded. "This is your new foster home. It is where you are going to be staying. These good people have agreed to take care of you."

Apple squeezed Sister Henrietta's hand tighter. Harold, the foster father, roared for Apple to listen to the nun. Janet, the foster mother, guided Apple to a bedroom she would be sharing with the other kids.

The screen door slammed shut as Sister Henrietta exited the foster home for the four-hour drive to Charlottetown.

"Don't touch my stuff or I will beat the tar out of you," warned one of the seven children and pinched Apple in the arm. Apple began crying. An older boy, Paddy picked on the younger children and blamed Apple. The foster mother threatened the kids with a beating if they did not behave. Apple hid under the bed and waited for the commotion to settle down. The bickering continued throughout the three-month placement.

Sister Henrietta returned to collect Apple. The foster home placement had been too much for the foster mother. "My nerves are bad. I have enough children and a husband to care for without an orphan in the house," the foster mother explained as she sipped hot tea laced with valium.

"What good is a foster child when she is in school instead of helping with taking care of the babies?" Janet asked Sister Henrietta. "The money we're getting is not worth the trouble. The girl cannot get along with the other kids. They fight with each other like alley cats."

Apple ran to the car and locked the back door while Sister Henrietta paid the foster parents.

❋

Apple had been living with a foster family near Tignish for almost three years. It was her fourth foster family since entering the system.

The foster father, Charlie, fished in the summer and found employment on farms picking and grading potatoes in the fall.

His wife Martha fished with him while Apple cared for a set of twins.

Apple hated being saddled with babysitting in the heat of the summer. But at least in the heat there were no schoolkids to torment her.

The few school friends she had never visited during summer vacation. Sometimes, she would sneak away and join a couple of girls from school for an afternoon of fun diving off a wharf. Summer passed and it was time for school.

A group of schoolkids circled Apple and pushed each other towards her. The kid who touched Apple yelled out "Germ!" and pretended to drop dead on the ground. The winner of the game would be the last kid standing.

Apple stood frozen waiting for the game to end. A boy punched her in the stomach. "You're just a dirty germ."

An older student approached a teary-eyed Apple. He pulled a tiny knife out of a blue denim pocket and popped open a bottle of Coke. A bottle of Coke was a luxury item many students could not afford.

"Come on, take a drink." He held out the bottle of Coke. The foster mother had packed the usual bologna sandwich and a mason jar of watered-down Kool-Aid. More than anything Apple wanted to take a long swig of the Coke. "Come on, take a drink," he repeated.

Apple studied the smiling face trying to figure him out. He never played the Germ game. He was never nice to her, but he was never mean.

Apple reached for the bottle. The boy turned the pop bottle upside down until it was empty. The school kids howled like a pack of laughing hyenas. Apple raced out of the schoolyard for home.

The foster mother was in the house waiting for Apple. A set of five-year old twins were circling her and kicking up a fuss.

"Get changed out of your school clothes," Martha demanded. "I need you to watch the twins and put them to bed. It's bingo night in the village and there is a big jackpot up for grabs."

The twins never stopped moving and were messy eaters like their father.

She was in no mood to babysit while Martha played bingo with a bunch of old biddies.

"I am not babysitting tonight. I hate living here. I hate school and I am not going back."

The bulky six-foot foster mother ripped down the switch and moved towards Apple. "How dare you speak to me like that? We took you in and gave you a bed to sleep in when no one else wanted you. I am going to bingo, and you are going to watch the twins."

Apple bolted out of the house and stayed outdoors until night settled on the land. She snuck indoors only to be confronted by the foster father waiting in darkness with the switch.

❅

Apple packed the battered brown suitcase and waited for the familiar long black car. Sister Henrietta was not pleased Apple had been kicked out of yet another foster home.

"If you mess up one more time, it will not be a foster home you'll be going to," Sister Henrietta threatened. "Charlottetown is your last stop. Any more trouble and you will be crossing the strait to a reform school for delinquent girls till you are eighteen."

Apple heeded the warning. The sting of the words triggered memories of being carried into a monstrous building believing it would gobble her up and she would never be seen again.

The memories tormented her in the dream world as well. They'd locked her in a padded room with only a mattress on the floor and a piss pot in the corner the first night she arrived. She would never forget the powerlessness of unwanted touching or the feeling of abandonment by Nana, who never came to rescue her.

Sister Henrietta held great power and could easily make nightmares become real, as sure as the moon and stars glowed in the night sky.

She knew the nun would be happy to ship her across the strait. Apple wanted to be as far away as possible from the torture of school bullies, changing diapers, babysitting, and putting kids to bed. Who knows, she thought as she watched the landscape pass by in the backseat, perhaps she might luck out and get foster parents without young children. The suspense of not knowing if the next foster home had youngsters became too much. She had to ask.

"Are there any little kids where I'm going?" The nun ignored the question. The car buzzed down the road. "Are there any little kids where I'm going?" Apple repeated with a tone of anger.

"You'll find out soon enough. I am warning you. This will be your last stop. You mess up and you are crossing the strait. I can make it happen."

An exhausted Apple curled up in the warmth of the back seat of the car and drifted into the dreamworld.

Nana was bathing her in the big washtub in the kitchen next to the woodstove. The water was dirty with red clay. Nana was scrubbing away the fun of making mud pies behind the house. The kitchen door swung open. Crows stood in the doorway screeching. Caw-caw-caw. Apple woke up screaming, "Nana, Nana, don't let the crows take me. Don't let them take me."

Her body jerked awake in the back seat. Where was she? Where was she going? Why had Nana let the crow take her away? Her fingers touched the Saint Anne's chain on her neck. It was the one possession she had managed to hold on to while bouncing around foster homes. Nana had said Saint Anne would keep her safe. But Saint Anne had done a lousy job.

Sister Henrietta paid no attention to the nightmarish shouts coming from the back seat. The grandmother was dead. No one wanted the child. How did Gladys repay her kindness of finding good homes? With violent outbursts, setting a house on fire, talking back, and being too lazy to help the foster mothers. She had five more years of tolerating the ungrateful girl—unless Gladys ended up in a reform school. Then she would become someone else's problem.

CHAPTER 7

A pple had never been to Charlottetown. Her life had consisted of being farmed out to foster families living near seaside villages or in the countryside. Charlottetown was a new world with rows of houses, brick buildings, bustling traffic, and the never-ending concrete sidewalks that linked street after street. Apple was mystified how the Island landscape could change from quiet rural communities to a fast-moving town within a four-hour drive.

Questions rumbled through her head. Who lived in the houses? Were they friendly? Would there be girls her age? Would she be able to find her way around or get lost and not know where to go? A mixture of excitement and anxiety caused stomach pains.

The sleek black car came to a stop at a two-storey dwelling on a street with side-by-side houses. You could step off the sidewalk into the front doors of homes. Apple had just turned thirteen and had lived in foster homes since she was nine. She had developed a knack of knowing what she would be tackling on the inside of a foster home over the years. But today, she had no idea what waited on the other side of the door.

Stan and Hilda were a childless couple in their early forties. Being a barren woman was one of Hilda's greatest disappointments in life. She envied the mothers living in the neighbourhood. The women in the neighbourhood envied Hilda who could go anywhere for the day, if she wanted, with no kids bawling at home. Hilda, they figured, could spend money on bingo night rather than buy groceries for hungry mouths.

But Hilda, with her dark purple, twisted varicose veins zig-zagging up and down her stout legs, could no longer tolerate standing long hours cooking in kitchen restaurants. Stan earned a meagre salary loading turnips and potatoes on boats and sweeping city streets to pay the rent and put groceries in the cupboard.

The couple, devout Catholics, attended Mass every Sunday and would go to confession once a month. They had approached Sister Henrietta with a request to foster a child. Hilda had learned of fostering through a friend of a friend. Foster parents, she was told, received a monthly allowance and a clothing allowance for the child. It seemed to be the answer to their financial problems.

They promised to be good to the child. They had a spare bedroom. There was a school nearby. They would take the foster child to Mass every Sunday. The timing could not have been more perfect for Stan and Hilda.

"Do you have any experience caring for children of any age?" Sister Henrietta quizzed Stan and Hilda. "I have a teenage girl in need of a foster home. She is no angel. She is mouthy and can be lazy. You will need to be strict with her. You'll receive fifty dollars a month along with a clothing allowance every six months until she's eighteen."

The extra fifty dollars would be a blessing for Stan and Hilda. The money would put more food on the table and bills would get paid on time. They could open a bank account and start saving money instead of living paycheque to paycheque.

Hilda and Stan needed fast cash and the money would be a motivator for accepting a wildcard of a foster kid, figured Sister Henrietta. Gladys would spin circles around the couple. Sister

Henrietta would give the foster home placement less than a month before getting the call to come fetch Gladys.

"We have no experience taking care of kids. It wasn't in God's plans for us to have children," Stan answered. "But Hilda here, she is right good with the neighbourhood kids. Bakes them cookies, she does. Don't you, Hilda?"

Sister Henrietta smiled. Stan and Hilda were the perfect couple. Gladys would be exiting the foster system before too long and heading across the strait to reform school to become someone else's problem.

The nun rang the doorbell and waited. Apple glanced across the street and noticed someone watching from behind a curtain in one of the houses. Apple stood behind Sister Henrietta as if she were a shield.

A short, tubby woman with a broad smile answered the door. Apple forced a smile and mumbled "hello" when introduced to Hilda. Apple glanced behind Hilda, expecting to see curious children.

"Well, isn't she a pretty little thing? Come on in, honey. You must be tired. Tignish is a long way to come from. Do you like cookies? There is a fresh batch in the kitchen. Come down this way."

Apple and Sister Henrietta shadowed Hilda down the narrow hallway to a small kitchen in the back of the house. She motioned Apple to sit down at the table and offered a glass of milk. The crammed kitchen had enough space for a table and four chairs, a stove, a fridge, and a sink with a window above it. A string of cupboards crossed the length of the room. A print of the Last Supper was nailed on the wall above the table. A side door opened to a picket fenced backyard with a clothesline and a tool shed.

Apple watched Hilda trying to figure her out. Had Hilda taken a dose of valium? One of the foster mothers swallowed valium when her nerves were bad. The little white pills made the foster mother sluggish. But Hilda was not moving slow. Perhaps she was sipping moonshine. One of the foster fathers would get hammered on moonshine and Apple would hide under the bed.

A baffled Apple could not figure it out. If it was not moonshine or valium then what was up with Hilda? She was being too nice, too kind. She acted differently from the other foster parents who looked her up and down as if she were a piece of furniture they were buying. They would comment about her being fat and be concerned how much food she would eat.

"Thank you," Apple mumbled.

"What nice manners she has," said Hilda, beaming. "Such a dear little pet."

Sister Henrietta sat at the table with a smug expression. The reform school was just a telephone call away. "I have business at the office and will be back in a couple of weeks to check up on how things are going."

Hilda walked the nun to the door. Apple did not dare budge from the kitchen table. She sat and waited with the brown suitcase next to her.

"Follow me and I will show you to your room, Gladys." Hilda led the way upstairs to a bedroom that faced the backyard. "Stan put a fresh coat of paint on the walls when we heard you were coming. We know girls like pink."

Apple gasped as they entered the bedroom. The walls, ceiling, and a dresser were painted hot pink. A large bed had a painted pink headboard. Who were these strange people? She would be sure to keep a pair of scissors under a pillow while she was sleeping.

"You put your things away and rest. The bathroom is down the hallway. I put out fresh towels and a bottle of pink bubble bath."

Hilda had done research on teenagers through conversations with women in the neighbourhood. "I heard young girls enjoy taking bubble baths."

The country foster homes had a slop-pail in a corner of the bedrooms. It had been her job to dump the pails in an outhouse. She tuned out the chitter-chatter coming from Hilda. A vision of soaking for the first time in a tub of hot bubbles occupied her thoughts.

"I'm going to start supper. Stan likes his tea to be ready when he gets home from work. You let me know if there is anything you need." The pink walls closed in on a bewildered Apple.

A neighbour called Irene had been watching from behind a window curtain. She and Hilda had lived across the street from each other for years. Irene watched Sister Henrietta leaving Hilda's house. A minute later, Irene was banging on Hilda's door.

"What do you mean by taking a foster child in?" Irene blurted. "Is that why you were asking questions about what teen girls like to do? Are you crazy, taking in a teenage girl? And from Tignish, of all places. I heard Tignish girls are wild and nothing but trouble. She will rob you blind or burn the house down while you are sleeping in your bed."

Hilda scanned the living room cluttered with junk Stan found in the trash while cleaning the streets. An aged black-and-white floor model television and radio were the only luxury items they owned.

"What would the girl steal?" Hilda rebutted. "I couldn't pay a person to take some of the junk Stan keeps bringing home. I don't get a family allowance like you do for that tribe of kids you and Ivan have. Me and Stan could use the money we will be getting for fostering. We plan to take good care of her and provide her with a good Christian home. Tignish girls are no different than Charlottetown girls. I bet the mothers in Tignish warn their daughters not to hang around Charlottetown girls."

Irene fished for as much information as she could get which she planned to share with anyone willing to listen. "Do you know anything about her? Why is she a foster child? What about her own family?"

Hilda looked up the stairway to make certain Gladys was not in earshot before responding.

Apple tip-toed down the hallway and discovered the bathroom. She locked the door and looked about the room in amazement. Water gushed out of the tap as if it were a magic trick. A smile crossed her lips. She undressed, climbed into the claw-foot bathtub, stretched out and closed her eyes. Never had she imagined such luxury living in foster care.

The sudden noise of the oil furnace spooked her. She sat upright expecting Sister Henrietta to crash through the door and yell for her to get dressed and be ready to cross the strait to the reform school. She eyed the locked bathroom door to be certain no one could open it.

The twenty-minute glorious soak miraculously erased a mountain of tension and stress. She would have stayed in the tub longer if she had not been spooked. Apple yanked the plug, quickly dressed, hurried to the pink bedroom, and shut the door. She would wait another day before indulging in soaking in bath bubbles. When she was certain she'd be staying.

"She's got no family, the poor little thing," Hilda explained to Irene. "She is like a little orphan bird that tumbled out of a nest. I figure if we treat her right, she will treat us right. I will bring her over tomorrow for a visit. I was hoping your Millie would walk her to school. She could use a friend like Millie. They are about the same age."

Irene was about to tell Hilda no way she was going to allow a Tignish girl to befriend Millie and get her in trouble but changed her mind. Irene figured it would be better to meet the girl and let her know who was boss.

The kitchen clock struck five. The door burst opened. Stan had arrived home from street cleaning. "Where is she? What is she like? What did the nun say when she dropped her off? Did she leave any instructions?" Stan peppered Hilda with questions not waiting for a response.

"The girl didn't come with instructions," chuckled Hilda. "She's upstairs having a rest. Go get washed before she comes down for supper and get that dirt off. You will frighten the poor little thing. She seems right shy and nervous. She doesn't talk much. And don't go asking too many questions and scare her. We need the extra income."

Stan was short and stocky with hands the size of a baseball glove and fingers like thick, rounded sausages.

Stan approached Apple with an outstretched hand at the supper table. "Pleased to meet you, Missy."

Apple ignored the outstretched hand and mumbled, "hello," and helped with setting the table without being asked. Stan watched as Hilda smiled.

"Put an extra plate out," Hilda instructed. "You never know who will drop by during the supper hour."

The doorbell rang just as the food had been placed on the table. "I knew he'd come by," Stan said. "I best go let him in."

"This is Harry." Hilda introduced a burly man about thirty years old holding a lunchpail. "How did work go today, Harry?"

Harry had not worked a day since the accident more than ten years earlier. He had been knocked out senseless on the loading dock. "It could have easily been me," a tearful Stan often told Hilda. "I was standing right next to him. He picked up a potato sack and tripped on the hauling rope, smashed his head on a plank of steel and bled like a butchered pig. We all thought he was dead."

Harry survived the fall, but his brain did not. He walked around the neighbourhood with a lunchpail going to an imaginary job. He had the mind of a nine-year-old but was as strong and muscular as a moose.

Lunchbox Harry walked down one street and up another going around and around in circles.

Harry lived with an older sister, Thelma, and financially supported his family before the accident.

Thelma would tell people. "He gave every penny of his paycheque to our mother before the accident killed his brain. I promised Mother I would take good care of Harry before she passed away."

The neighbours called her a saint for taking care of the helpless brother rather than admitting him to an institution for the insane. But other people questioned why she didn't have him locked up. Parents warned their children to "stay away from the imbecile."

Apple figured she would be nice to Harry out of fear of upsetting the foster parents. She could never survive years in a reform school. But where in blazes had the old crow left her? She'd picked this couple for a reason. Sister Henrietta was up to no good, she was certain of it.

"Harry, this is Gladys. She is new to Charlottetown. And she is going to be living with us. She's going to be part of our family."

Lunchbox Harry took a seat at the kitchen table without being asked. He stared at the floor as if there were something of interest on it. "Where are you from, Gladys?"

Apple began to wonder what was on the floor that had caught his attention. "Everyone calls me Apple. Sometimes I forget my real name. I like it better than Gladys." She shot a look at Stan and Hilda hoping they would get the hint. "I grew up near Tignish." She forked food into her mouth and ignored what Hilda said about being family. She figured Hilda was a better liar than most foster parents she encountered. In the foster world, she was a paycheque, not family.

"Tignish!" Harry bellowed. "You came all the way from Tignish? I never met anyone from Tignish before. Do you want to be my girlfriend?"

Hilda quickly changed the subject. She would explain the accident to Apple after Harry had gone home. "There are a few funeral cookies in the cupboard if you want one, Harry."

"My gawd. Did someone die? Someone I know, Hilda?" He put the fork down on the table. Big tears smeared his face.

"It was Betty Sprigs on Dorchester Street. She almost made it to ninety years. I heard the family had planned a big birthday celebration. The good Lord called her home and ruined the birthday plans. Me and the women on the street got together and made sandwiches and cookies for the funeral lunch. There was a plateful of cookies left over. I took 'em home for Stan."

Apple declined the offer of a funeral cookie. Her tummy rolled with nausea as she watched Harry dunk the funeral cookie in a cup of hot tea. She would keep the scissors nearby when he was around. She was not going to take any chances with the dummy. Out of habit, she cleared the table without being asked.

"Thank you, dearie," smiled Hilda. How blessed she and Stan were for getting a thoughtful girl. They would reward their blessing with an extra dollar in the church envelope.

Apple ignored the thanks. Why was the foster mother being so darn nice when she did not have to be? Best not to let her guard down, not for a moment.

"Do you want to play checkers?" Lunchbox Harry asked Stan like an eager child. "I bet I can beat you." Stan got up from the table and got the checkerboard. He told Lunchbox Harry to go home after the game because his sister would be waiting for him.

"I will take you across the street tomorrow and introduce you to Millie," said Hilda. "She is about your age. You can walk to school with Millie after I get you registered. You will like Millie. She is a right sensible girl for her age. She never gives her parents any trouble at all."

Apple only half-listened to Hilda. The woman talked too much. She was too polite, too kind. It made Apple uneasy. "Can I be excused?" Hilda nodded yes and wished her a goodnight.

Apple rushed to the privacy of the pink bubble room. She would have rather been fostered in a home where she knew what to expect. Leaving the light on, she crawled into the bed and ducked under the blankets with one hand touching the scissors under a pillow.

"She's awfully skittish. Do you think she will like living with an old couple like us?" Stan asked Hilda.

"Give her a chance to settle in and get to know us," Hilda replied. "Give her time to come around."

❀

In the dreamworld, a crow tortured Apple. It pecked the bedroom window with its long black beak. The crow had found her the first night in Charlottetown. She woke up from the dreamworld, curled up in a ball under the bed, sobbing for Nana. Why did Nana let the crow take her away?

CHAPTER 8

M illie was pretty with saucer blue eyes, long brown hair that framed a creamy coloured complexion.

The house boomed with noise. The entire family talked as if they were in a shouting contest. Some things in life were just so unfair for Hilda. She envied Irene for having a house full of children while she remained childless.

Irene grabbed a broom and shooed a tribe of kids out the door. "Get outdoors till supper and stay out of trouble. Is this the girl you were jabbering about?" She looked Apple up and down. "She's chubby. It's going to cost you to feed her."

The comment angered Apple. She hated big-mouth people like Irene. There would be consequences if she said what she was thinking. Instead, she remained silent. Hilda spoke up.

"Stan and I are lucky to have her. She would be a good friend for your Millie. Give her a chance?"

Irene was not convinced but figured if the foster child was sly enough to worm her way into Stan and Hilda's home and gain their trust, the girl might be sneaky enough to befriend Millie without her knowing it.

"I don't put up with any nonsense. I've warned my Millie to stay out of trouble." She pointed a finger at Apple. "I will put the run to you if you give my Millie any wrong ideas."

Irene would have been the perfect predictable foster parent thought Apple as she and Millie strode upstairs to get to know each other in the privacy of a bedroom. Millie shared a bed with two sisters. Millie and an older sister slept at the head of the bed. Their younger sister slept at the foot of the bed. The sisters shared a dresser filled with hand-me-down clothing.

"What's it like being a foster kid?"

Apple glared at Millie for asking such a stupid question. Then Millie wanted to know if Apple had ever kissed a boy. Apple never answered. There was nothing to tell. Millie gossiped about the girls at school. She named girls who stuffed toilet paper in their bras and the girls who came to school with hickeys on their neck. Apple figured Millie was a blabbermouth like Irene. It would be best to be careful what she told Millie. She sat on the edge of the bed and listened to the gossip without interest.

Irene opened the bedroom door without knocking. "You girls better not be talking about boys." She threw a warning look at Apple. "Go downstairs. It is time to go. Hilda is leaving."

❀

Her worn-out suitcase was stuffed with underwear, socks, a prized blue denim jacket, second-hand clothing and a few personal toiletries. Apple packed the contents into the pink dresser.

Foster parents received an allowance to purchase clothing for foster children. It was obvious the last foster parent had not used the clothing allowance for its intended purpose.

Apple dressed in the same clothing every day. Hilda took pity on the girl for not having new clothing for the first day of a new school.

A hidden hatbox in a corner of a bedroom closet contained money Hilda had managed to save. She counted out a fistful of dollar bills and would replace the cash with the money Sister Henrietta would be giving her at the end of the month.

"Would you like to go shopping for school clothing? You can invite Millie and she can help you pick out a new outfit for school."

Apple didn't need any coaxing and raced across the street to see if Millie would accept the invitation before Hilda could change her mind.

Apple followed Hilda and Mille uptown like a confused, lost puppy. Charlottetown was a fast-paced world with honking horns, busy sidewalks and towering buildings, compared to the slower-paced seaside villages near Tignish.

Shopping for clothes was a new experience for Apple. The last foster mother would come home with a bag of hand-me-down clothing once a year. A girl at school had teased Apple for wearing a dress that had once belonged to her.

Hilda spied a rack of girls' clothing, but Apple had no idea what to select. There were too many choices.

"Millie will help you pick out what the other girls at school are wearing. I am going to check out the sales while you two do some shopping." She disappeared for almost an hour while Millie and Apple explored racks of clothing. The girls ripped through the clothing in search of styles and sizes.

A wide-eyed Millie observed Hilda counting crumpled bills to pay for a skirt, a blouse, knee stockings, and penny loafers. A jab of jealousy poked Millie who wore hand-me-down clothing. Her parents had too many kids to feed and dress to spoil her with a shopping spree. The shopping trip ended with a treat at the lunch counter at the back of the store. Apple tasted a milkshake for the first time. Millie could not wait to blab to Irene the money Hilda forked out for new clothes, including a pair of expensive penny loafers. Millie knew the foolishness of wasteful spending on a foster kid would shock Irene. Millie silently swore her children would never wear second-hand clothing. It would become her mission in life to marry a wealthy man.

❄

Sister Henrietta visited on occasion. Stan and Hilda would reward the visit with an extra dollar in the Sunday collection. Apple took great pleasure eyeing Sister Henrietta sipping tea and eating funeral cookies. Hilda raved about Apple being a great girl and a wonderful help around the house. The old nun did not buy any of it. Apple sneered at the crow and politely offered her more tea. It forced the old nun to answer nicely. It was a game Apple and Sister Henrietta played, taunting each other. Hilda never caught on.

A nervous Apple trailed behind Millie on the first day of school. Millie strode through the familiar hallways of school unaware of the discomfort Apple was experiencing.

In the mid-sixties, a rebellious generation of young people were discovering freedom. The teachers and the principal of the school cracked down on anyone they considered rebellious. Teachers considered them troublemakers and they were not welcomed at the school.

Apple entered the office for a class schedule and was greeted by a stern receptionist who handed her a sheet with room numbers, subjects, and teachers.

The middle-aged receptionist wore a stiff blue skirt that covered her knees and a snow-white blouse buttoned to the neck. She was aware that Stan and Hilda were fostering a thirteen-year-old girl who would be attending school and suspected the foster child would be a wildcard.

"You're the foster child living with Stan and Hilda," said the receptionist with a frown. "We expect students to be respectful while on school property. Students are here to learn, and trouble will not be tolerated."

First day of school and she was labelled the foster child thought Apple as she walked through the school in search of her homeroom class.

Apple had never attended such a large school. There were different classrooms and teachers for every subject. She did not fit in with the other students, but she did not stand out and no one played the Germ game at the new school.

Millie and Apple walked to and from school and hung out most Saturdays. Millie had the responsibility of taking care of her younger siblings. Millie and Apple would take the kids to the playground. Millie would disappear leaving Apple to watch the kids. A conniving Millie warned Apple, "If Mom finds out I left the kids with you, she will not let us hang out." Apple remained quiet. A friendship with strings attached was better than no friendship at all.

CHAPTER 9

Apple became accustomed to Lunchbox Harry coming to the house. She played checkers with him out of boredom. She and Lunchbox Harry were not that different, she mused. They were misfits in need of acceptance and friendship.

"I won. I won. I won," Lunchbox Harry declared.

"Time for you to go home."

"Can we play one more game?" Harry begged and began setting up the checkerboard. "This time you can have the red checkers, Apple," which were his 'favourite'.

"One more game Harry and then you go home." There was more goodness in Harry, she reckoned, than the people who drifted in and out of her life. Apple won the game knowing Lunchbox Harry had let her.

Many of the teenage girls on the street had been friends since childhood. They grew up playing and arguing. They were drama queens who shared girly secrets with each other, gossiped, and ratted on friends. Apple had been living in Charlottetown for almost a year and was still considered the foster kid from Tignish. Apple hung out in her bedroom listening to music when Millie socialized with her other friends. She yearned to be one of the popular girls and be included.

✼

"Apple, Apple!" a familiar voice shouted as she and Millie walked home. "Wait for me."

"Finished work for the day, Lunchbox Harry?" Millie teased. "Were you late for work? You will get fired if you are late." Millie snickered. "He is such a dummy."

Apple stopped walking and turned to face Lunchbox. "You better get home, Harry. Your sister is waiting for you. Go on. Get home."

Lunchbox Harry began to sniffle thinking his girlfriend was mad at him.

"You can come over later and we'll play checkers." Lunchbox Harry lumbered down the street with his head down.

"There's no need for teasing him," Apple scolded Millie. "He's slow in the head, but that don't mean you have to make fun of him."

Millie stopped in her tracks. She did not care for being lectured. "Why do you stick up for him? Everyone teases Lunchbox Harry. He's a nutcase."

Apple knew the sting of being bullied. "People can be so friggin' cruel. I don't want any part of it."

The kids teasing Lunchbox Harry were no different than her tormenters at the last school. Hilda and Stan were an odd couple but kind to her. It was a good deal and one she was not going to risk messing up. She no longer slept with the scissors under the pillow and with the light on. The crows seldom pecked at the bedroom window.

Millie sulked the rest of the way home. Apple finally broke the silence. "Listen, Millie, I know what it is liked to be teased by a bunch of snotty kids who think they are better. If I make fun of

Harry, it is like saying it was okay for those kids to tease me. Harry doesn't even know he's being laughed at, but I did."

Millie did not change her tune. The kids on the west side of town teased her, but it was expected because of where she lived. Some kids in school had the bad luck of being born poor on the east side of the railroad tracks. There were kids born to a more privileged lifestyle who lived on the west side of the tracks. The railroad tracks separated the wealthier kids from the poorer kids. It was that simple.

Apple lived with foster parents, a rented kid. She was lower than Millie in the pecking order, and Lunchbox Harry was even lower than Apple. The foster kid had no right to lecture her.

It was like the times Apple had witnessed her lifting her dress for a cabbie for a fistful of change and lectured her. "All the girls on the street do it," Millie argued when Apple told her it was a disgusting thing to do. "All he sees is my bloomers for a few seconds. What is the big deal?" Millie began spreading gossip the foster kid thought she was better than her and the other girls on the street.

"Come on, you are not still mad at me, are you, Millie?" Apple inquired. Millie never said a word and the two girls walked in silence.

A young man stepped out of an alleyway in front of the girls. People called him, Sneakers, a foster kid who had bounced around from home to home. He exited the foster care system at eighteen. Welfare provided him with a bedsitting room and a living allowance. He had a reputation of being clever and dishonest. If you wanted something, Sneakers could get it for a price, no questions asked. He lived his life on his own terms and did what was necessary to survive.

Millie might be considered poor white trash by the elite kids, but Apple and Sneakers considered Millie privileged compared to their upbringing.

Millie froze as Sneakers approached her. "Come on, Millie, let's take a walk down to Dead Man's Pond and make out. You know you want to."

Millie flinched. Sneakers stepped closer. Apple jumped in front of Millie like a shield and screamed, "Leave her alone!"

A fearful Millie stood on the sidewalk unable to move. Apple grabbed her hand and led her up the street. The door was unlocked. Apple pushed it open and yanked Millie inside. "You can stay with me, and I will walk you home later. Let's go upstairs and listen to music," Apple suggested, to calm her friend.

Millie looked over at Apple with a newfound respect for standing up to Sneakers and protecting her. It would be the talk of the street before long.

❋

A flu bug circulated through the school and many of the students became ill. Hilda cooked heaping plates of vegetables and insisted Apple drink orange juice to avoid getting ill. "A healthy diet will save you from the misery of being home sick," she said. Millie faked being sick to stay home in bed. The school enrollment dropped, with students home sick or faking sickness. Millie didn't see the point of achieving an education. "I don't need schooling 'cause I am smart enough to find me a rich husband to take care of me and the babies," she once told Apple.

Apple had graduated grade eight with high marks and was rewarded with a ten-dollar bill from Stan and Hilda. The monetary gift was a strong motivator for Apple to ace an upcoming math test. Chances were Stan and Hilda would reward her again if she did well in the exam. She planned to put the reward money to good use and buy a tube of lipstick at one of the most expensive stores in town.

Apple walked to and from school alone while Millie recovered from a fake illness. She encountered Sneakers walking home from school alone one day. Apple never noticed him until he reached out and touched her. She jumped and screamed.

"Keep your lid on. I am not going to hurt you. I just want to talk without that blabbermouth friend listening. I heard you're from a village near Tignish. I used to be fostered out to a family in Tignish. The foster mother was decent. Her old man was a different story."

Apple considered making a dash for home but figured Sneakers would outrun her. Foster homes had taught her the best way to deal with a bully was to remain silent. There was no one on the street as she stood quivering with fear.

"The foster parents told me to pack my stuff and threw me out of the house the day I turned eighteen. The foster father grabbed my arm and told me to get out, so I cut his hand with a pocketknife. I guess he didn't call the cops because he was glad to see the end of me. But I was lucky he never called the police."

The rumours were true about Sneakers attacking a foster parent with a knife, but Millie hadn't told the entire story. A surge of pity for Sneakers washed over Apple as she envisioned him standing outside the foster home with a garbage bag full of clothing and nowhere to go. It could easily be her on the street at eighteen if it were not for the kindness of Stan and Hilda. The fear of him hurting her began fading as she came to realize they had common ground of being disposable with little value to the people who were paid to care and protect them.

"Do you smoke?" He offered a cigarette. Apple declined. Most of the people in the neighbourhood smoked, but not Hilda and

Stan. She did not need to start an expensive habit that she could not afford. "Stan and Hilda foster you. I know who they are. They're not bad people, better than most people around here."

Sneakers was not the street thug Millie had made him out to be. Millie considered him a bad boy and not to be trusted. But Apple noticed a hint of kindness in his voice.

"Hilda never yells at me. She takes me shopping and buys me decent clothes. She said I could stay after I turn eighteen. I am going to get a job and help with the rent."

A carload of older boys drove by and honked the horn at Sneakers. He waved. Apple recognized the car and had seen it around. The boys were rough looking and gave her the creeps. Sneakers read her mind. "No worries about that crew. It's the hockey boys to watch out for. They can do stuff and get away with it just because of who they are."

The kids in school were afraid of Sneakers. They were afraid of people outside of their tight little circles. But they used street-smart people like Sneakers to do their dirty work.

A few classmates were walking up the street. Apple shouted out hello. They ignored her. She lowered her head in embarrassment. Sneakers scrunched his face in anger and snarled. They were the same little shitheads who paid him to buy their cheap wine because they were underage. It was the hockey players he detested more than the little shitheads. The hockey players were treated like kings. They relied on Sneakers to do their thieving for them in exchange for money. They were too gutless to get their hands dirty. If they were caught stealing it could ruin their fantasy of becoming a hockey legend. Sneakers saw no sense in chasing a puck up and down the ice. There were better things he could do with his time.

"I am going to give you some free advice. Don't ever think you are as good as the other kids in school, and never trust them.

They'll turn on you like a pack of dogs." The day would come Apple would regret not heeding his warning.

CHAPTER 10

It was Friday morning, no different than any other Friday. Apple soaked in the tub, got dressed for school, and dragged her feet downstairs for breakfast. Hilda quizzed her. "Do you know what day it is? I will give you a hint. It's a very special day for all of us."

What could be special about an ordinary Friday? It was just another dull day at school. She would hang out with Millie after school. They would head over to the rec centre in the evening and go bowling.

"It's your first-year anniversary with us," Hilda blurted with a big smile. "To celebrate, Stan and I are going to treat you to a fancy restaurant meal."

Surprises were fun for Hilda and Stan, but not for Apple. She had freaked the time Hilda and Stan surprised her with a birthday cake and candles when she turned fourteen earlier in the year. She had gawked at the two-layer cake with pink candles poked into a layer of pink icing. She mustered a quick thank-you and dashed upstairs to the pink bubble room. Hilda had to coax Apple to open the bedroom door and return to the kitchen. "Open my present first," Stan asked handing Apple a small box with a silly grin. She unwrapped the gift to discover a pink wristwatch. "I know you girls like pink," he'd said, just as Hilda had said when she first arrived.

She did not have the heart to tell either of them pink was her least favourite colour. Then she'd opened Hilda's gift and screeched with excitement: inside was a record player and an envelope with money to buy records.

"Who's coming with us to the restaurant?" Apple wondered, envisioning Sister Henrietta being invited, and frowned.

"Just the three of us."

Apple stood in the kitchen not knowing how to respond to their kindness that conjured up memories of her loving Nana.

No one had told her that Nana had died. But she knew it was unlikely she would still be living.

Nana had been too old to take care of a child. But why hadn't an aunt or uncle or even a cousin taken her in? Perhaps they did not want to be saddled with another child. Babysitting in foster homes had taught Apple children were exhausting.

Apple dashed to the safety of her room and cried without really knowing why. Her emotions were all over the place. She missed Nana and was upset a relative never claimed her. She was feeling protected and loved for the first time since going into foster care. Hilda and Stan were not blood relatives, but they were the best family she could ever hope for.

❋

Trouble in school started for fifteen-year-old Apple when she developed a crush on Wayne, a hockey star and one of the most popular boys in school. Being a star hockey player came with privileges. The players were able to get away with bad behaviour. Some teachers ignored the shenanigans because winning games and school trophies were just as important as getting good grades.

Wayne and his buddies hung out at the community recreation centre, a dull brick building a few blocks away from the street he lived on. The wealthier students hung out at clubhouses where their parents played golf. A rich girlfriend was the answer to Wayne's wish for an invitation to a clubhouse.

Mary-Lou, the most popular and prettiest girl in school, had been blessed with a Barbie-doll figure. Budding pointed breasts pushed through pink cashmere sweaters. Mary-Lou dressed the best because she was the daughter of a prominent lawyer. And when she flounced down the school hallway, a golden taffy-brown ponytail bobbed with each step. Male hormones fired up like shots of electricity as she paraded around the school with a group of giggling girlfriends.

Wayne raced down the hallway to catch up with Mary-Lou before heading to the hockey rink. "Wait up, Mary-Lou." She ignored him. A game of teasing began. He shouted louder, "Wait up, Mary-Lou."

She spun around. "What?"

He invited Mary-Lou to a house party. "I could pick you up after hockey."

Her friends gawked at Wayne, waiting for an answer. "No, I am busy tonight."

She liked Wayne more than any of the boys in class. But appearing eager would ruin a reputation of being able to have any boy she wanted. She waited for Wayne to ask if she had plans for Saturday night. She would think about it for a few minutes before saying yes. To her surprise, he did not ask about Saturday night or any night. Another boy would have begged for a date. That fool Wayne let the opportunity slip by. Her cheeks glowed red with embarrassment waiting for a question he did not ask.

Wayne was not the smartest boy in class. What he lacked in smarts he made up for in good looks. He had been blessed with towering height for his age. He was athletic and muscular, with eyes as black as coal and black curly hair framing a handsome face. He was cocky and charming which made him popular with teachers and with girls.

His family lived on the east side of the railroad tracks. Mary-Lou had been born into a white-collar privileged world on the west side. His face burned with anger at the rejection.

Apple strolled down the hallway into the pathway of a fuming Wayne late for hockey. Earlier in the day, Apple had daydreamed about him in English class, imagining playfully tugging his curly hair and whispering girlish silliness in his ear. She had snapped out of daydreaming when the English teacher repeated her name. "Gladys. I am waiting for you to give me an example of a subordinate clause in a sentence." Apple jumped in her seat.

Mr. Pencil Head had earned the nickname because of a crop of hair sticking to the top of his head as if it had been glued on. He had a stretched-out neck like that of a giraffe stuck to his pencil-thin body. The shirt sleeves and pants he wore were too short for his dangling arms and legs.

Was she still daydreaming? Was it real? Had Wayne stopped to chat with her? "Hey, Apple, what's the big hurry? Some of the crew is getting together for a party on Fitzroy Street. Would you like to come? I could meet you at the party after hockey practice. Give me your pen," he commanded.

She pulled one out of a book, unable to utter even a word.

He scribbled the house number on Fitzroy Street. "Meet me at eight-thirty," and winked at her.

Apple watched Wayne rush away. She had the house number memorized before she exited the school doors.

Wayne was late. The game had started. The coach was peeved, but Wayne did not care. He had big plans for the night. He boasted to his rink buddies about taking a big bite of Apple and laughed.

Apple tripped on a sidewalk crack in a hurry to get home to get ready for a date with the most popular boy in class. Millie caught up to Apple speeding down the street. "What's the big rush?"

Apple blurted out the date plans with Wayne. A stunned Millie listened. Wayne, the most popular boy in school, had a date with…the foster kid?

Millie, too, hated the snobbish, haughty girls from the west side of the railroad tracks who paraded around the school with their snickering, whispering, and silly giggling. But the west end girls were the most popular students in school, and they knew it. "The gossip around the school is that Wayne likes Mary-Lou. He is a hockey jock and can get any girl he wants. Why would he ask you out?"

Apple wanted desperately to tell Millie to mind her own business figuring Millie was jealous because Wayne had asked her instead of Millie. A date with Wayne could earn new friends.

"Mary-Lou only dates the rich west side boys. I'm an east ender like Wayne," Apple argued. "I am not going to turn down the chance to date the most popular boy in class."

The two friends walked the rest of the way home in silence. Millie thought Apple to be a fool if she believed for a moment Wayne had a romantic interest in her. Guys like Wayne did not date girls like her and Apple. The hockey players could have their choice of girls.

❀

"Please do not tell Hilda I have a date with Wayne," Apple pleaded. She will ask too many questions and ruin everything."

Millie agreed. She owed Apple for saving her from Sneakers. Irene would beat the tar out of Millie if she knew the truth about the dress lifting and stealing lipstick from Eaton's. Any romantic notions Millie had with Walter, a boy she had a crush on, would be dead in the water.

Walter was a pimply faced geek with bifocals that slid off his nose and dressed in hand-me-down clothing. He was unpopular but intelligent and crafty.

Walter's father worked with Stan cleaning the city streets. He was no prize catch, but he was smart, figured Millie. She craved financial security, not a marriage to a man who escaped the house to drink with buddies at the Legion like her father. How many nights had she huddled with siblings, listening to their parents in a yelling match? Millie had big plans for a better future than being married to a street cleaner and a drunk. She recognized that Walter shared her ambition of getting off the street and doing better than their parents.

Walter was Millie's ticket to marriage and crossing the tracks to the west side of the town. And Apple knew a conniving Millie was not about to have her plans ruined.

❋

Apple was hungry for romance from reading True Romance magazines and watching late afternoon soap operas with Hilda. Her ideas of being loved were images of women being seduced by strong handsome men as the women moaned with passion and desire.

"I'm going to a movie with a couple of girls from school," she lied to Hilda when she got home.

Hilda smiled, pleased Apple was making friends at school. "Come right home after the movie." She pressed a fistful of coins in Apple's hand.

Hilda and Stan were the best deal she had going. They did not ask for much and treated her decently. The walls of the pink bedroom were now decorated with posters of teen idols. She wore nice store-bought clothes. She had three more years in the system before independent living. Hilda and Stan were not in a financial position to keep her after she turned eighteen unless she was working and helping with the household expenses.

Apple rummaged through a stuffed dresser and tried on blouses, skirts, and jumpers before deciding on a flouncy red skirt and a black frilly blouse. She applied rouge on her rounded cheeks and rubbed perfume on her wrists and tied a scarf around her neck for the final touch.

True to his word, Wayne was waiting for her outside the house on Fitzroy Street. He grabbed Apple by the hand, led her inside and down the darkened steps of a basement. Schoolkids were drinking beer and listening to music in semi-darkness. A few teenagers were necking in corners.

Apple searched the room. She knew the faces but not the people. They were the teenagers who snubbed her in the school hallway. Wayne took a long swallow of a beer. He handed the bottle to Apple. She hesitated.

"Come on, take a swig." He gazed at Apple with the same charismatic smile that charmed the schoolgirls and teachers.

She tipped the bottle to her lips and gagged on the warm, fizzy liquid.

"Let me show you how to drink beer." He downed a mouthful. "You need to practice." He laughed and handed the bottle back to her. This time, she sipped the beer, tiny sips. Wayne grinned, which convinced Apple he liked her. The kids at the party would not ignore her now. They would want to be her friend now that she and Wayne were dating.

"How was the game? Did you win? Can I watch the next time you play?" She asked, slurring.

He did not answer. A few of the teenagers watched as he grabbed Apple by the hand. She did not pull away as he led her to a darkened room and shut the door. Apple closed her eyes for the expected romantic kiss. Wayne squeezed her breasts till she moaned with unexpected pain. He lifted the flouncy skirt and tugged at her underwear. Moments later, a surge of pain shot through her as he rammed his penis into her vagina. She did not try to stop him. Her face flushed with excitement. A powerful hockey star liked her. She was the chosen one. The school kids would have to like her if she and Wayne were dating. They would stop calling her the foster kid. She would be in with the popular crowd.

Her virginity had been stolen long before the encounter with Wayne, before her first blood which had spared Apple from pregnancy. She had been an eleven-year-old and the village lad was eighteen. Earlier in the week, he'd offered Apple a chocolate bar and told her she was special.

No one had ever said she was special. She grabbed the bar and hid behind a shed to enjoy the pleasure of eating it.

A few days later he'd offered her a bottle of pop as she walked home from school. She gagged on greedy mouthfuls until the bottle was empty. He said not to tell anyone.

He approached Apple when no one was around and told her he knew a place where there were horses in a field. She followed him through the woods. He grabbed her, pushed her to the ground, pulled down her underwear, and mounted her. There were no horses. He had tricked her. She screamed but he muffled the noise with a hand over her mouth. It took her breath away. Apple would run and hide with a pounding heart anytime she saw the attacker in the village.

Wayne zipped up his pants without saying a word. Apple pulled up her panties.

Wayne strutted out of the room with a tell-tale smirk on his face that screamed the hockey star had scored. She followed Wayne outside. He told her it was time to go home. The party was over.

Millie was on Apple's doorstep the next day for party details. Apple did not invite her in saying she'd promised to help Hilda with the grocery shopping because visitors were coming to the house.

It wasn't exactly a lie. Hilda was a member of a religious organization composed mostly of middle-aged women. They were having a meeting at Hilda's house to discuss charitable work within the parish. Apple had agreed to help with the luncheon.

"Did he kiss you? Who was at the party? Did he take you home? I watched out my bedroom window but did not see you or Wayne. Did you come home late? It was almost midnight before I gave up and went to bed."

Apple figured Millie would be watching out the window; she'd done it before. So, Apple had cut through backyards, climbed the fence, and ducked in the back door without being noticed hours before midnight.

"Of course he walked me home, and he gave me a big smooch on the lips. It was past midnight. I must go and help with the cleaning before our company arrives. It is too much work for Hilda, and I promised I would help."

Millie was not convinced as she trotted across the street to her house.

Gossip about the party circulated the school on Monday. Who was at the party? Who was necking? Who was drinking? Who got lucky with a girl? And the rumour was Wayne took the foster kid to the party and scored.

Apple ignored the gossip. "He didn't score with me," she later told Millie. It was a wasted school day for Apple. Her concentration was challenged as she recalled details of the party. The romance magazines she read described men lusting for the women they loved. She was his girl now and would not allow school gossip to ruin it. However, the nagging feeling of doubt deep within her kept surfacing to the top.

Wayne collided with Mary-Lou and a gaggle of smirking girlfriends on the way to class. The loudest mouth in the pack shouted out to Wayne, "I heard you took that foster kid to a party Friday night. You must be desperate." The girls locked arms and pranced down the hallway like prize poodles in a dog show.

Walter wished he could play hockey but was too poor to buy hockey equipment and too unpopular to make the team even if he could acquire disposable cash for gear. He was always on the hunt for ways to impress Wayne and the other players, who tolerated him enough to let him do their homework and run their errands.

"I heard my sister talking with her friends from school," Walter informed Wayne. "They said you insulted Mary-Lou by dating the foster kid. And Mary-Lou was mad as heck you did not go chasing after her like the other boys do. Mary-Lou said you'd rather been seen with a tramp than a lady."

Walter was always hungry for gossip that would impress Wayne and the guys. Gossip was a popular pastime in the school. Walter played dumb and would pretend to be reading a book in the school cafeteria. All the time, his ears were tuned in to what was being said and who was saying it. No one wanted him as a friend. The hockey jocks used him and made fun of him when he was not around.

"Thanks, Buddy." Wayne rewarded Walter with a jolly slap on the back. "Let me know if you hear anything more. I'll tell the guys to treat you good at the rink."

Mary-Lou was no different from the other girls, figured Wayne. She might not want him, but she did not want another girl to have him. She was jealous. He planned to give her something to be jealous about. He strolled through the school in search of Apple to invite her to a hockey game. The entire school knew about the hockey invitation, including Mary-Lou, before the end of the day.

The students were easily distracted and paid little attention in English class. Who cared about a long dead poet or the complete works of Shakespeare? Mr. Pencil Head noticed Wayne slipping a note to Apple. Her face flushed red and nodded, yes. Wayne was cocky and a user, figured the English teacher, just like his own boyhood tormenters.

"Wayne," he shouted. "You have not passed in the writing assignment I gave the class last week. You have till tomorrow to pass it in or else detention for a week."

Apple spied Mary-Lou at a locker. It was payback time for the little snot. "I'm going to watch Wayne play hockey tonight," Apple announced loud enough for Mary-Lou to hear. "We are going to hangout after the game." Mary-Lou pretended not to be listening. Apple passed Mary-Lou with her head held high in the air as if she had been crowned the Homecoming Queen.

"I'll teach the little tramp a lesson she will not forget," Mary-Lou murmured to the girlfriends trailing her. Apple and Millie locked arms and trotted down the hallway with the victory of sticking it to Mary-Lou and her pack of snickering girlfriends.

CHAPTER 11

A pple had never been to a hockey game. The players all looked the same in their hockey gear, except for the numbers on the back of their hockey jerseys. Wayne was number nine. Her eyes followed number nine skating towards the net with the puck. The crowd went wild, screaming, "Go number nine. GO!" Wayne whacked the puck and scored. Apple stood with the crowd and cheered.

She could have a million days and nights, but this was an evening Apple was certain she would never forget. She was no longer just a foster kid in a system controlled by crows. She was now dating a hockey star. All the girls in school would be mad with jealousy. Any negative thoughts of the earlier sexual encounter at the party on Fitzroy Street dissolved. It was what fellows do to girlfriends justifying the rough sexual encounter.

"Let's go down to Dead Man's Pond," Wayne suggested after the game. The leaves rustled as they tripped on the narrow pathway that led through the woods, near the edge of town where teenagers were known to go to make out.

His tight blue jeans bulged with eagerness. He zipped down his pants, took her head, and pushed it down on him. She pulled away from his grip. "Come on, if you really like me, you will do it. All the girls do it to the guys." She got down on her knees. He moaned with pleasure as semen spurted down her throat. Apple gagged and threw up. A teardrop trickled down her face under the night sky.

A shadow in the darkness watched Apple stumble through the woods with Wayne.

"This is my street," Wayne said. "I will see you at school tomorrow." He turned and walked in the opposite direction without kissing her goodnight. Apple hurried home, four blocks away.

The shadow snuck closer and closer to the hockey star. The street was quiet, with no one around except Wayne trotting down the street. A punch to the back of the head knocked Wayne to the sidewalk. He groaned with pain. The shadow disappeared like a fathom in the dark.

"Hey, Apple," Sneakers called out. "Let me walk you home." She turned and faced Sneakers. Where had he come from? Sneakers seemed to have the ability to appear and disappear without being heard. Apple figured it was probably a survival skill he developed in foster homes. She did not want Sneakers or anyone to look at her. She just wanted to be alone and declined the invitation. Sneakers followed from a distance until Apple arrived safely home.

Millie watched the street through a bedroom window. She spied Apple coming up the street. It was late. They must have gone somewhere after the game. Wayne was not with her. There were too many roughnecks this time of night for a girl to be walking alone. Millie figured Wayne was using Apple.

❀

Millie shared her opinion on their usual morning walk to school. "He's using you. That is what the other kids are saying. I might not be popular, but I would know if a guy used me."

Why did Millie always have to listen to gossip? Who cared what the other kids said? It was what Apple knew that really mattered: Wayne liked her, and she liked him. They were dating. "Mary-Lou and that pack of girls she hangs out with are jealous and so are you. Wayne's my boyfriend."

Millie did not believe a word of it. Apple was fooling herself if she thought Wayne was her boyfriend.

"Look, Apple, I am no fancy catch, but I am going to marry a guy with ambition, get off this street, and have a houseful of kids," snapped Millie. "I am going to have three girls and three boys. I even have their names picked out. I know I am not going to be marrying no hockey jock or one of the popular boys. I'm going to marry Walter. I know he hates being poor as much as I do."

Apple knew it would be best not to tell Millie about the invitation to Wayne's house while his parents were out for the evening.

The two friends walked the rest of the way to school in silence.

❧

An angry Wayne hobbled with pain around the school from the street attack. He bragged to his friends he got banged up at hockey. He took one for the team, he boasted. His friends clapped him on the back.

Lunchbox Harry had the bad luck of crossing paths with Wayne. It could have been Lunchbox that attacked him in the dark, fumed Wayne. He grabbed Lunchbox Harry by the arm and demanded if he'd been out late the night before. Lunchbox Harry whimpered in fear. Wayne stood in his way and would not let him go by. "Hey, big dummy," he taunted. "I'm going to beat the crap out of you."

A voice yelled out in the distance. "Get away from him." Stan rushed up the street. "One day, you and those hoodlums you hang out with are going to go too far with teasing Harry."

Wayne sneered at Stan with disgust. "What are you going to do about it, old man?"

"Go home, Harry," Stan demanded. "You stay away from this fellow. He is nothing but trouble." Then Stan turned to Wayne. "You leave Harry alone or I will stop by the rink and have a talk with the hockey coach. I bet he'd like to know how the big hockey star treats a harmless soul like Harry."

"Fuck you, old man," Wayne sneered, consumed with rage. He swore to beat up the dummy when no one was around.

❄

The Sadie Hawkins Dance dominated school gossip. It would be an opportunity for the girls to ask the boys for a date instead of waiting for a boy to do the asking. Notes were slipped to each other in class. Groups of teenagers huddled together with news of who'd been asking whom. Apple and Millie had been to a school dance before, but no one had asked them to dance. They'd stood near a door and watched the more popular girls being asked. They dared not dance together like they did while listening to music at Apple's house. They left before the dance was over.

Millie asked her older sister to check with Walter's older sister to see if he'd been asked to the dance. No one had apparently so Millie did. Walter figured it would be better to go with Millie than being bored at home.

"I got myself a date for the Sadie Hawkins Dance," Millie announced with glee as if she'd just won first prize in a baking contest.

"Did you ask Wayne?" Millie tied Apple's red scarf around her neck with the intention of borrowing it.

"Not yet. I haven't had a chance to. That old mean Mr. Pencil Head has been keeping him in detention all week just because he did not have a class project finished. I'm going to ask him before class. We can all hang out together at the dance: me and Wayne, and you and Walter." The two friends danced around the pink bubble bedroom like excited children on Christmas morning.

Millie dashed across the street early the next morning. Stan answered the banging on the door. She ran upstairs and banged on the bedroom door.

"Open the door," demanded Millie.

"Come in," shouted Apple.

Millie stepped into the bedroom and her jaw dropped open.

Apple was dressed in a satin red blouse, a leather black skirt, and knee-high leather boots that Stan and Hilda gave her the first Christmas she lived in town.

Millie and Irene spread gossip Stan and Hilda were spoiling the foster kid with extravagant gifts. They said it was money that could have been used for groceries.

"Wow. You're dressed foxy like you're going to a fancy party," Millie declared, the words poisoned with jealousy. She had to beg an older sister to loan her a dress suitable for the dance while the foster kid wore fancy store-bought clothing and fashionable boots.

"Do you think Wayne will notice I got dressed up just for him? I am going to ask him to the dance, and I want to look sexy."

The teenagers bounced around the room with excitement and rushed by Hilda before she could ask questions.

They headed up the street looking more like they were going to a party than school. They turned the corner and encountered Lunchbox Harry.

Millie yelled out, "Going to work Lunchbox Harry?"

Apple did not bother to scold her. She would not allow anything to ruin what would be the most perfect day.

Apple searched the school hallway for Wayne and noticed him leaning against a locker, laughing with Mary-Lou.

Mary-Lou waited for Apple to get close enough to hear before asking Wayne to go to the dance. He said yes and kissed her on the cheek. They held hands and strolled passed Apple as if she were invisible.

Apple never made it to class. She rushed for home in an outburst of confusion and tears. She had been a fool for thinking she was Wayne's girl.

❅

The nightmares of crows pecking at her bedroom window had been idle for months. Now, the black crows returned to torture her.

She screamed for Nana not to let the crows take her away. For one quick moment, the nightmare tricked Apple. Nana had arms wrapped around her, protecting her from the crows. A startled Apple opened her eyes and jumped. Her arms were hooked around Hilda and not Nana.

"Please don't send me to school," sobbed Apple.

"Did you and Millie have a fight? Did she say something to hurt you?" Hilda waited for answers. But Apple remained silent. Hilda must never know about Wayne. She turned to face the wall, communicating she preferred to be alone to soak in misery. "Goodnight, sweetie," Hilda said and quietly closed the bedroom door behind her.

"I will cross the street tomorrow," Hilda whispered in the dark bedroom to Stan. "I will talk to Irene and see if Millie and Apple had a falling out."

The school dance was a hot topic when the classes resumed the following week. The circulated stories cut Apple to the bone with sadness and depression. Millie was right. She had been a fool for believing she was Wayne's girl.

Irene had no idea if Millie and Apple had a fight but was secretly glad the girls were no longer friends, and she told Hilda she didn't care enough to find out.

Mary-Lou and Wayne flaunted their friendship in front of Apple. Out of desperation, she passed Wayne a note in class. She thought he owed her an explanation. He crumpled the note and tossed it in the air. He would soon be invited to the clubhouse and taste the wealth he had been denied living in a blue-collar district. He was on the way to becoming a bigshot, schmoozing with the sons and daughters of the elite. Wayne angrily warned Apple to stop bugging him. She raced out of the school for home and disappeared into the pink bubble bedroom for the night.

"Leave her alone," Stan suggested to Hilda. "She will come around in time." Hilda ignored the advice and knocked on the bedroom door. Apple refused to come out for supper. A distraught Hilda couldn't eat not knowing what was going on with Apple. But she knew Stan was right. It was best to leave Apple alone and wait till she was ready to talk.

Apple spied Millie going into a shop with a fistful of coins she'd earned lifting her skirt for a cabbie. She waited till Millie came out and approached her friend, hoping they could walk to school together.

Millie jabbered nonstop about a house party she had gone to with Walter. She dropped the names of the popular students who'd been at the party with the hockey jocks. She bragged how Walter received an invitation to a party on the west side of the tracks where the rich lived. And she was going with him. But Walter didn't tell Millie he'd promised to do a big school assignment for the classmate in exchange for the invitation.

Apple only half-listened. She had no interest in Millie's romantic life and wished the sidewalk would crack open and swallow her rather than go to school.

"I'm meeting Walter after school," Millie explained. "So, I won't be walking home with you." The teenagers parted ways. Apple rushed to class to avoid meeting Mary-Lou and Wayne holding hands.

CHAPTER 12

It started with Apple rushing to the bathroom in the morning and vomiting. "I'm not hungry," she told Hilda. "I must have the stomach flu. Please don't send me to school."

Apple was still feeling poorly and unable to keep food down at the end of the week. Hilda made an appointment with Dr. Jay much to Apple's horror. She tried to convince Hilda bedrest was all she required to get better.

Hilda insisted and splurged on a cab for the ten-minute drive to the clinic.

The doctor pushed down on her belly and poked a finger in Apple's uterus and inquired when her last period was. "I can't remember because I am not regular," she answered.

"Get dressed and the nurse will take you to my office."

Hilda was waiting in the doctor's office with a worried look on her face. Out-of-control thoughts that Apple might have cancer or something just as terrible occupied her mind. She had watched enough afternoon soap operas to know it was bad news if the doctor talked privately to you in his office.

"Gladys is about three months pregnant," he announced. A dumfounded Hilda sat speechless. It was not the diagnosis she was expecting.

"What? She can't be. There must be a mistake." She grabbed Apple's hand and searched her face for answers.

The doctor repeated, "She is almost three months pregnant."

Apple listened in disbelief. Her life had changed forever in less than a minute.

She would not get pregnant, she thought, if she took a hot bath and the sperm washed out of her within twenty-four hours of having sex.

"Did a boy hurt you?" Hilda demanded. But Apple had no words as she tried to digest the news. The doctor responded. "Gladys will need regular appointments. You can see the nurse on the way out."

Apple didn't want to step inside the examining room and have the doctor poke her private parts, ever again. The thought disgusted her. She pleaded for Hilda to take her home.

Hilda began to cry. What would Stan say? How would he react? Would he go searching for the guy in a fit of rage?

Dr. Jay placed a call after Hilda and Apple left his office. "Hello Sister Henrietta. You better come to my office. I have information about a teenage girl. She is almost three months pregnant, and she's one of your foster girls."

Dr. Jay and Sister Henrietta were good friends. They worked together finding homes for babies born to unwed mothers. Judge Tweedy, also a friend, signed the legal documents. The babies were delivered to Catholic families in the United States. Sister Henrietta had close contacts with American parish priests who referred families. The families were willing to give the required donations for healthy babies.

"I'm leaving to deliver a baby to a New Jersey couple. I will visit when I am back in Canada," Sister Henrietta replied.

✳

A confused Hilda sat at the kitchen table with Apple. The truth had to be told. She did not have a boyfriend. She did not date. A boy had never called at the house for her. Apple had never lied to her or Stan. She did not seem to be boy crazy or even show an interest in boys. Someone had got her girl in trouble. Who?

"Did one of the lads at school get you? You will have to tell me who did this to you. Stan will be home soon. He is going to have to know. We can't keep it from him."

Apple broke down in tears and blurted it was a boy from school. "He didn't get me. I let him do it to me. I wanted him to love me."

Apple soaked in a hot bath. But the soapy water could not calm her. Hilda told Harry to go home when he knocked on the door. She had a headache. He could come back another night. Supper never got cooked. A tearful Hilda broke the news to Stan as soon as he walked through the doorway.

Stan locked the door and dimmed the lights. He and Hilda talked in low whispers. Stan had an idea. Apple could stay. They could be grandparents to the baby. This could be their miracle baby. He could find extra work doing odd jobs in the evenings and the weekends. Apple could find work after the baby was born and help with the rent. And Hilda would look after the baby while she worked. It seemed like the perfect plan; what could go wrong?

"Hilda and I have been talking," Stan said when Apple finally came downstairs. "You can stay with us for as long as you want. You can keep the baby and find a job. Hilda and I can be grandparents to your baby. It is up to you. What do you want to do?"

Apple did not want to be a mother, changing diapers and chasing a toddler. She had diapered too many stinky bums in foster homes. She was fifteen years old, too young to be a mother.

Apple knew how much work it was taking care of toddlers. She wanted to be a teenager and have fun before being saddled with babies.

"I'm not sure I want to be a mother," Apple said carefully. "I want to stay here. I have no place to go. I'll get a job and Hilda you can be a mommy to my baby. I know you and Stan would be wonderful parents."

❀

Sister Henrietta had her own plans when she learned about the pregnancy. Dr. and Mrs. Brooks lived in New York. The childless couple were wealthy and considered good candidates for adopting an infant. She would arrange a meeting with the couple. But first she had the task of getting Apple settled in a home for unwed mothers operated by the Catholic Church. The Charlottetown haven Apple had been fostered into would soon crumble.

❀

Apple announced she was not going back to school. "I will be good. I will stay in my room and behave. I will not leave the house unless you know where I am going. Please don't send me back to school."

Stan and Hilda agreed to the arrangement without giving it much thought. God was good. The good Lord had blessed them with Apple to care for and now He'd blessed them with a baby. They would contact Sister Henrietta and share their good news. They began to make plans to convert an empty room upstairs into a nursery. The couple sat at the kitchen table and rehearsed what they would tell Sister Henrietta. They knew the nun would be coming and soon.

"Listen, dear. These things happen to girls. We will tell Sister Henrietta that me and Stan will raise the baby as our own flesh and blood and that you are going to be staying with us."

Hilda and Stan were not rich, but they were good people she could trust. The baby would be loved and cared for. Apple confessed the name of the daddy in a blurry of tears and shame.

"His name is Wayne. I never had a boyfriend before. I wanted him to love me. I thought I was his girl. He got what he wanted and then dumped me for a rich girl at school."

Hilda blessed herself with the sign of the cross. The good Lord had answered her prayers. She was going to be blessed with a baby. Her age did not matter, or perhaps she had not calculated the years. She would be in her mid-fifties chasing an active ten-year-old around the neighbourhood. But she and Stan would make it work. They would make certain the child would grow up a good Catholic. They would groom the child at an early age to enter the priesthood or the sisterhood. It would be their way of giving back to the good Lord for bestowing the gift of parenting.

Hilda did not sleep that night. She thought about baby names, sewing cloth diapers, and knitting little baby booties. Apple went to bed grateful her baby would not be growing up with strangers and would never experience living in foster homes. The crows allowed Apple to sleep in peace knowing they would return when life became miserable. And it would.

Stan had confronted Wayne and his parents about the pregnancy. They denied responsibility. It was easier for the parents to believe lies than accept the truth. He was their golden boy with a chance of a hockey career. His parents scrimped and saved for years to enroll him in a prestigious hockey school. Two sons and a daughter would probably end up with back-breaking jobs. Wayne was an investment in their future if he landed a contract with the NHL.

Stan left their house angry as hell. The hockey star showed no remorse for his actions that had landed Apple in trouble. But at least he knew Wayne's parents were not interested in becoming grandparents. He and Hilda could sleep at night knowing they could raise the baby without any interference from Wayne or his parents.

❀

The house came alive with noise early Saturday morning with Stan working on the baby room and Hilda giving directions. Apple ignored the commotion as she raced to the bathroom and puked into the toilet bowl.

"Are you okay?" Hilda tapped the bathroom door.

Apple opened the door and stepped into Hilda's waiting arms. Fresh tears were streaming down her drained face. "I am as weak as a kitten from morning sickness. It's never going to end. I just know it. I will be puking my guts out till the baby is born."

Stan stopped wallpapering and disappeared downstairs. Woman talk made him uncomfortable.

"All women go through morning sickness. It will stop soon," Hilda reassured Apple, while wishing she could have experienced morning sickness, swollen ankles, and stretch marks on a bulging belly. "Stop your crying. It can't be good for the baby growing in your belly. I will make a fresh pot of tea and dry toast. Then you'll feel better."

Apple, wrapped in a blanket, watched Hilda manoeuvre around the kitchen. She waited for Hilda to sit at the kitchen table before discussing what had been on her mind since Hilda and Stan agreed to raise her baby.

"I heard you and Stan talking about baby names. You have every right to name the baby. But...I have foggy memories of my parents except for what Nana told me. She said my papa adored me, treated me like gold, and my mama spoiled me. Could we name the baby Elmer after my father?"

She nibbled on the dry toast. Was she asking too much? Stan and Hilda were willing to raise the child and yet she wanted the privilege of naming him or her.

Hilda reflected on what Apple was sharing with her. How different life would have been for Apple had the parents lived. But then she and Stan would never have been blessed with Apple. And now they were being blessed with a baby. A pang of guilt pinched Hilda for such selfish thoughts.

"I will talk to Stan, but I don't think he will mind if you name the baby." Stan came barrelling through the door with a bottle of ginger ale. "This will make you feel better," he said and opened the bottle and poured a drink for Apple.

"I best get back upstairs and get back to wallpapering the baby room." He slipped a five-dollar bill to Hilda. "Go buy the prettiest curtains you can find."

The doorbell rang just as Hilda set the table. It was probably Lunchbox Harry early for supper. "Go let Harry in, Apple. I'm busy mashing the potatoes."

The door swung open, but it was not Harry. A speechless Apple gawked at Mr. Pencil Head standing on the doorstep. "Hello Gladys. Are Hilda and Stan home?" Apple would not have been more surprised if a little green man from outer space had landed on the doorstep. She had no idea how Mr. Pencil Head knew where she lived. Stan came whistling down the street. He bellowed out a joyful greeting to Mr. Pencil Head.

"Come in, Gerald." He shook his hand. "We haven't seen you around these parts in ages. It is about time you came for a visit. Hilda will be pleased to see you."

Mr. Pencil Head stepped into the house and walked by a startled Apple. Why was Mr. Pencil Head at her house?

Supper could wait. They had company. Stan and Hilda were as much surprised as Apple.

Gearld grew up nearby, Hilda explained to Apple. His parents lived at the end of the street.

"They were hardworking folks. Good people. Gerald used to be a paper boy delivering the papers all over town."

Apple could not imagine Mr. Pencil Head ever being a little boy delivering papers. "Are your parents still on the west coast?" Hilda asked and placed the pot of mashed potatoes on the back of the stove to keep it warm. Then she started brewing a fresh pot of tea.

"Yes. My parents live in Vancouver with my brother, Vince, and his wife, Nancy."

"What's Vince doing out west?" inquired Stan.

"He's teaching at the university. My parents plan to stay on the coast. The climate is more favourable with not much snow compared to winter on PEI."

Apple listened with distrust. It was strange to see Mr. Pencil Head in her home. She began to suspect the visit had something to do with her. Would he try to talk Stan and Hilda into sending her back to school? She would run away before going back.

"You have done well for an east ender. We heard you were engaged. Congratulations."

Mr. Pencil Head engaged? She would never have believed it even if the news had been splashed on the front page of an Island newspaper. It was news Millie and Irene probably had not heard.

She gloated at knowing something that would shock Millie and Irene. The mother and daughter were walking newspapers.

"How are you, Gladys? You haven't been in school for the last few weeks." The teacher sat at the table sipping tea, waiting for an answer.

Stan answered before Apple could speak. "She's not going back to school, Gerald. She is going to stay home with us. Apple is in the family way. There is no need for us trying to hide it, Hilda."

The stories circulating the school were true. Mr. Pencil Head lowered his head as if he were in prayer. He was sure the father was the smartass hockey star who strutted through the hallways with the rich girl as if she were a personal trophy. "Will you be coming back to school after the baby is born?"

Apple eyed him with suspicion. What did he care? Why would it matter if she returned to school or not?

But Gerald did care. He knew what it was like to grow up with a label. His father was a janitor and his mother a cleaner. He had been an easy target for bullies.

The courage to dream and a good education had been tickets to a teaching career.

He recognized that Gladys was smart. Any person kicked about from one home to the next and still able to have top marks had the potential to do well in life.

"Apple is going to stay with us. She is going to get a job after the baby is born. Hilda and I are going to raise her baby."

It bothered Gerald greatly to see Gladys throw away an education that could open the doors of opportunity just as it had for him. "Gladys is the smartest student in my class. The other teachers have commented that she is a brilliant student." He gathered his thoughts. "The world can be a cruel place especially for youth trying to fit in. A person can be robbed of their self-esteem and confidence. But an education is earned, and no one can take it from you. An education unlocks the doors of poverty."

Stan and Hilda glanced at each other not knowing what to say. They knew Gerald and his brothers had sacrificed their youth working at back-breaking jobs to pay for their educations. But not everyone had the luxury of working and saving. Stan had never finished grade eight like most of the people he knew. Parents expected older kids to go to work to help put food on the table so the younger kids would not go hungry.

Stan thought Gerald had lost touch with the reality of living on the east side of the tracks. "No need for Apple to go back to school. A big education might be important to some people, but it is not for everyone. I get by and I never saw the inside of a high school." Stan stood up, indicating the visit was over.

❀

It was noticeable when a student dropped out of school with a population of about five hundred. And many of the students drop out before graduation especially in the less advantaged side of town. Sons would leave school to work and help their parents support the family. The girls desiring the latest clothing styles would dropout of school in search of employment in restaurants and a sweatshop laundromat that employed about fifty people washing and ironing mostly hotel and hospital sheets.

And then there were the pregnant girls who disappeared from school and the neighbourhood. They would return home broken-hearted and without their babies. Apple didn't quit school to go to work which created suspicion.

The tongues began to wag. Why did she drop out? Was she pregnant?

Irene spotted Hilda walking with Apple. She made it her business to stop Hilda and inquire where they were going. Before Hilda could answer, Irene blurted Millie had not seen Apple in class for weeks.

"Apple is finished school." Hilda kept walking with Apple.

Irene smirked. The rumours about the foster girl being pregnant were true. She had been right; the Tignish girl was nothing but trouble.

Irene marched across the street and banged on Hilda's door one evening. Not waiting for an invitation, Irene stepped into the house. She spied Apple going upstairs wearing a loose-fitting top to cover an obvious rounded pregnant belly.

"You keep that pregnant hussy away from my dear little Millie," Irene barked, pointing at Apple. "You and Stan were foolish to foster a teenager. I told you it would bring you nothing but trouble."

Hilda shouted for Irene to go home and never come back.

CHAPTER 13

Hilda had been up all night with diarrhea. It had been Mr. Jones's wake the day before and she blamed the funeral food for her illness.

She begged Apple to go to the pharmacy to end the emergency trips to the bathroom as Stan would not be home till evening. Hilda could not wait that long. She swore to never eat another funeral lunch if she survived the diarrhea attack.

Apple would have given Hilda a kidney if she asked for it. She would be at the mercy of Sister Henrietta and facing the constant threat of crossing the strait to a reform school if it were not for Hilda and Stan.

It was a good twenty-minute walk to the pharmacy. Apple bundled up against the cold and at almost five months pregnant, walked as fast as she could to the pharmacy.

It was close to the noon hour and the streets would soon be flooded with school kids.

She grabbed a bottle of the much-needed medicine to stop the diarrhea attack. She counted the change to pay for it and scrammed out of the pharmacy—right into the pathway of Wayne and Mary-Lou.

Wayne whispered to Mary-Lou that he would meet her back at school. Mary-Lou noticed Apple's bulging belly and snickered. It was perfect timing for Wayne. It was a window of opportunity to scare Apple into shutting up about the baby being his. Apple clutched the bottle of medicine that Hilda desperately needed as she rushed for home. Wayne caught up to her.

"What's the rush? Are you in a hurry to see your boyfriend? I heard Lunchbox Harry got you knocked up." He grabbed Apple by the arm and spun her around. "I heard you were telling people that's my kid," he said, observing her rounded belly. "You keep your mouth shut. That is not my kid. It's that dummy's kid."

There was no one on the street to come to her aid. Wayne grabbed her arm. "You opened your legs for Lunchbox, didn't you? He took a big bite out of the Apple." Lunchbox Harry came around the corner when he heard Apple's hysteric cries for Wayne to let go of her.

"Don't you hurt my girlfriend," he shouted at Wayne. Lunchbox Harry stepped closer. Wayne laughed with a face twisted with madness as if possessed by the Devil. "I heard you got Apple knocked up, dummy. I bet she liked that big dick of yours being poked into her. Couldn't get enough of it, could you, Apple?"

Apple shouted for Harry to go home to his sister. He did not budge and kept shouting at Wayne to leave his girlfriend alone.

"You let go of her." He took another step towards Wayne.

"What are you going to do about it, dummy? Are you going to be a hero and beat me up? Oh, look at me. I'm shaking in my boots."

Wayne pushed Apple. She stumbled backwards and tumbled to the sidewalk.

Harry cracked Wayne on the side of the head with his steel lunch can. Blood gushed down Wayne's face. The blow stunned him. Harry pushed Wayne and knocked him down. He pounced on Wayne and pummelled him with the lunchbox. The snowy sidewalk became beet red with blood.

Apple attempted to pull Harry off Wayne. Lunchbox Harry had the mind of a child but the power of a grown man. Apple screamed and screamed. The commotion attracted the attention of a corner shop owner. His strength was no match for a riled Lunchbox. Police cars arrived. The officers failed to pull Lunchbox Harry off the lifeless body. A few cracks of a policeman's steel baton to the back of the head shattered what was left of Harry's injured brain. He slumped over the bloodied body of the hockey star, a stream of blood oozing from his head.

Apple ran for home like a chased animal and burst through the door screaming for Hilda. "Harry has gone crazy!" A dumfounded Hilda grabbed Apple and tried to calm her down. "What are you talking about? What happened? Where is Harry?"

Apple flopped on the sofa, screaming and crying, repeating, "Harry has gone crazy!"

Hilda looked out the door and searched the street for clues. The piercing sound of an ambulance could be heard in the distance. "What's happening?" she yelled out to people gathering on the street.

A neighbour yelled back: "Oh, my god, Lunchbox Harry was in a street bawl and killed someone." Hilda stumbled back into the house and almost fainted.

The news of the street fight travelled like a bushfire. Stan learned what happened while at work. Police cars lined the street. People were milling around doorways, each with a story of what happened to Wayne, the hockey star.

Millie watched from the bedroom window. Her mother had been right about Apple being trouble waiting to happen. Millie blessed herself with the sign of the cross for being spared witnessing the gory tragedy. Everyone in school had known Apple was a fool to think Wayne was her boyfriend. But Apple had been too dumb to figure it out, thought Millie.

Officers rapped on the front door. Apple fled upstairs to the bedroom. Hilda invited the police officers inside. They asked to speak with Gladys. The officers sat at the kitchen table and waited. Hilda climbed the stairway and knocked on the bedroom door. No answer.

"The police are here. They want to speak with you. Just tell the police what you told me. You can't hide all day. They're not going away until they talk to you."

Apple opened the door and followed Hilda downstairs.

The police questioned Apple. They repeated the same questions over and over. Her answers never changed through fits of hysterical sobs.

"Wayne was teasing Harry. He was being mean to Harry. I told Wayne to leave Harry alone. He would not listen. I told Harry to go home. Wayne got rough and pushed me down on the sidewalk. Harry went crazy. I tried to pull him off Wayne, but I wasn't strong enough." She choked on tears and grabbed Hilda by the arm. "Don't let them take me away," she begged. "Please don't let them take me away. It wasn't my fault."

The police officers jotted notes. Hilda offered a clump of tissue paper to Apple. The officers listened with stone-cold eyes without any sign of believing Apple.

Hilda excused herself and rushed to the bathroom. The diarrhea medicine had been left on the street where Apple had dropped it.

The attack on the hockey star became a national newsmaker. The story referred to Harry as a retarded male who viciously attacked a teenager in the streets of Charlottetown. The reporter wrote that the unprovoked attack had left a hockey star in a coma. There was no mention of the details Apple provided to the police.

Stan and Hilda, arm-in-arm, dragged their feet as they walked to the hospital to visit Harry.

"If only I had not insisted she go to the pharmacy, none of this would have happened. I am to blame not Apple. She did not want to leave the house because of that cowardly boy who got her in trouble."

A group of teenagers including Millie and Walter heading to the hospital pushed passed Stan and Hilda. One of the lads recognized Stan and shouted, "Apple is a boy-crazy whore!"

Hilda pulled a wad of toilet paper out of a pocket as snotty tears dripped out of her nostrils. Stan gently guided her down the street.

The hospital reeked of unpleasant disinfectant odours that made Stan gag. He and Hilda peered inside Harry's room. Stan gasped. The head bandages triggered memories of the accident on the waterfront that had left Harry brain damaged.

His sister, Thelma, was kneeling below the bed, clutching a rosary. Hilda and Stan waited till she finished praying. They hugged. They cried. They comforted each other.

"Harry will be locked in an institution for the insane if he comes out of the coma," Thelma said, choking on the words.

Hilda begged Thelma for forgiveness. Stan knew the institution for the insane would be a slow death sentence for Harry.

"I am not blaming you or Gladys for what happened to Harry. Gladys has been a good friend to my brother. She was kind to him. It was the other kids around town who tormented my dear brother."

Harry slipped away a few hours later after being given the last rites by the parish priest. Death had spared him from decaying in an institution.

❀

A group of schoolkids and hockey players kept a vigil outside the hospital. Crazy talk about getting revenge on Lunchbox Harry fuelled anger. Sneakers huddled with the crowd. Without being noticed, he disappeared into the night.

Apple ignored the banging on the back door. Hilda and Stan were still at the hospital. She was alone in the house. The knocking got louder. She cracked the door open to see who was standing there. Sneakers did not wait for an invitation. He stepped into the kitchen and cut straight to the point.

"Don't go out on the streets alone. The hockey guys are out to get you. They are blaming you for what happened to Wayne. They are saying Lunchbox went crazy because of you."

Apple cupped her belly.

"They don't care if you're knocked-up with Wayne's baby," as if he'd knew her thoughts. "They want revenge and Lunchbox is dead."

The words echoed in her head. She staggered across the kitchen floor consumed with fear and sorrow. She plunked on a chair fearful of passing out. "Wayne is a bad cat, but he will not let the hockey guys get me. He'd never allow it to happen." She said it with such conviction to make it believable.

"Have you not heard? Wayne has traded places with Lunchbox Harry. Lunchbox cracked Wayne's head open. His brain is nothing but sawdust. He will never lace up his skates again. Wayne will do good if he remembers his own name. The hockey boys are planning a gang rape."

The memory of being tricked and raped by the village lad resurfaced with this threat. She'd rather die than have a lifetime memory of fighting a group of vengeful hockey players. The baby thrashed about in the womb as if it, too, had been threatened.

Apple wrapped her arms around herself as if to protect the baby growing inside of her. She would not survive a gang rape, and neither would the baby; she was sure of it.

Apple collapsed on a chair unable to move, trying to breathe. She had to get, as far away as possible, but where and how?

Sneakers advised Apple to keep the doors locked and the lights out before disappearing into the darkness of the night. Apple double-checked the doors to make certain they were locked. She crawled into bed and bawled with grief. Her friend was dead. There was no escaping the crows in the dream world. They pecked the bedroom window and cawed most of the night. The crows had no mercy.

Dr. Jay contacted a parish priest in New York who tracked down Sister Henrietta with the news of the street brawl. She drove non-stop back to the Island. It was midmorning when she landed on Stan's doorstep. She got right to the point.

"It's a shame what happened to that young man. He has been robbed of a bright future. I visited his family yesterday afternoon. They are devastated. Their son will never go back to school or play hockey. Thelma should have committed her brother years ago. Instead, she allowed him to walk around town like an idiot with a lunchpail pretending to go to work. Her brother is dead and a teenager from a good family has been robbed of a normal life."

Hilda and Stan were expecting a lecture. They would allow the nun to finish before sharing their plans to raise Apple's baby.

"I know about the pregnancy," the Sister continued. "Wayne's parents said Gladys pointed the finger at their boy. A good Catholic family's name is being ruined by accusations. As if the family did not have enough to grieve over. Their boy has the mind of an eight-year-old because of Gladys. His parents are considering having him put away, so he won't harm anyone like that feeble-minded Harry."

Tears streamed down Hilda's face. She would never have sent Apple to the pharmacy if she could rewind the clock. Harry would still be alive. Wayne would be home with his family.

"Where's Gladys?"

Hilda climbed the stairway in agony with each step. She pleaded from behind the bedroom door. "Come out. Sister Henrietta is waiting in the kitchen."

Apple followed Hilda downstairs to the kitchen one slow step at a time to delay the encounter with the crow.

"Get your clothes packed," Sister Henrietta demanded. "We're leaving today for the mainland." Apple jumped up from the kitchen chair. She would rather be dead than cross the strait to a reform school. A shocked Stan and Hilda eyed each other. "Apple isn't leaving for the mainland. She is staying with us. Hilda and I are going to raise the baby."

"Such foolish talk!" Sister Henrietta screeched. "Gladys is still in the foster care system. I control where she lives and who will be adopting the baby."

Stan interrupted the nun from ranting. "It's already been decided that Hilda and I will raise the baby. Apple wants us to have the baby. She can stay here and get a job and help with the rent."

Apple stood in the middle of the kitchen and screamed, "I am not going to a reform school! I am staying here and giving my baby to Hilda and Stan."

Sister Henrietta screamed back for Gladys to march upstairs and pack a suitcase. She was taking her to a home for unwed mothers in Halifax. In a few short sentences, she explained the home would take care of her until the baby was born and then

Gladys would be on her own. Sister Henrietta would have no more control where she lived or what she did after the birth of the baby.

"How are you are going to raise a baby to be a good Catholic if you couldn't keep Gladys from getting pregnant? Wayne's parents do not need a living reminder of Gladys's wicked ways. It does not matter what the truth is. People are gossiping their son is the father." Her voice softened. "You've been good to Gladys. She ruined it by being boy crazy; that landed her in trouble. I will provide the baby with the opportunity to grow up without being ridiculed about having a braindead father and a fallen woman for a mother. I will find a good, God-fearing home for the infant."

Hilda cried, "We'd be good parents to the child, as good as any parent could be and better." She begged the nun not to take Apple.

The nun closed her eyes as if in prayer before speaking. "It's not going to happen."

"Why send her to Halifax?" Stan inquired with suspicion. "We all know there is a home for unmarried girls expecting a baby right here in Charlottetown. We could visit Apple. She could stay with us on the weekends. Why send her away? If she goes to Halifax, we will not be able to see her."

Hilda became hysterical at the thought of losing Apple and the baby. Stan reached across the table and held her hand to calm her down.

"Apple is like a daughter to us. She is a good girl," Hilda told the nun. "She wanted a boyfriend like the other girls in school. That hockey boy took advantage of Apple and got her in trouble. He treated our Apple as if she were dirt. He tormented poor Harry. And you know it, Sister Henrietta. You know it."

Stan guessed Sister Henrietta probably had an American family lined up to adopt the infant. And all the begging and pleading would never change her mind. He felt his anger bubble up over the unfairness of it all and how much it was hurting his wife and Apple.

"We all know what happens to those babies born to girls at that home," he shouted, taking himself by surprise. We all know why those Americans flock to town. How much do those Yankees pay for the babies you say you find good God-fearing homes for? I saw a woman who works at the home for unwed mothers with a bundled baby in a parking lot we were cleaning up. She gave it to a couple. I saw the United States plates on the car. Everyone in town knows what happens to those babies. God strike me dead right here in the kitchen if I am lying."

"How dare you?" Sister Henrietta sputtered. "You profited from fostering."

Hilda pleaded for the nun to let Apple stay in Charlottetown. "Stan didn't mean what he said. He is just upset. We all are. We will give all the money back to you, a little at a time, if you let her stay. Please, Sister Henrietta. If you want, I will get down on my hands and knees and beg. Please don't take our girl from us."

Sister Henrietta ignored Hilda. Stan had gone too far. No one questioned her authority, especially a blue-collar street cleaner. She would make certain he would pay for what he'd said.

"I am calling the police and will have you both arrested if Gladys is not in the back seat of my car in fifteen minutes." The nun exited the home, sat in the car, and waited with the engine running.

❋

Hilda and Stan stood on the sidewalk and watched with sorrow as the car pulled away from the curb with Apple in the back seat.

Apple had never been off the Island. But ever since Sneakers had warned her about the plan to gang rape her, and even before that—hiding the pregnancy—she'd been locked up in the house. It felt like she was going crazy. At least at the home for unwed mothers in Halifax she'd be safe from the hockey team. She could settle on the mainland after the pregnancy until the hockey team grew up and moved on and Wayne was old news.

The baby was not due for five months. It would give her time to cook up a plan to reunite with Stan and Hilda and let them raise the baby while she laid low in Halifax. She vowed Sister Henrietta would never get her baby.

Millie watched Apple leaving the street from behind a bedroom curtain. She and Walter were dating and hanging out at the hockey rink. Everyone in school—including Millie—believed Apple was to blame for the fight that destroyed a hockey career. Irene warned Millie, if Walter wanted the milk, he'd better be prepared to buy the cow. Millie pledged to never allow Walter to screw her and risk an unwanted pregnancy. She would not become a disgraced woman like Apple.

CHAPTER 14

Sister Henrietta journeyed to New Jersey to meet the Brooks family.

"Dr. and Mrs. Brooks are interested in adopting a healthy baby," Father Regan explained to Sister Henrietta in a telephone conversation. "I told the Brooks family about the homes for unwed mothers you operate and the success of arranging adoptions. They put a hundred-dollar bill in their church envelope last Sunday after our conversation. I'm able to arrange a meeting as early as next week."

No stranger to luxuries, Sister Henrietta arrived at the airport to a waiting limousine. She often visited the American families to check on "her babies." The families treated her like royalty. She wined and dined with wealthy people and pocketed a generous donation with each home visit.

The limousine arrived at the sprawling estate. A butler answered the door and guided the nun to where Father Regan and Dr. and Mrs. Brooks were waiting.

The middle-aged couple were living the American dream of prosperity, but all their money and status could not produce a biological baby. The childless couple turned to adoption and discovered the procedure was complicated and could take years. Sister Henrietta's adoption services did not require home visits by social workers to determine the stability of the home environment, nor was there a waiting list.

"What if the mother changes her mind and decides to keep the baby?" Mrs. Brooks glanced at her husband. Dr. and Mrs. Brooks were generous parishioners. Father Regan would not have the family disappointed by uncertainties. He shot a look at Sister Henrietta with an unspoken message to convince the family the mother would not change her mind and keep the baby.

"The parents are teenagers in high school. It is a small town where people gossip. The girl had to leave town to have her baby in another province. The parents of the teenagers are ashamed and want nothing to do with the baby. It will grow up in an orphanage if I cannot find a good Catholic home. The young girl has been living at a maternity home where she has been well cared for. The baby will be examined by a medical doctor after the birth to ensure the infant is healthy. The young girl has reddish hair, like you, Dr. Brooks. The father is athletic with plans to attend medical school. He got tangled up with a girl trying to trap him into a bad marriage."

Sister Henrietta glanced at Father Regan. His sheepish smiled expressed satisfaction. Father Regan would know for certain if the couple were convinced with the cooked-up story after the Sunday church collection.

"I could have a lawyer start the legal work before the baby is born. You could take the baby home after the birth," Sister Henrietta suggested.

Mrs. Brooks was only half listening. She was being blessed with a baby. Her mind filled with plans of decorating a nursery and shopping for baby accessories and clothing. Father Regan would christen the baby at St. Michael's Basilica followed by a catered reception.

Dr. Brooks motioned Sister Henrietta to join him in the study. The walls were lined with bookshelves and artwork. Large bay windows gave a view of acres of manicured lawn. A gardener was busily watering prized flowerbeds. A large bronze crucifix hung over the doorway of the study. The crucifix Jesus witnessed Dr. Brooks opening a chequebook.

Sister Henrietta gasped at the amount of the cheque. It was more than she'd anticipated. Her voice crackled with emotion, thanking the good doctor for his generosity. Dr. Brooks eyed the sister. He was a respected surgeon, born into a world of privilege, a scholar, and a world traveller. He would not be thought a fool by a silver-tongued fox.

"I will not have my wife denied the opportunity to become a mother. And I am willing to double the amount and pay the legal fees. My wife is an intelligent person but vulnerable to fairy tales out of her desperation for motherhood."

The doctor was aware of the price tag from friends who'd adopted through Father Regan and Sister Henrietta. Father Regan and the nun were not good Samaritans securing good homes for babies born to unwed mothers. The truth did not matter to him. In his world, money had no conscience, just like Sister Henrietta and Father Regan.

"I've seen the sadness in her eyes when friends boast about their children. I watched my wife sink deeper and deeper into a dark hole of depression when she learned she could not have children. She had to be hospitalized and treated for depression. Her mental health would be questioned by an adoption agency. It would only add to the shame and guilt for not being able to conceive. I know of colleagues who've adopted through you and Father Regan. They have been faithful in their continuous generous financial contributions. It would be a shame to have it end if the teenager you speak of changes her mind and decides to keep the baby."

Sister Henrietta smiled at knowing Mrs. Brooks would most likely never experience motherhood without adopting through the church.

"I will not take up any more of your time. You must have several families to visit while in the country." It was her cue to leave; he had no more to say. She stepped out of the study without so much as a thought of the weeping Jesus hanging on the cross over the doorway.

❋

Stan and Hilda had not answered any of her letters. Apple wondered if they had changed their minds about raising the baby. It never dawned on her that the nuns were trashing the letters.

Dear Hilda and Stan, I wish you could visit me. But the nuns would never allow it. The baby is kicking all the time. It must be a boy to be so active. Did you get my last letter? I will never sleep at night if strangers adopt my baby. The baby will be born in another month. You must come soon to be here when the baby is born so you can take him back to the Island. I miss you. Love, Apple

Apple shared a bedroom with seventeen-year-old, Jackie. Apple and Jackie were expecting to deliver around the same time. The two teenagers forged a bond.

Jackie had no intention of giving her baby up for adoption. She was determined to raise the baby with Scott, her boyfriend. They would move in together. Scott would go to university. They would marry after he walked across the stage to accept an engineering degree.

The plan didn't include how he would pay the rent and university fees while supporting a family. Scott's family were more than eager to have their eighteen-year-old son attend university and secure a career. It was not in their plans for him to be saddled with a baby and a girlfriend.

Jackie had been sitting in class when her mother and the parish priest arrived at the high school. Her mother said they were going for a drive. Jackie had no idea where they were going. They arrived at the home for unwed mothers two hours later.

"When I saw the priest, I thought something horrible had happened to Dad. I kept asking Mom where we were going, but she would not answer. I am pretty sure Scott has no idea where I am. And none of my letters are getting to him."

Jackie and Apple approached the office for permission to go for a walk. They promised not to venture far from the home.

"Rules are not to be broken," the administrator warned the pair. "Did you finish all of your chores?"

They assured the administrator they had finished the list of chores. The administrator glared at the teenagers, certain they were telling lies, but was too busy with paperwork to check.

Chores were a daily part of their routine at the three-storey home on a corner of a busy intersection. Beds were to be made, dishes washed and put away, meals prepared, floors swept and scrubbed, laundry and ironing.

Apple hated standing on swollen feet ironing bedsheets. It made little sense to her to iron bedsheets that would just get wrinkled when she slept on them.

A girl had gone into labour while scrubbing a floor on hands and knees. Her water broke. She curled up on the floor and screeched in terror. Jackie and Apple watched not knowing what to do. Fear shot down their spines. Is this what labour would be like? The tormented girl had screamed like a rabbit being skinned alive.

The housemother came tearing into the room from the first floor. She dragged the tearful teenager to her feet. A couple of office staff assisted the housemother. They whisked the young girl to the hospital next door where she gave birth. The young girl never returned to the home for unwed mothers.

Jackie and Apple had speculated in the privacy of the bedroom what had happened. Where did she go after the birth? What had happened to her? Did she get to take her baby when she left the hospital? They stayed up late whispering in the dark. It was long after midnight before drowsiness ended their chatter. The images of the girl screaming in labour haunted their sleep.

❀

The country girls staying at the home hated the congested traffic and the blaring horns of impatient drivers. They cautiously manoeuvred across the pedestrian crossing, fearful of getting hit as they waddled to a nearby park.

Apple didn't stray too far from the home for unwed mothers out of fear of becoming lost. The hilly streets were challenging as the pregnancy progressed.

She and Jackie being small town girls were not accustomed to a fast-paced Halifax. They linked arms and an unexpected surge of excitement encouraged the pregnant teens to explore the city. It was their first feeling of freedom since arriving in Halifax.

"I see a post office up ahead. I will not trust the nuns to mail my letters to Hilda and I just know they will come and take the baby back home with them."

Jackie pulled a letter out of a pocket. "Do you have any money to buy stamps? I don't. Mom said there would be no need for money where I was going."

Apple fished a handful of coins out of a pocket for Jackie.

"I will give you my parents' address and we can keep in touch," Jackie said.

Apple promised to write as well, once she got settled. "What are you going to call your baby?"

Apple didn't have to think before answering. Hilda and Stan had agreed she could name the baby. "I am going to call him Elmer, or Mary-Jane if it's a girl."

Jackie rubbed her belly when Apple asked if she had a name for the baby.

"I'm going to wait to see what Scott wants to call the baby."

Hilda gave Apple an envelope with forty dollars the day Sister Henrietta took her away and warned her not to let the nuns know or they might take it. Apple had pinned the envelope inside her bra where the nuns would never find it. She kept it on her all the time, even while sleeping.

Jackie mailed letters to a girlfriend with instructions to pass the letters on to Scott. She would get word to Scott about where she was staying so he could come and rescue her.

"Let's find a Woolworth's store and treat ourselves to cheese-cake and Cokes," Apple offered. "But don't tell anyone."

❈

Three weeks had passed since the trip to the post office to mail letters and still no word from Scott.

Jackie searched the street below from the third-floor bed-room of the home for unwed mothers with the eye of a hawk. Constant questions nagged her. Why wasn't he coming? Did he know where she was? Had her friend passed on the letter to Scott?

❊

Sister Henrietta grabbed the telephone on the second ring. The voice of Dr. Jay boomed out of the receiver. "An Indian girl had been seen pregnant around Charlottetown, a pretty, dark-eyed Indian with golden brown skin. A social worker visited the girl and learned the father was white."

The social worker had contacted Dr. Jay and scheduled a checkup for the young pregnant woman.

"How far along is she? Do you know if she's on the bottle?" Sister Henrietta asked, suspicious of all Indigenous people. "I do know of an Italian family looking to adopt, but the infant needs to be healthy. Are you certain the father is white?"

Father Florian, a parish priest, had contacted Sister Henrietta earlier with news of an Italian family interested in adopting a dark-haired infant with an olive complexion who could pass as family. Sister Henrietta had arranged adoptions to parishioners in his parish before. They were doing God's work. The babies were going to good and deserving homes. The families were willing to give generous donations to the parish and to the good Sister Henrietta. The donations were their reward for saving babies born to unwed mothers, reckoned Father Florian.

The young Mi'kmaq woman they were talking about, Jean-Anne had moved to Charlottetown with the dream of enrolling in nursing school. She planned to return to the reserve to administer health care to the community with the assistance of Elders using traditional medicines.

Then, on that day, in full daylight, she was attacked. A car had pulled up to the curb and she had been thrown into the back seat. Although she'd fought hard, she could not ward off the two male attackers. They then dumped her on a country back road and sped out of sight. Terrified, she was grateful her life had been spared.

She did not report the attack. In her experience, the police were not to be trusted. The police had threatened to jail her parents when they refused to send Jean-Anne to an Indian residential school in another province.

"The social worker says the girl is sober and living in a boarding house in town to be closer to a hospital," Dr Jay reported to Sister Henrietta "She told the social worker, she is going back to the reserve on the west side of the Island after the baby is born around Easter. She claims the Indian Agent for the band will find a home for her and the baby on the reserve."

"I was told she was nothing but trouble at the residential school, running away and talking back to the nuns, a real wildcat. It is not surprising she got pregnant, but I will make certain her baby-making days are done before she goes back to the reserve."

Jean-Anne would not be the first "Indian" the doctor would sterilize without consent.

"Let the Indian go back to the reserve," Sister Henrietta, racist to the core, told Dr. Jay. "We'll wait till the baby is born and then bring the police with us to the reserve and take the infant."

"I will contact Father Florian and let him know we will have a baby ready for adoption at Easter. It will be an Easter miracle for the Rossi family. The Italians are generous people. In my experience, money can be found for anything that is considered worthwhile by the right people."

❋

Sister Henrietta received a telephone call midafternoon. Another girl had gone into labour. She booked an early-morning flight to Halifax.

The labour started after midnight. A hysterical Jackie woke up Apple. It was too early for the baby to come. "I can't have the baby yet. Scott is not here. He is supposed to come get me. We are going to get married and have more babies after he graduates from university."

She muffled her cries to avoid attention. She had to hold on till Scott came. "He'll be here. He's not late; the baby is early."

The pains were coming quicker and sharper. The young girl squirmed in the bed with agony. "Where's Scott?" she kept repeating as if Apple had the answer. Apple waddled down the three flights of stairs to the apartment of the housemother.

"Can I go with her to the hospital?" Apple begged. "She wants me to go with her. I told her I would." The request was denied. It was against the rules. "You will be crossing the street soon enough to the hospital," was the reply.

The labour pains were intense. Jackie begged for relief, becoming delirious. "It's killing me. Please, I am begging you." The nurse ignored the cries. Sister Henrietta had told the nurse that suffering would redeem the girls from their sin of getting pregnant outside of the sacrament of matrimony. The nun gave strict instructions the unwed mothers were to be denied pain medication. After birth, a prick of a needle would lull the mothers into a drugged sleep. They would wake hours later dazed and confused.

Jackie gave one final scream that announced a newborn had entered the world. A nurse washed the wailing newborn where Jackie could not see her. "Please, give me my baby," she slurred in a weakened tone of voice. A stab of a needle lulled Jackie into a deep medicated sleep.

Scott never came to her rescue. Throughout the pregnancy, Jackie never gave up hope that Scott would find her, and they would be a family of three. The slight tinge of hope she'd clung to was quickly fading.

A couple of days had passed without news of Jackie. Apple snuck out of the home and crossed the street to the hospital. She wobbled through the maternity ward in search of her friend. A nun spotted Apple and alerted security. A burly security guard grabbed Apple by the arm and escorted her across the street to the home for unwed mothers.

"You're not to leave the house," a nun from the home warned her. "If you try to leave, I will be forced to lock you in your room until the baby is born."

The doctor had been summoned to examine Apple after the struggle with the security guard to ensure a healthy birth.

"Keep an eye on her," he told the housemother in charge of the pregnant girls. "She should deliver any day."

A puddle of clear yellow water splashed to the floor as Apple trudged slowly to the bathroom in the early morning. The baby was coming.

The birthing pain was brutal, and it triggered a memory of Agnes screaming from behind the bedroom door. Panic kicked in. Would she die too, like Agnes? The pain ripped through her body with each contraction.

A voice in her head kept telling Apple to push hard. In a bewildered state, delirious with unimaginable pain, a vision of Nana appeared. Apple obeyed the vision and pushed with every ounce of strength she had. Moments later, a son was born, and the vision disappeared.

A nurse drugged Apple after the delivery which dulled the cries of her newborn. It would be a couple of hours before a drowsy Apple woke up in a hospital bed.

❀

Sister Henrietta was still in Halifax and had been summoned to the hospital. Two of the mothers from the home had given birth: one to a girl, the other to a boy. Doctor and Mrs. Brooks were scheduled to arrive and would have the choice to adopt a boy or a girl.

Apple demanded to see her baby. The request was denied. A nurse explained it was better not to see or hold the infant since he was being put up for adoption. Apple experienced a surge of joy discovering she gave birth to a boy. "Please," she begged, "I need to hold my baby."

She hobbled towards the nursery in search of her baby boy. She would not be signing any adoption papers. Apple was determined the nuns were not getting near her precious baby.

"Your baby is not in the nursery," snickered a nurse. "He's gone to a foster home before adoption." Apple screamed and dropped to the floor in agony and tears. Jackie heard the commotion. She helped Apple to get off the floor and guided her to a room.

"They took my baby, too," Jackie sobbed. "I didn't even get to hold her. They said I had a baby girl, and she was healthy. That's all they would tell me." The two friends clung to each other. This was not how their story was supposed to end.

Scott never came to the rescue. He had plans that did not include Jackie and a baby. Her parents would not take her home if she refused to sign the adoption papers.

"I told Sister Henrietta I am going to keep the baby and raise her on my own. I told her I planned to get a job and find someone to take care of my baby while I worked." Jackie stopped talking. Big gulps of cries burst out of her gut. "Sister Henrietta laughed and said, go ahead, leave, and I will have someone bring you the infant. And we will see how far you get with a crying newborn. You'll not make it to the end of the street."

Apple shook her head in disgust.

"She was right. I had nowhere to go and no money for milk or diapers. I begged to hold the baby, just once. But she said, no. She's bringing the papers tomorrow for me to sign. She says there is a Catholic family interested in adopting Eden. I named her Eden. It is an uncommon name, and it will make it easier to find her someday. But I am not signing any papers till I've held her."

The two friends comforted each other with stories about finding jobs, getting a place of their own, and searching for Eden. Apple swore she too would refuse to sign adoption papers. Stan and Hilda were going to raise Elmer.

❀

Apple dressed and hurried to the nursery with a plan to find her baby and leave the hospital before anyone noticed. She did not believe the infant had been sent to a foster home. She'd vowed to protect him from being raised in foster homes when he wiggled in her belly. The baby had to still be in the nursery.

Sister Henrietta discovered Apple at the nursery window looking at the newborns.

"I will not sign the adoption papers. You are not getting my baby. I'm taking him back to the Island to Hilda and Stan," Apple shouted before Sister Henrietta had a chance to speak.

Sister Henrietta had enough drama for one day with Jackie. Why could she not be grateful the baby would be adopted by a good family? But no, it was not enough. She had to be selfish and make demands to hold the infant. She had no rights to the infant. Rights were for married women not for a selfish little sinner.

Sister Henrietta figured it was time for Gladys to get a good dose of the reality of the consequences of being a bad girl for getting pregnant just as Jackie had received earlier. The unwed mothers were weak for giving in to the temptation of sin and this justified the nun's actions.

"You stupid girl," she hissed. "I didn't need your signature on the adoption papers. The infant will be going home with his adoptive parents. You are a minor and under the care of foster services, under my care. My advice is to get as far away from me as possible before I change my mind and contact the reform school and book you a room."

The anger bottled up inside over being mistreated throughout the years exploded like a bomb. The nun was not expecting the slap across her face. "I hate you!" Apple screamed. The nun staggered as Apple pushed her with all the strength she could muster. Sister Henrietta tripped and stumbled to the floor. The hysterical teenager repeatedly kicked the nun in the gut like a mad person.

Apple swore at the heap on the floor curled up in a ball. She gave the nun one final kick in the head and fled the hospital.

"I will not press charges," Sister Henrietta later told a security guard. "She will pay for her crime if she ever crosses my path. Girls like Gladys never learn from their mistakes. She will get tangled up with another lad and end up pregnant. I will have her arrested and the child will go into care."

❄

Dr. and Mrs. Brooks met Sister Henrietta at the airport and learned the good news that two babies were ready for adoption. They would have their choice of a boy or a girl. Mrs. Brooks insisted on driving directly to the foster home where the two babies were staying until adoption.

The baby girl slept while the infant boy squirmed in a bassinet. He was ready for a feeding. "Would you like to give him his bottle, Mrs. Brooks?" She traced the infant's delicate head with a finger. The doctor watched Mrs. Brooks feed their miracle bundle as if she had been doing it for years. "He has a tuft of reddish hair." Dr. Brooks smiled. The nun had been telling the truth about the birth mother having the same hair colour as his. A red-haired child would make it easier for Dr. Brooks to raise him as if he were his own flesh and blood and not an infant born out of wedlock that he had purchased.

"When can we take Joseph home?" she whispered, not to disturb his feeding.

Dr. Brooks glanced at Sister Henrietta for a response.

"He can go home today," she replied. Dr. Brooks asked if the baby had been examined. Sister Henrietta assured the couple the baby had been examined and the doctor declared the infant to be in perfect health.

"He'll be christened Joseph, the patron saint of families and fathers," Mrs. Brooks announced. "My beautiful baby Joseph." She kissed the crown of his head.

Mrs. Brooks counted his toes and fingers and marvelled at the length of the baby; a sign he would grow tall. "Let me try and burp you." She carefully wrapped Joseph in a receiving blanket. She gently patted his back as if he were breakable. The infant rewarded the efforts with a coarse burping sound. Dr. and Mrs. Brooks chuckled.

The infant would soon be boarding the Baby Train to the United States.

CHAPTER 15

Rosa had been born in the hills of Mexico to a plantation worker. It had been her duty to care for seven younger siblings while her parents worked. Her father toiled under a blazing sun to provide for the family. Her mother sold crafts to tourists in the marketplace.

At sixteen, Rosa received a letter from a cousin, Maria, working in the United States. Maria wrote about employment prospects with wealthy families. Rosa convinced her parents that her working in the United States would be an answer to their hardships. It took a year to save enough money to pay a guide to escort Rosa across the Mexican border.

Maria supplied Rosa with travelling instructions to a boarding house that rented to illegal immigrants in the state of New York. She had suggested Rosa try and learn English in preparation for the journey to a new life in America. With false confidence, Maria purchased a bus ticket in English and sat at the back in silence. Her stomach growled, a reminder she had eaten very little since crossing the American border. She fished out crumpled bills from a pouch tied around her neck at a rest stop and purchased strange-tasting American food.

Maria worked as a maid for the Cohen family for years. Mr. Cohen would ask his employees if they could recommend a relative for employment. The employee who recommended a family member would be reprimanded or even fired if the relative had to be dismissed.

Maria recommended Rosa for the position when she learned of a nanny position through her employer.

She assured Mr. Cohen that Rosa had years of experience caring for siblings while her parents worked at a coffee plantation. And her cousin came from the same village. Maria vowed Rosa would be a trusted and loyal employee.

Mrs. Cohen inquired whether Rosa could speak English and was told her English was limited but she was a fast and willing learner. The nanny position required obedience and loyalty secondary to speaking English well explained, Mrs. Cohen. Mrs. Cohen agreed to speak with Mrs. Brooks and recommend hiring Rosa based on recommendations from Maria, her maid. "Mr. and Mrs. Brooks are dear friends. I will not be pleased if your cousin disappoints them." Maria nodded that she understood the consequences.

Illegal immigrants arrived in the United States hungry for work. Mrs. Cohen and close friends were aware of the desperation of the immigrants in need of employment. The Cohen and the Brooks families were wealthy employers, and their staff of mostly illegal immigrants were powerless to argue or speak out if they were dissatisfied with working conditions.

Maria contacted Rosa with the good news of a job offer that came with warnings. She instructed Rosa never to complain or gossip about the family to the Spanish-speaking staff, and never to offer unsolicited childcare advice to Joseph's parents.

She also suggested Rosa bathe every night and not to worry about wasting water like she would back home. "Stay clean and tidy and have a fresh uniform to wear every day. Never pick up things to admire. The rich take their wealth for granted. But do not take anything thinking they will not miss it because they have so much. Everything is catalogued by a maid. You will never earn their trust. Also, the job will end in grief if you become attached to the child. It's important to remember this is a position that you are being paid for."

❀

Rosa packed a few belongings at the rooming house she had been living at since arriving in the country a month earlier. It had been arranged for the driver, Carlos, to pick her up in the family limousine.

Rows of tall trees on both sides of a paved driveway led to a three-storey mansion with towering white pillars at the entrance. A twelve-foot stone fountain with a life-sized statue of an angel stood guard in front of the mansion as if it were a protector of the wealth.

Acres of manicured lawn, rows of rosebushes, and neatly trimmed hedges greeted an astonished Rosa. What would her family think of living in such riches? She knew they skipped meals so their children could have more food to eat. A sudden rush of guilt upset her stomach. The nanny income would be able to support the family back home. This would become the motivation for keeping the job no matter what and relieve her of any guilt about living in wealth while her family struggled.

She asked the driver a question in Spanish, but he answered in English. "A maid is waiting for you and will take you to your room. You are to wait there till Dr. and Mrs. Brooks are ready to meet you." Rosa nodded she understood. "You need to practice speaking English. The family will be suspicious if they hear you speak Spanish to the other staff." A faint smile crossed her face realizing Carlos would become a good friend she could trust.

Rosa stepped across the threshold to a world of wealth. She gasped. Never could she have imagined such wealth even existed and would never have believed it unless she saw it. For one fleeting moment, she wanted to be back in Mexico with her family. But it was too late to think about returning home as she followed the maid to the room next to the nursery. She had no choice but to adapt.

Rosa tried on the blue nanny uniform hanging in a closet. There were other similar style uniforms: cotton blue and white shirts and matching below-the-knee skirts, a couple of blue dresses, a pair of flat brown shoes, and a pair of flat blue shoes. She was provided with white nylons, an outdoor jacket, and blue and white scarves. The clothing fit perfectly. She would later learn Maria had provided Mrs. Brooks with sizes. But the colours were dull in comparison to the colourful Mexican clothing she was used to wearing in her homeland.

The floor-length mirror reflected an image of a slender eighteen-year-old Mexican girl with raven black waist-length hair. A knock on the door signalled Mrs. Brooks was ready to meet her.

Mrs. Brooks provided Rosa with a list of duties that included nighttime feedings and the daily care of Joseph. The family would provide room and board and forty dollars weekly for the first year of service. If the position worked out, she would receive an annual increase and a bonus at Christmas. The monthly wage would be more than what Rosa's father earned in months working for plantation owners.

The nursery had a crib fashioned in the shape of a swan with white padding over the mattress and trimmed with blue satin and silky material. A cushioned wicker rocking chair had been placed next to the crib. On the wall was a gold-framed painting of Jesus with laughing children gathered around Him. Volumes of children's classics lined a bookshelf. A life-sized smiling yellow giraffe stood in a corner. Stuffed animals and teddy bears were everywhere. A large toy box in the shape of a pirate's treasure chest with the letter J for Joseph had been placed in a corner of the room.

Plush yellow and brown rugs covered the hardwood floor. The walls were a soft white colour with a mural of storybook characters hand-painted on one side of the room. Blue floor-length curtains with images of Peter Pan characters covered a bay window.

A shocked Rosa would not have believed the luxuries if she had not seen them. Her family home of clay-based soil and cement supported by a wood frame could easily fit it inside the nursery and the bedsitting room. She walked about the nursery too intimidated to touch anything.

The money Rosa would be sending home to her parents would make life easier. There would be more food on the table. Her father could buy a plot of land and grow vegetables at the marketplace and no longer be at the mercy of plantation owners. The money would allow her siblings to be educated.

Rosa gently picked up and admired one of the many brown plush teddy bears. Her four-year-old sister, Adella, had never seen a teddy bear. The thought of sending a teddy bear to Adella was tempting. But Rosa remembered Maria's warning and put the stuffed toy down. Instead, she'd purchase teddy bears and mail the stuffies to Adella and young cousins living in the hills of Mexico.

The private bedsitting room with a door to the baby's room had a walk-in closet and a private bathroom. It had been furnished with a queen-sized bed. This would be the first time in her life she would not have to share a bed with siblings.

She dropped to her knees, blessed herself with the sign of the cross, and thanked God she'd safely crossed the United States border as other Mexicans fleeing the country in search of employment had not been as fortunate. Rosa praised Jesus for answering her prayers for finding employment that would benefit her family. She prayed for protection from the sin of greed in this new world, the land of the wealthy, and to someday return home to the hills of Mexico.

❀

Baby Joseph woke up for feedings throughout the night. Rosa bathed Joseph morning and evening. She would take the baby to Mrs. Brooks around midmorning and escape to the bedsitting room to nap until Mrs. Brooks returned Joseph to the nursery. Rosa would hum melodies and rock Joseph to sleep. She took Joseph for strolls in a baby carriage along the many pathways around the property that were bordered by flowers, trees, and manicured shrubs. Joseph snoozed in the carriage while Rosa rested on benches next to ponds teeming with goldfish and exotic flora.

"Would you please change Joseph into the new sailor outfit and bring him downstairs before lunch is served? I am expecting a group of women who belong to the Catholic Daughters of America. Make sure the baby is not fussing or drooling. I don't want my friends wondering if something's wrong with him."

Mrs. Brooks was alarmed that Joseph might be intellectually slow because of the drooling. Dr. Brooks had tried to assure his wife that he was just teething, but she still fretted.

Rosa passed Joseph to Mrs. Brooks. The women circled Mrs. Brooks to peer at six-month-old Joseph. The Catholic Daughters of America complimented what a loving mother Mrs. Brooks must be to be blessed with a beautiful, healthy child.

Rosa noticed Joseph becoming fidgety. She feared the baby would start drooling, or crying, knowing this would upset Mrs.

Brooks. "It's time for Joseph's nap," Rosa said with nervousness. Mrs. Brooks was basking in the glow of compliments and wanted to keep Joseph on her knee. His chubby face scrunched into a frown. Rosa knew he was about to burst into tears.

The maid entered and announced lunch was ready. Mrs. Brooks cuddled Joseph close to her bosom. "My sweet little pet. It's time for your nap. Mother will take you for a stroll in the carriage when you wake up. We will feed the goldfish in the pond."

Rosa hurried with Joseph out of the room. She poked a finger into his mouth to act as a soother in case he began crying on the way to the nursery.

Rosa later approached Mrs. Brooks about taking Joseph for a stroll, but she declined. The meeting with the Catholic Daughters of America and organizing the luncheon had tired her.

❊

Joseph was a thumb sucker. It had been rather cute when he was a baby. But now that he was older Mrs. Brooks feared he would be bucktoothed. She told Rosa thumb sucking was as bad a habit as nose picking. People might think Joseph was insecure which would reflect on her parenting abilities. "Do not let him suck his thumb," she instructed Rosa.

Rosa remembered how her younger brother Miguel sucked his thumb, and his teeth were perfectly fine. Her parents never corrected him.

"He just needs a little more love," Father would say. Mother would hug Miguel and whisper in his ear, "You're my special little boy." Before long, Miguel began to feel more secure and stopped thumb sucking.

Rosa never shared how her parents got Miguel to stop sucking his thumb. Such interference could have consequences. Mrs.

Brooks often reminded Rosa that she was hired as the nanny. She reprimanded Rosa. "You are never to hug or cuddle Joseph and steal my little boy's affection."

Dr. Brooks arrived home from the hospital earlier than usual. "You should go upstairs and surprise Joseph before he goes to sleep," Mrs. Brooks suggested. Dr. Brooks opened the bedroom door to see if Joseph was still up. He was sitting up in bed waiting for Nanny to read a storybook. She was busy putting toys away and had not noticed Joseph sucking his thumb.

Father walked out of the room and came back with adhesive tape. "Hold out your hands," he commanded. Joseph began to cry. Rosa could not watch what was going to happen. She quietly exited the room with her heart filled with sorrow. Father taped Joseph's fingers and thumbs together for the night.

❁

Joseph enrolled in kindergarten while his parents took a two-month European vacation. They usually vacationed in the Swiss Alps every year for a few weeks. The mountain air agreed with Mrs. Brooks who had bad spells of depression. Dr. Brooks took advantage of skiing at nearby resorts. They decided to extend their vacation.

It had been arranged for Joseph to have a birthday celebration when his parents returned to the States. Mrs. Brooks reassured a tearful Joseph he would have the best birthday party with miniature horses and a petting zoo, a magician, and all his friends from kindergarten. His mother promised a birthday cake as tall as he was. Father would arrange for fireworks in the evening.

"Father and I will bring home a special birthday gift for you," Mrs. Brooks said.

Joseph began to pout. Tears welled in his eyes. He did not want to wait for a birthday party. "Joseph, you're a big boy," his father scolded. "You are too old for crocodile tears. We will celebrate your birthday, but not until we return from holiday. Mother works hard taking care of you and needs a vacation. I work long hours at the hospital to provide a good home for you and Mother. Don't be such a selfish little boy."

Joseph stood quivering. Father put him in the corner for being disobedient. He would stand in the corner for a long time trying not to cry. "Yes, Father," he muttered. "I will be a good boy and wait for my party."

Dr. Brooks smiled at the response. His father had been strict with him and his brother. Father figured with strict discipline, Joseph, too, would be successful in life.

In the village Rosa came from everyone celebrated a birthday. Early morning, the noise of firecrackers announced a birthday in the village. There would be mariachi music, kid-sized sombreros, maracas for the children, a challenge to see who could break the piñata first, and games.

Rosa wondered how any parent could expect a little boy excited to be turning six to wait weeks to celebrate. Joseph had childhood riches her siblings could only dream about, but her family was richer than Joseph in many other ways. Her heart ached for the unhappy little boy trying not to cry.

"This is the schedule for Joseph. Be certain the maid has his blazer, a white shirt, and black pants ready for Sunday Mass." Rosa glanced at the schedule for piano lessons, horseback riding lessons, and soccer games. "We will telephone once a week before his bedtime."

The maid had been instructed to serve Joseph meals in the dining room. He was used to eating alone. Father worked late most nights and Mother would take meals in her room if she were feeling poorly. But it was different on his birthday. He was moping about the mansion feeling sad and lonely when Nanny approached him.

"You will have dinner in the kitchen with us this evening," Nanny said. He followed her to the back of the house to the kitchen area where the employees ate.

"Happy birthday!" a choir of staff voices shouted. Joseph's face lit up like a ball of sunshine.

The household staff had decorated the kitchen with balloons and colourful streamers. A string of coloured lights dangled across the ceiling. A two-layer birthday cake with blue icing and six long candles graced the decorated table. On a setting table were birthday gifts from the household staff. Carlos took a guitar from a case. Everyone sang "Happy Birthday." "Make a wish and blow out the candles," laughed Nanny. The little boy closed his eyes as if in a deep state of concentration. "What did you wish for? Did you wish for a new pony?" she asked.

"I wasted my wish," he mumbled. "It can never come true."

Nanny broke the no-hugging rule for the first time since arriving at the mansion. Joseph welcomed the comfort of her arms. He dared not say aloud that he had wished she were his mom.

"I wished for another pony," he fibbed.

They toasted marshmallows in a fire pit in the backyard. Joseph had never tasted a hotdog before and savoured the flavour. Carlos lit firecrackers as he would have back home in Mexico to announce a birthday in his village. The sound of merriment, laughter, and fun echoed through the evening air.

Nanny tied a piñata to a tree limb. A blindfolded Joseph twirled around three times and was handed a stick to hit the piñata. He screamed with laughter as he swiped the air with the stick. Nanny allowed him to stay up past his bedtime. Darkness settled and a full moon brightened the night sky. Joseph plunked down on a padded lawn chair mesmerized by the flickering flames in the fire pit. It would be a birthday celebration he would never forget. He wrapped his arms around Nanny at bedtime not wanting to let go.

❋

Carlos stepped out of the limousine and opened the back door for Joseph. Nanny was waiting. "Have a pleasant evening, Master Joseph," said Carlos. Joseph replied with a polite "thank you" as he did every day.

Joseph recognized the car in the driveway. It belonged to the doctor who cared for his mother. It could only mean Mother had another one of her spells.

"Is Mother feeling well?" he inquired in too serious a tone of voice for an eight-year-old child.

"She is feeling poorly," Nanny replied. "You can see her tomorrow if she is feeling better."

Joseph followed Nanny along the pathway of manicured shrubs towards the front door. "Will Father be late getting home from work?" He looked up at Nanny with jet-black eyes begging for the answer he wanted to hear.

"Dr. Brooks will be home in time for dinner. Mrs. Brooks needs her rest. She will be having dinner in her room. You must hurry and change out of your school uniform. You have a piano lesson before dinner."

Joseph could count on Nanny to tell the truth. He wanted to reach out and hold her hand as they walked along, but he was not allowed. Mother had told him not to hold Nanny's hand unless it was for safety reasons.

"Do you think Father will play chess after dinner? Father has been instructing me. I am rather good at the game."

The young lad would rather study the chessboard set up in his bedroom than play the piano. His father was a fierce competitor. Joseph desired more than anything to win not only the game but his father's admiration. Father always won no matter how long he studied the chessboard.

"Dr. Brooks enjoys a good game of chess. He will play another time if he is too busy tonight."

Joseph looked up at Nanny and smiled. His little world was a safe place with her nearby.

❄

Dr. Brooks admired the competitiveness Joseph thrived on. His adopted son was blessed with natural athletic ability that he lacked as a youngster. His own father never encouraged him to participate in sports. Excelling in academics was more important to the family than playing hockey or soccer and sports took away time better spent on studying.

An eleven-year-old Joseph earned the position of team captain of the football team at the Holy Trinity private school he attended. He was a star soccer and basketball player, but hockey was his favourite sport.

Joseph would not be punished for checking another player and he did not have to be polite. Hockey released the anger inside of him of being punished by his father and the frustration of being a little gentleman for his mother. The crowds would go wild the harder he hit and the faster he skated. The reddish curls earned Joseph the name Big Red at school.

He would skate down the ice with speed, slap the puck and score. Hockey was too rough of a sport for Mrs. Brooks to attend. Joseph tried to please his dad for finding the time to watch him. He played harder than usual and with more passion. Joseph would look up at the crowd at his dad. But it was Carlos who drove him home from the game. Carlos would be up early to drive Joseph to the hockey practices and then drive him to and from school.

The private school enrolled privileged students of professional families. Joseph had a particular interest in sciences and math which pleased Dr. Brooks. He would lend Joseph expensive medical books from the study to encourage an interest in Joseph becoming a doctor. It became a duty to groom his son just as his father had groomed him to become a medical doctor.

Joseph cut a striking figure with eyes as black as coal and trickling reddish curls. The navy school blazer complemented his flame-coloured hair. People commented how much he and Joseph looked alike. Dr. Brooks would gush with pride. Joseph had been adopted, but he was his son, his legacy. He would make certain another generation would be successful.

Christmas Day was less than a couple of weeks away. Mrs. Brooks hired professionals to decorate the mansion with Christmas trees, bells, lights, garland, wreaths, angels, snow globes, and nativity scenes. The home was transformed into a Christmas village. Mrs. Brooks became busy planning the annual holiday celebration. It was one of the most talked about Christmas celebrations within elite social circles.

She hired Christmas carollers wearing Victorian apparel to entertain guests, and a professional dressed in a classic holiday Santa Claus suit. The hired Santa would arrive with a red satin bag bursting with presents of expensive bottles of perfume wrapped in glittery pink tissue, chocolates, miniature bottles of champagne, and cigars wrapped in blue tissue for a roomful of people.

Tables were lined with plates piled high with ham and turkey, baby potatoes simmering in creamy sauce and spices, platters of seafood and salads, Christmas puddings, an assortment of appetizers, and bottles of champagne and wine.

The guest list consisted of close friends, hospital colleagues, judges, lawyers, politicians, and the parish priest.

Sister Henrietta was on the guest list because Mrs. Brooks considered her a close family friend.

Extra staff were hired the evening of the party. Rosa was responsible for watching Joseph. "Don't touch anything," Mrs. Brooks warned Joseph days leading up to the party. "Don't go near the tree. Do not touch the ornaments. Stay out of the way."

Rosa was instructed to stay with Joseph in the bedroom in case he wandered downstairs during the Christmas party. "The party is for adults, not for an active eleven-year-old child," she told Joseph. "Your mother is hosting a Christmas party for you and your schoolmates next week."

His mother rented a hall for his Christmas party with hired staff. There would be plates of food, games, prizes, gifts, and entertainment, but it was different from the lavish Christmas party at the mansion. His parties were never celebrated at his home. His mother said the mansion was no place for a group of children running wild.

Joseph wished, just for once, his mother would trust him to behave instead of treating him like a little kid.

He'd snuck out of his bedroom while Nanny was asleep when he was much younger. The Christmas party was in full swing with guests singing and toasting champagne. His mother was mortified when she noticed him standing in the ballroom acting "silly" in front of the guests and wearing only a pair of boxer shorts.

He got punished and Nanny got a warning never to let it happen again, or else.

Joseph drifted to sleep about midnight. The clock struck two-thirty in the morning when Mrs. Brooks had the maid notify Rosa all the guests had gone home.

❀

A mountain of beautifully wrapped gifts had been scattered under a twelve-foot Christmas tree covered with hundreds of twinkling lights and vintage ornaments. Several outdoor trees were gaily dressed for the Christmas season.

Rooms were decorated with ropes of garland, poinsettias in full bloom, a holiday collection of a Christmas village graced table-tops, and a stream of red-and-white satin ribbons crisscrossed ceilings. A life-sized figure of Santa stood in front of one of the several Christmas trees throughout the mansion. Musical glass angels dangled from windows and Christmas wreaths hung on doors. Advent candles stood next to a hand-carved nativity scene on a marble table in the centre of a room. Six decorative five-foot toy soldiers lined the hallway leading to the parlour.

Rosa was shocked the first Christmas she worked for the family. She never dreamed such luxuries existed.

Christmas in Mexico was a religious holiday. There was no Christmas tree with presents. The village children led a procession to church and placed a figure of the Christ Child in a nativity scene. Rosa and her family attended midnight Mass. The family would gather for traditional food, music, and dancing.

The American Christmas did not bring joy to Rosa. She yearned to listen to Spanish-speaking relatives laughing and sharing food and stories. But village celebrations ended for Rosa the day she crossed the Mexican border.

Rosa could never return to Mexico for a visit and risk being denied entrance back into the United States.

Her siblings were now in their teens. Her parents had aged. The money she wired home had been put to good use. It built a new home for her family with more rooms than the two-room shelter. Her father had purchased land to grow vegetables for the family. Her wages allowed her siblings to be educated.

Rosa traced a photograph of the family with a finger. Tears spilled from her eyes. The siblings were smart-looking wearing school uniforms Rosa had paid for. An education in Mexico was rare for the children of plantation workers. Being educated allowed her siblings to have better employment opportunities than slaving in coffee fields or working in wealthy American homes.

The Brooks family would be jetting to visit relatives in Miami after Christmas Day. Rosa had travelled with the family to Miami in the past, but this year she would not be joining them. They would be vacationing with a family living in Miami who had their own Nanny.

The resort trips were not a paid vacation but work caring for Joseph. This year, she would enjoy the freedom of reading, writing letters, and going for long walks without interruption. She planned to visit Maria, the cousin who recommended her for the nanny position with the Brooks family.

"Rosa," Mrs. Brooks said as they were packing up. "You and Joseph are to bag toys to donate to charities. He has a roomful of toys he no longer plays with. Christmas is coming. He'll need the space for the gifts he will be receiving."

Rosa and Joseph looked around the room not knowing where to start.

"We will pile the toys you want to keep in this corner," Rosa instructed. "We'll put the ones you don't want to keep in boxes for charity."

Joseph watched as Rosa examined an action figure Joseph seldom played with. The toy would have entertained Rosa's young cousins for hours along with the boxes of toys destined for the charity bins.

"I'm going to keep this one." Joseph put the action figure with the pile in the corner along with a dozen more action toys.

"What do you want for Christmas, Joseph?"

He shrugged and replied, "I don't know. What do you want for Christmas, Nanny?"

Rosa did not dare share her Christmas wish was to go home and be with family. "Christmas is the season for giving and not just receiving," she said as she glanced at the discarded toys waiting for eager little children. "You're giving away toys to children who might not have gifts Christmas morning. What you are doing is very special and in the true spirit of Christmas." Rosa smiled at Joseph.

Joseph wished he could hug Nanny. He had no use for the toys being donated to charity, but Nanny made him feel special for giving them away.

"What will you give away this Christmas?" Joseph inquired. "My mother gives clothing to charity."

Rosa thought before answering. She had few personal possessions worthy of giving away to the less fortunate. She wore uniforms and had little need for street clothes. The family provided her with a bedsitting room on the third floor. She received a household allowance separate from her wages.

He overheard Mother say Rosa had adjusted well to living with the family despite being uneducated and coming from nothing. He thought Nanny was very smart and kind. It did not matter to Joseph if Nanny came from nothing, as his mother proclaimed. He guessed Rosa did not have extra stuff like his mother to donate to charity. He changed the subject and talked about hockey.

Rosa helped Joseph carry suitcases downstairs the day the Brooks family were leaving for Miami.

"I forgot a book in my room to read on the plane." Joseph bolted up the stairs two at a time and pulled out a box from under the bed. He raced up the back stairs to the third floor and dropped the box in front of Nanny's room with a note.

Rosa discovered the box outside the door with her name on it. With curiosity, she opened it and found the twelve action figures she had admired. Had Joseph discovered the true meaning of giving at Christmas?

She would have Carlos drive her to the post office later in the day with the box of action figures destined for children living in the hills of Mexico, and not as charity but as gifts from her heart.

❈

The Brooks family attended Mass every Sunday and the family, including Rosa, went to confession every month. Thirteen-year-old Joseph had little to confess and hated whispering boyish sins to a priest listening behind a small screen in the dark. But the teachers at the private Catholic school he attended said God sees everything you do, the good and the bad. And telling the priest sins was the same as telling God. An embarrassed Joseph confessed to not listening to his parents, lying to the teachers, and misbehaving at home.

Schooldays began with prayer and attending Mass in the school chapel. Religious courses were part of the school curriculum. Mother had groomed him to join the priesthood since he could remember. It would make her the envy of the members of the Catholic Daughters of America of which she held the esteemed role as president.

✾

A familiar black Cadillac with a Canadian license plate parked in the circular driveway could only mean Sister Henrietta was visiting. Every year, the adoptive families received a Christmas card from Sister Henrietta. She drove to the States from Canada at Christmas to visit with the adoptive families and would leave with a generous monetary donation.

Mrs. Brooks treated the visitor like royalty and orchestrated every detail in preparation for the visit. Cleaning staff worked extra hours to ensure the mansion was gleaming.

Joseph learned at an early age to be on his best behaviour when the nun visited. His mother would reward him with a spending trip to a sporting store.

✾

Nanny escorted thirteen-year-old Joseph into the drawing room where visitors were entertained. Sister Henrietta stood and greeted Joseph. "You've grown tall since my last visit. You are the image of your father with that mop of reddish hair. Tell me, Joseph, do you enjoy school?"

Mrs. Brooks answered for Joseph. She glowed with pride and bragged about his academic achievements. "Tell Sister Henrietta what you are going to be when you grow up."

He glanced at Dr. Brooks. Father expected Joseph to attend medical school. On rare occasions, he allowed Joseph to enter the study with strict instructions to sit, listen, and not touch anything. Dr. Brooks talked about the importance of his job at the hospital that earned respect from colleagues. On occasion, Joseph accompanied Father to work. He would be fascinated by patient monitors, surgical tables, EKGs, anesthesia machines, electrosurgical units, and other necessary pieces of hospital equipment. Father would explain the purpose and use of the equipment to an interested Joseph. Father would tell Joseph he, too, could become a doctor someday. Joseph would nod in agreement.

"I'm going to be a priest someday," he said as Mother gushed with pride.

Mrs. Brooks had Joseph recite the Apostles' Creed in Latin for Sister Henrietta followed by reciting the Ten Commandments. Sister Henrietta clapped with delight. Dr. Brooks frowned.

"Play for us before lunch is served, darling." Joseph played Mozart on a grand piano in a corner of the room. His mother had studied music and had been an accomplished pianist in university. Joseph had mastered the keys but had no interest in playing. He played only to make Mother happy.

❀

For the church to grow and prosper in the future required more priests and nuns. A family Sister Henrietta had visited earlier in the week had adopted an infant the nun arranged. The now eighteen-year-old girl planned to enter the convent.

Sister Henrietta had devoted her life to being a servant of the church and to God. She bragged about saving countless lost little souls from the sins of their unmarried mothers by finding good American homes that could provide the comforts of privilege and the guidance of religion. The priesthood and sisterhood would be their redemption from being conceived out of sin.

"Lunch is served in the dining area," announced a maid. She served a platter of lobster, a silver bowl with jumbo shrimp on a bed of ice, brown rice mixed with slices of tender beef, heaping bowls of roasted seasoned vegetables, mashed potatoes, tossed salads, and warm bread served on a silver tray. For dessert, the maid served a tray of white-chocolate-dipped strawberries with specialty teas and rich gourmet coffee.

Dr. Brooks invited Sister Henrietta to his study after they finished dining. She thanked Mrs. Brooks for the luncheon and wished Joseph success with his studies.

"Joseph is doing well," Sister Henrietta remarked once they were in the study. "You and Mrs. Brooks are obviously proud of your son, and rightfully so. He is a credit to both of you."

Dr. Brooks remained silent. Mrs. Brooks enjoyed such flattery, but he had no time for it. He suspected Sister Henrietta had been encouraging Mrs. Brooks to groom Joseph for priesthood as payment for arranging the adoption. It was obvious from their exchanged expressions when Joseph announced he wanted to become a priest. He knew of an elite Italian family that had adopted a boy through Sister Henrietta. The adoptive father told Dr. Brooks he had sworn to God their son would become a priest. He owed it to the good sister for arranging the adoption. There was no higher honour than a son entering the priesthood, he told Dr. Brooks.

"My son will not be the sacrificial lamb for the church in exchange for the privilege of parenthood," he later informed a shocked Sister Henrietta. "Joseph is being raised with privileges that he would never have if it were not for me. He will do what I tell him to do. What better legacy than to have a son walk in his father's footsteps? Joseph will respect my decision just as I respected my father's wishes; he will enter medical school."

His tolerance of Sister Henrietta had been growing thinner with each visit. Dr. Brooks took out a chequebook. Sister Henrietta scanned the amount. She fumed with anger and slapped the cheque on the desk.

"There will be no more visits to my home." He motioned her to leave.

"What would Mrs. Brooks say knowing you threw a woman of God out of your home?" Sister Henrietta asked with a smug expression. "Without me, you would never have been able to adopt a baby, with her medical records of being institutionalized for depression and mental illness. She knows this and will keep the promise she made and groom Joseph to become a priest."

Dr. Brooks opened a desk drawer and removed a key. The key opened a steel box concealed inside a filing cabinet. Inside were returned personal cheques he wrote to Sister Henrietta that tallied more than two hundred thousand dollars.

"I have powerful allies. It would be a shame if it were to leak to the authorities the extortion of money in exchange for Joseph. Child trafficking is illegal. Not even the Pope would be able to protect you if I were to go public. You are to leave my home and never return. I am sure you have other families to visit while you are in the country."

Sister Henrietta slammed the cheque on the desk and stomped out of the study. Dr. Brooks took the cheque for one dollar and placed it in the steel box.

CHAPTER 16

It had been two years since Apple attacked Sister Henrietta at the hospital. Hilda and Stan left Charlottetown and moved to Saint John, New Brunswick and rented a three-bedroom house. Apple and Sneakers pitched in with their share of the rent and filled the fridge with groceries. They settled in a new city where no one knew their history with Sister Henrietta.

The wind and the rain battered the house at the end of a quiet street in Saint John. Apple cuddled next to Sneakers in bed. She could hear the rhythm of his breathing in the dark. She felt protected for the first time in a long time. The nightmares of crows pecking at the bedroom window were becoming less frequent.

Apple announced the unplanned pregnancy to Hilda before telling Sneakers. She shared with Hilda the fear of Sneakers leaving and the fear of having another baby snatched at birth. "I will die if I lose another baby," she sobbed. "I don't want Sneakers or you to think I got pregnant to replace my baby boy. My arms ache for him, and I could never replace him if I had a dozen more babies."

Hilda listened with empathy. She, too, shared Apple's fear. Sister Henrietta had robbed her of becoming a parent to Apple's baby. "You have to tell him before he figures it out," she told Apple. "You will not be alone as long as Stan and I are breathing."

Apple risked whispering the baby news after a night of sweet lovemaking. Her body stiffened, preparing for rejection.

Sneakers reached out and pulled Apple close and smothered her in kisses in the darkness of the night.

The preparations began. Stan purchased paint to transform a room into a nursery. Hilda purchased knitting needles and wool. It would be a winter baby in need of warm clothing.

The days and weeks passed, but Apple refused to go to a doctor.

"I will not risk going to doctor appointments," she told Hilda. "Sneakers will take me to the hospital when I am ready to deliver. I will have the baby and leave. Sneakers gave me a wedding ring to wear, and we are going to pretend we are married. We will use a phoney address so no one can track us down. Sneakers has it all planned."

Hilda agreed with the arrangement. It was better than causing suspicion or a trail for people like Sister Henrietta to follow.

Frankie was born in the dead of winter in the early seventies.

Sneakers took Apple to the hospital in a cab and never left her side. Hilda and Stan waited at home for the baby news. They were finally going to be grandparents.

"She's a girl. Why do you want to give her a boy's name?" Apple quizzed Sneakers at the hospital.

Sneakers had been named Frank after his father who had been killed in a car accident when he was a boy. His mother had had no means of caring for Frank Junior and his older siblings. The siblings had been farmed out to neighbours looking for extra workhands on farms or in households. Frank Junior had been too old for adoption and too young to be farmed out. He entered the foster system in the fourth grade.

"Frankie is a tough name to give a girl. If she has a tough name, she will not become a sissy and be bullied. What's wrong with naming our daughter after me?"

Sneakers would cradle the infant in his arms long after she had gone to sleep. "Daddy's little girl," he would whisper. "My sleeping little Tinker Bell."

❀

Four-month-old Frankie snoozed in a crib across the hallway in a bedroom with enough space for a crib, a dresser, and a changing table. Stan had painted the room in a creamy colour with blue trim. Sneakers had tacked a kite to the wall and glued the long, colourful tail of the kite across one side of the bedroom. Apple had decorated the room with cut-out images of the Disney character, Tinker Bell.

But nightmares of losing her firstborn plagued Apple. Most nights, she would get out of bed and check on Frankie. One night she peeked into Frankie's room and screamed. Frankie was not in her crib. Sneakers came running. "She's gone. The baby is gone."

Hilda staggered up the stairs out of breath holding Frankie. She had gone downstairs to warm a bottle of milk and taken Frankie with her. Trembling, Apple grabbed Frankie.

"No one is ever going to take Frankie from us. I promise." Sneakers guided Apple back to the bedroom. "She's our baby girl. We're a family."

The crows pecked the bedroom window and cawed without mercy. Deep in sleep, she dreamed Sister Henrietta was lurking downstairs in the dark searching for Frankie. Her screams for help woke the baby sleeping between them.

Sneakers cursed Sister Henrietta under his breath for traumatizing Apple. He whispered in the darkness of the night, "Go back to sleep. The nuns will never take Frankie from us. I promise. Close your eyes, and sleep."

Apple came downstairs with Frankie early the next morning. Hilda was buzzing around the kitchen preparing a plate of food for Stan.

"I am right sorry for scaring you last night. I got up to go to the bathroom and stopped to check on the baby. She was just waking up for a feeding. And I took her downstairs to let you sleep." Big tears rolled down her face. "That dirty old nun will never get near that little bundle of happiness in your arms."

Apple looked like a racoon with big black circles under her eyes from lack of sleep. Hilda placed a strong cup of tea and toast on the table for Apple. "Would you hold the baby for me while I sip my tea?" It was her way of communicating she still trusted Hilda.

❅

It was Frankie's first Christmas, and the house was filled with excitement. There would be baking, cleaning, wrapping, and hiding presents. Stan came home after work as excited as a kid. "What's in the bag?" Hilda eyed up a bulging brown bag with curiosity. "That's for me to know and you to find out," he joked. Hilda hid wrapped gifts in the hall closet. Sneakers hid unwrapped gifts under the bed. Apple hid presents in a bedroom closet. Stan stuffed gifts in a dresser. He would pick up Frankie and bellow, "Ho, ho, ho! Santa is coming soon."

Stan and Hilda took a row of film of ten-month-old Frankie sitting under a Christmas tree mesmerized by twinkling strings of lights. On Christmas Eve, the family gathered in the living room. The doorbell rang. Stan checked his watch. "I'll get it," he said and winked at Hilda. In came Santa with a burlap sack over a shoulder. He roared. "Ho, ho, ho. Have you been a good little girl?" Santa placed the sack next to Frankie. He pulled out a rag doll larger than Frankie that Stan had purchased earlier in the week and passed on to "Santa" (his friend, Jack), along with candy canes and chewy chocolates. The fat little man had a fake beard and was dressed in a red Santa coat with white trim, a red stocking hat, black rubber boots, black workpants, and a pair of white potato gloves. Apple became concerned the strange-looking Santa would frighten Frankie, but she grabbed the dolly and smiled at the chubby little man.

Stan had asked Sneakers and Apple for permission for Santa to visit Christmas Eve. He explained Jack worked on the docks and played Santa for those who could afford to pay five bucks. "He has a big family to feed. He's not even Catholic, has no connections to the church. It is Frankie's first Christmas. What's Christmas without a visit from Santa?"

Apple reluctantly agreed. The fear of losing a second baby caused her not to trust anyone, not even Santa. All week, she had been thinking of her other baby, Elmer. Where was he? Who had adopted him? What kind of Christmas would he have? Would there be gifts under the tree for him?

She had hated foster-home Christmases; she had been treated like a rented kid. The parents bought their own kids the nicer presents and they would open their gifts first. She would receive socks and mittens. It disturbed her greatly that Elmer might be treated like a rented kid, like she was.

She never forgot the year a "real kid" got a music box for Christmas. A tiny ballet dancer twirled as twinkling music played. Apple had waited till the real kid got tired of playing with it and put it back under the tree. Apple picked up the music box. The real kid punched Apple in the arm for touching it.

"Santa must have a busy night ahead of him." Stan walked the fat little man to the door. "Here you go, Jack." He slipped a five-dollar bill into Jack's outreached hand.

Christmas gifts mysteriously appeared under the tree. Most of the gifts were for Frankie bought at a downtown discount store.

Hilda and Stan did not go to church in Saint John out of fear of encountering someone connected to Sister Henrietta. What if she called the police and charged Apple with assault? If she did, the police might arrest Apple. It was just too risky for the couple to attend Mass.

But on Christmas Eve, warm memories of attending midnight Mass occupied Hilda's thoughts. "Let us go to midnight Mass. There is a church not far away. Please, Stan. It does not seem right not to go. Even the Protestants attend midnight Mass Christmas Eve," begged Hilda.

Stan agreed. They bundled up against the cold and walked arm-in-arm to midnight Mass, a good twenty-minute walk in the snow and cold.

Apple and Sneakers cuddled on the sofa. Craziness and hoodlums sneaked around late at night even on Christmas Eve. Mass would not be over until about one in the morning and an older couple like Stan and Hilda would be easy targets walking home long after midnight. Sneakers did not want harm to come to the couple. It was his duty to protect Stan and Hilda from people much like himself, prowling the streets late at night looking for opportunity. He planned to meet Hilda and Stan outside of the church and safely escort the couple home.

"Do you think we will always be happy, Sneakers? I never want our happiness to end."

His arms tightened around her plump waist. She accepted him on his terms. She never questioned the late nights he came home with a pocketful of cash. Or the times he stashed cartons of cigarettes under the bed, to be sold on the illegal market. Even Stan and Hilda ignored any shenanigans if he did not bring trouble home.

The woman nestled in his arms never drilled him with questions the night he came home with a blood-soaked shirt. Apple had simply sponged his back with warm water and bandaged the knife wound. Sneakers considered Apple a prized catch. No other girl could ever match her. "We'll have a thousand Christmases together." He planted a kiss on her head as she drifted peacefully to sleep in his arms.

❄

The next morning, the house came alive with the magic of Christmas. "Santa came last night!" yelled an excited Apple. "Get out of bed, everyone. Christmas is here. Come on, Sneakers, get out of bed! It's Christmas morning. It's time to open the gifts." She dashed downstairs carrying Frankie. "Grab the camera, Hilda. It's Frankie's first Christmas."

The family gathered under the Christmas tree. The adults encouraged Frankie to unwrap gifts and she screeched with delight as she ripped the wrapping paper.

Sneakers had stocked the fridge with holiday food that Hilda and Stan could not afford to buy. Hilda and Apple buzzed about the kitchen preparing a feast. Stan strummed a guitar and sang one Christmas song after another while Sneakers and Frankie played with the Christmas toys.

❄

Hilda bustled about the kitchen, packing a lunch for Stan on a Monday morning in early spring. Dishes clattered. A tea kettle hissed on the back stove burner. Stan was in a hurry to get down to the docks to load the fishing boats that were due to arrive.

Fourteen-month-old Frankie sat in the highchair. Bright blue eyes followed Hilda around the kitchen. "Be good for Nana." Stan plunked a kiss on her forehead. "Gramps will bring you home a surprise."

"She's always good, aren't you, darling? Now, get to work, Gramps," teased Hilda. "You're going to be late for the docks."

Hilda locked the door behind him. The front and back doors were kept locked even while someone was at home. No one could enter without a key. The house rule gave the family a sense of security knowing no one could enter their home without permission.

❄

Sneakers was still sleeping when Apple came rushing down the stairs. She popped bread in the toaster. She did not have to be at Woolworth's for a half hour.

"Sneakers got our share of the rent money." She plunked fifty dollars on the table.

Sneakers worked nights at a popular bootlegging joint. On the outside, the place had an appearance of a well-kept home and not what one might expect of a bootlegging establishment. Inside were a pool table, a bar, tables and chairs, and a back room for poker games. The owner, known only as Muskrat, was a no-nonsense type of guy who kept a pistol under the bar. The illegal drinking establishment was located smack in the middle of Saint John and attracted all sorts: the blue-collar workers, welfare people, the middle class, and the wealthier folks.

Sneakers had been working for Muskrat since arriving in Saint John. He was right for the job. He had the ability to recognize an undercover police officer and wasn't afraid to get hurt throwing troublemakers out the door. Sneakers served alcohol and was bold enough to confront agitated drunks wanting to drink now and pay later.

Muskrat paid Sneakers thirty in cash at the end of the night. On occasion, Muskrat gave Sneakers an extra twenty-dollar tip.

Hilda and Stan never questioned Sneakers when he gave the couple a new toaster or other merchandise. They now had a colour television, thanks to Sneakers. Where and how he got money and merchandise were none of their business. But Apple knew. She had witnessed Sneakers on many occasions leaving a shopping mall with unpaid merchandise and food.

The thieving did not bother Apple. She rationalized the stealing as compensation for the times she and Sneakers had been robbed of being protected or valued. And the many times fostering payments were not used for much-needed clothing and new shoes and winter boots. If the system had done its job and provided better opportunities when they aged out of foster care, Sneakers would not have to steal.

He was her protector and took loving care of her and Frankie. And he was better than the "law-fearing" people she had encountered in life.

It was noon when Sneakers came downstairs. He grabbed Frankie out of a playpen set up in the living room. She screamed with delight as he twirled her around in the air.

"Daddy got paid last night. He is going out and buying his baby girl a new dolly." He pretended to be a dog and chased a toddling Frankie who screamed with laughter.

"You're going to get her too excited, and she won't nap," Hilda told him. "It's a nice day to take her out for a ride in the stroller."

Sneakers ignored Hilda. Why wait to play with Frankie when she wanted to play now? He would not be around later to take her outdoors for a stroll.

"Would you like Daddy to bring you home a big dolly? Daddy will find the biggest dolly in the city."

"You and Stan are going to spoil her, you will. Apple takes home more stuff from work than Frankie could ever use."

She placed Frankie in a playpen and picked up an armful of stuffed animals scattered around the floor and flung them in with her. Frankie hurled a stuffed toy out of the playpen. Sneakers chuckled. He picked it up and threw it back in the playpen. Frankie threw the stuffed toy back at Sneakers in a fit of giggles.

"Me and Apple grew up with nothing. Things are going to be different for our Frankie."

❀

Stan and Hilda were pleasant to the neighbours but did not socialize with anyone on the street. With spring in the air, mothers were out pushing baby strollers in the warm sunshine. Hilda treasured the days of pushing Frankie in a stroller. The baby had been a true blessing. If Stan was home, he and Hilda argued about who was going to push the stroller. They came to a mutual agreement. Stan would push the stroller downtown and Hilda would push the stroller back home.

❀

Hilda and Stan had not returned to church since Christmas Eve, but Catholic guilt gnawed at their conscience which caused sleepless nights. "I can feel the heat of the Devil next to me in bed, Stan, tormenting my soul for not attending Mass."

It was a huge church the couple surmised. They could sit at the back. Be the last people in and the first people out.

Father Pat had been at the back of the church greeting parishioners. Hilda and Stan could not escape the parish priest. He made it his business to know the congregation.

"Welcome." The priest extended a hand. Stan shook it and introduced himself and Hilda.

He seemed nice and friendly thought Hilda. With a slight smile, she shook the extended hand. The priest could not remember seeing the couple at church.

"Are you new to the parish?" The question hung in the air as Hilda waited for Stan to answer. "Yes, Father. We are," he stammered, wishing the priest would greet another parishioner. But the priest became suspicious that Stan was acting edgy. The one-sided conversation continued.

"Where are you from?" The priest inquired in a demanding tone of voice.

Priests held great power and demanded respect when entering a room. People stood taller and were careful with their words when speaking with priests. And parents hushed children with warnings to behave and not to make a sound. People agreed with the priest regardless of their own opinions or thoughts; to do otherwise was disrespectful.

The priest was a holy person with religious connections to a God that determined who entered the Kingdom of Paradise or the fires of hell.

Hilda began silently praying Stan would not say "Charlottetown." But he did.

A husband and wife approached the priest with their eight-month-old baby requesting the priest to bless their son. It was as an opportunity for Stan and Hilda to escape.

"Why did you tell him where we are from? What if he knows Sister Henrietta?"

A defeated Stan tried to comfort Hilda "We will sit in the middle of the church next Sunday and exit through the back entrance. If we stop going it will look like we are trying to hide something."

The next Sunday Hilda and Stan blended in surrounded by the other parishioners. They snuck out the back exit at the end of mass while Father Pat greeted parishioners at the front of the church.

Hilda encountered Father Pat as she was pulling the stroller out of the house later in the week. He had been in the neighbourhood visiting a shut-in and recognized Hilda and approached her. Bright-eyed Frankie smiled at the priest when he stopped to chat.

"Who's this little angel?" He asked with curiosity.

"This is my granddaughter," replied Hilda. It was not the truth, but nor was it a lie. Frankie was not blood, but she and Stan were considered grandparents. "I take care of her while her parents are at work." Too much information, but it was too late.

"What's her name?"

"Frankie."

"Frankie," Father Pat repeated. "Is it a nickname?"

Hilda told a lie to a priest for the first time in her life. "Frankie is short for Francesca."

Father Pat could not recall seeing the baby or her parents at church. There were three Catholic churches in the town. He wondered if the parents were Protestants, or perhaps the parents did not attend church which was considered a deadly sin.

"What church do they go to?"

The truth would have shocked the priest. Sneakers said he would rather be beaten to death than have his sweet little girl enter any church.

"Where did they have the baby baptized?"

Hilda told more lies to a priest.

"She was baptized in Halifax. Her parents moved to Saint John for better paying jobs."

Father Pat did not seem convinced. The lies continued to flow. "Her parents plan to take her to church when she's older. She would only fuss and disturb people right now."

Father Pat leaned down and blessed Frankie with the sign of the cross on her forehead with his thumb. He took note of the reddish hair under a bright orange bonnet. A ginger baby, he mused.

Hilda pushed the stroller down the street as far away from Father Pat as possible. She reached the corner and glanced back at Father Pat watching her.

She now had a deadly sin on her soul for telling a pack of lies to a priest and was in desperate need to go to confession—but not to Father Pat.

Father Pat noted that Hilda acted nervously and had been anxious to get going. Grandparents raved about their grandchildren, but this couple had never mentioned a granddaughter or having family living in the city when he greeted Stan and Hilda after Mass. He became suspicious Hilda was hiding something, but what?

It would be best, Hilda figured, not to mention the encounter with Father Pat to Sneakers and Apple. She and Stan would figure out what to say to Father Pat should he ever ask about their granddaughter or ask questions about her parents.

Hilda and Stan decided not to attend church the following Sunday. It would be a sin to take Holy Communion because she didn't go to confession. Father Pat might wonder why she did not go to communion and become suspicious.

It was challenging for Hilda and Stan to separate their religious beliefs from personal values. They didn't want to stop going to church nor did they want to encounter Father Pat out of fear of him asking more questions about Frankie and her parents. Dealing with Sister Henrietta had taught Hilda and Stan that the church lacked mercy and understanding for removing Apple from their home and for denying the opportunity to adopt Apple's baby.

"Let's attend Mass at another church," Stan suggested.

"Father Pat might find out and wonder why," replied Hilda. "He knows where we live, and we can't risk having him show up on our doorstep. What are we going to do?"

Panic kicked in. "I will not sleep a wink at night with a mortal sin on my soul. What if I were to have a heart attack and not have gone to confession?"

Stan and Hilda hiked across the city to a Catholic church later in the week. Hilda slipped into a darkened confessional box. Teary-eyed, voice cracking with emotion, she whispered to the listening priest. "Please forgive me, Father, for telling lies to a priest." There was no need to give details, but the listening ears probed for more information. "What lies did you tell?" A trapped Hilda replied. "I lied to protect my family," she replied, sniffling. The elderly priest had a demanding workday, feeling exhausted, he gave absolution and penance without probing for more information. A hot meal and a warm bed were waiting for him.

People in the province endured months of a harsh Atlantic winter and welcomed the spring season.

The warmer days melted stubborn patches of snow. Bright spring flowers popped up on lawns. Animals came out of hibernation in search of food and a mate. The Canadian geese came home. The days were longer, and the air warmer.

Spring arrived in all its glories with a promise of new beginnings and transformations. But an unwelcome new beginning lurked in the shadows waiting to pounce on an unsuspecting Apple and Sneakers.

Sunday was family day for Sneakers. It was also a busy day for bootleggers. The establishment owners offered to pay extra for Sneakers to work the door—but he declined and devoted Sunday to Apple and Frankie.

Sunday was playtime at the park or spending time exploring the city. They would end the day with a stop for milkshakes, burgers, and fries. Sneakers and Apple would laugh at the antics of Frankie dipping fries into a mountain of ketchup. The toddler would make funny faces as she slurped mouthfuls of a milkshake. Sneakers and Apple would bathe Frankie and tuck her into her crib in the early evening. Sneakers would later guide Apple to their bedroom and close the door. "I love you, Sneakers," Apple whispered under the bedcovers as they embraced.

Hilda and Stan thought it best not to mention the blessing Father Pat had bestowed on Frankie to Sneakers and Apple. There was no point, they figured, in upsetting the parents.

Sneakers and Apple got Frankie ready for a trip to the park a couple of weeks after Father Pat had blessed their baby girl.

Instead of pushing Frankie in a stroller, Sneakers carried her on his shoulders. Their laughter echoed through the air as they strolled through the streets. A cat sprang out of an alley. Frankie went wild with excitement. "No, she can't have a cat," Sneakers answered before Apple could ask. "We're too busy to take care of a pet and it would be extra work for Hilda."

Father Pat had been visiting a shut-in after church near the street Hilda and Stan lived on. He saw a couple with a toddler riding on the shoulders of the man and recognized Frankie with her ginger hair and wearing an orange bonnet. He judged the man to be scruffy with stringy, dirty hair, wearing a black leather jacket, worn out blue jeans, and noticeable stubble on his face.

The woman had reddish hair like the child. They had to be the parents of Hilda's granddaughter. He stepped across the street and walked behind the couple.

"Pretend Daddy is a horsey and yank his hair to make him go faster." The child grabbed a fistful of hair, much to the delight of the woman.

"Cut it out," the man said when Apple playfully pulled his hair.

"Don't be such a sissy. I'm only having fun."

"That's a cute little angel on your shoulder," Father Pat said to Sneakers. Apple turned and noticed the white clerical collar. Father Pat read the fear in her startled eyes.

"We're minding our own business, and you should do the same," Sneakers snarled with stone-cold eyes. He grabbed Apple by the hand. "Let's go back home," Apple begged. Sneakers took long strides towards the park.

"We're taking Frankie to the park to play on the swings like we said we would."

Father Pat stood on the street and watched the couple. He wondered why the young mother feared him. He recalled how Hilda acted cagey, perhaps out of shame. Perhaps the couple were living in sin. The father dressed like a common thug. The mother had to be in her teens. Perhaps the baby had not been baptized after all. He would make it his business to learn the truth about Stan and Hilda.

❀

Sneakers entered the kitchen without making a sound as Hilda washed dishes. She turned around and jumped. "For pity's sake, don't sneak up on me like that."

Sneakers picked Frankie up out of the highchair. "Hey, baby girl, you be good for Grandma while Daddy is out working, and I'll bring you home a surprise."

Sneakers hugged the toddler. She screamed with delight as he spun her around the room.

Sneakers had grown up as tough as old army boots and would fight the Devil if he had to, but Frankie had him wrapped around her little finger. "Stay, Daddy." Big fat tears rolled down a chubby face.

He cuddled Frankie till the sobbing stopped. "Tell Grandma to give you a cookie." It worked. Frankie held out her arms for Hilda. Sneakers disappeared while Hilda distracted Frankie with a treat.

Sneakers forgot to lock the front door behind him in his haste to leave.

Hilda placed Frankie in a wooden playpen in the living room. The toddler snuggled under a blanket with a bottle of milk while Hilda cleaned the bathroom and collected dirty laundry.

Hilda heard the front door open and close. Apple would still be working unless she was not feeling well. Stan worked the docks till five. If it were Sneakers, you would see him long before you heard him.

"Is that you, Apple?" No answer. She heard Frankie screaming. Her heart pumped faster and faster. Hilda raced down the stairs and encountered a living nightmare standing in the living room.

"Put her down. NOW. Put her down!" Hilda yelled. She reached out to grab a hysterical Frankie.

"I know Gladys and Frank are shacked up and living in sin under the same roof as you and Stan," Sister Henrietta hissed. "You should be ashamed of yourself. Father Pat was shocked when he found out. He thought you and Stan were good-living people attending Mass every Sunday, but not anymore."

It would be impossible to fight the nun without hurting Frankie. "Please give the baby to me. She's frightened."

Sister Henrietta held a squirming Frankie tighter. "I will come back with the police if you don't get out of my way. This poor little soul will be spared a life with heathens for parents. Gladys and Frank are not fit to raise a child. Father Pat has found a good Catholic family willing to adopt the child."

It bothered Sneakers his little girl had been upset and decided to return home. He would take the toddler to Woolworth's and surprise Apple with an unexpected visit. He would work the doors of a bootlegger establishment when Frankie had gone to bed, and she would never know he was gone.

He heard Frankie screaming as he approached the house. Panic kicked in. He burst through the door into the house and saw his little girl in the arms of a dreaded monster.

"DADDY!" Frankie cried out. Sneakers grabbed Frankie from the nun and passed the child to Hilda. Sister Henrietta stumbled backwards.

"Take her upstairs, now," Sneakers commanded. "And wait in one of the bedrooms for me."

Sister Henrietta now wished the police had escorted her to the house. She had waited in a car parked near the house until she was certain Stan and Sneakers were gone and could easily take the child. The plan backfired but she was determined not to leave without the child. A decent family was waiting for the toddler and the nun could pocket a donation in the process.

"I will be back for the child with the police," Sister Henrietta stated with a smug look of victory on her face. But within a flash, a switchblade dug deep into her flesh and sliced her stomach wide open. The nun dropped to the floor.

A hysterical Frankie was crying for her Daddy from upstairs. Sneakers raced up the stairs two at a time. Frankie leaped into his arms, and he cradled her and bellowed commands to Hilda.

"Pack a suitcase for Frankie and Apple. I have friends in Toronto who will take care of Apple and Frankie. They need to get far away from the street before the police come."

"Police? What do you mean? What's happened?" A hysterical Hilda demanded.

"I stabbed her. The nun. She was going to come back with the police. I had to stop her." He passed Frankie to Hilda then pulled out a duffle bag stuffed with crumpled twenty-dollar bills under a cardboard box of clothing stored in a closet. "Give this to Apple." He wrote down the telephone number of the friends in Toronto. "They will hunt me down like an animal if I run. Jail time will be worth it if it means that bitch of a nun will let Apple and Frankie live in peace."

Hilda dropped a crying Frankie into the crib. She rushed about packing clothing in a suitcase.

"You tell the police that Apple has gone back to Prince Edward Island. They will never find her in Toronto. If she stays that miserable priest will come looking for Frankie."

A sobbing Hilda plopped down on a rocking chair. "Stan and I should have never risked going to church. It's our fault. I swear, I will never darken the doors of the church ever again."

Sneakers picked up Frankie and tried to calm her. He smothered Frankie's tear-stained face with kisses as she wrapped tiny arms around his neck.

"You and Stan did nothing wrong. That priest and nun are pure evil stealing children from their parents," he said, choking on tears. "Take the baby to Apple and tell her to leave as soon as she can." He handed Frankie to Hilda. The toddler screamed louder for "Daddy."

"You will always be a son to me and Stan." Hilda clumsily made her way down the stairs. She ignored the nun rolled up in a ball moaning with pain and exited through the back door with Frankie still screaming, "Daddy!"

There were few shoppers in the store when Hilda arrived with a squirming Frankie in her arms. The shocked expression on Hilda's face frightened Apple. Her mind raced. What had Sneakers done?

"Sister Henrietta is at the house. She tried to take Frankie. Sneakers hurt her." Hilda blurted before Apple could ask what was wrong.

Apple raced to the staff room, grabbed a coat, and rushed out of the store. The three headed for the docks with Apple rocking Frankie in her arms. Stan would know what to do.

❀

Blood seeped into the worn carpet. "Please help me," the nun begged in a low, gasping voice. She clutched the cross dangling around her neck and mouthed prayers.

"Who do you pray to, Sister Henrietta?" Sneakers mocked her. What God would listen to the prayers of a nun who kidnaps babies? I do not believe in God, but if there were a God, He would be on my side."

"You could not leave us alone, could you? I could walk out and leave you to bleed to death on the floor. It would serve you right. Because of you, I am not going to watch my baby girl grow up. I am going to make a pact with the Devil instead of running and hiding."

The pain was unbearable, and her black loose garment became soaked with blood. Sister Henrietta begged for mercy.

"I will save you from death if you make an oath to your God that you and the church will leave Apple and Frankie alone. Leave them in peace. You will lie to me, but hell-fearing Catholics like you would never break an oath to your God. Swear it. If you refuse, I will make a cup of coffee and watch you die like a dog on the floor. By the time Hilda gets back, I will have disappeared. The police will never find me."

Sister Henrietta curled up in a ball unable to move with the pain. You could almost mop the floor with the pool of blood oozing out of her.

She believed without a doubt he would watch her die and with pleasure. "I swear to God I will leave Gladys and the child alone only if you do time for the stabbing."

He agreed and the pact was sealed.

"I can be just as dangerous on the inside," he warned the nun. "I know people that would hunt you down and beat the crap out of you for a carton of cigarettes."

He phoned the police and waited to be certain she was still breathing when they arrived. She would be no good to him dead.

CHAPTER 17

S tan had a friend on the docks who agreed to hide Apple until travel to Toronto could be arranged. Stan and Hilda snuck out of their house late at night with a train ticket for Apple. "Stop that crying," Stan bellowed, holding back his own tears. "As soon as this all blows over, we will be reunited. We will start over someplace new."

Apple gave the couple the address of where she would be staying in Toronto. Stan and Hilda promised they would write every week.

"You be a good little girl for Mummy," and she smothered Frankie with kisses.

Stan embraced Apple. "You are the daughter we wished for," trying to hold back tears.

Apple clung to Stan not wanting to let him go. "That old nun has ruined everything," wept Apple. "She stole everything that was precious to me. My baby boy, Sneakers, and now you and Hilda."

Stan embraced a sobbing Apple. He pulled away. It was getting late and tomorrow would be a long day for everyone. "You take good care of yourself and our little Frankie. We will get this all sorted, and we will be a family again."

They embraced one last time and through fits of sobbing and tears they said a final goodbye.

Stan and Hilda bundled up and hurried through the streets to their little empty house.

He had arranged for a co-worker to drive Apple and Frankie to the train station. The next day, the train chugged slowly out of the station with Apple and Frankie heading to Toronto.

Father Pat made it his business to interrogate Stan and Hilda and find out where the mother and child were hiding. Hilda repeated the same story to Father Pat as she'd told the police: that the nun had tried to take the child. Sneakers was protecting Frankie and stabbed the nun. She took the child to Apple and then walked to the docks to let Stan know what had happened. She told the police and the priest that Apple had returned to Prince Edward Island with the child and was probably staying with friends. Stan nodded in agreement.

Father Pat was convinced Stan and Hilda were lying. He was certain they knew where the mother and child were, and their lies nagged him. He decided to return to the house with the police the next day, determined to learn the truth—but no one answered the door.

Stan and Hilda had packed what they could into a couple of suitcases leaving behind the furniture. They disappeared into the night to stay with Stan's friend from work. The next day they boarded a bus for Newfoundland where Stan could find work in processing plants.

Apple had never travelled outside of the Maritimes. It was late afternoon when the train arrived at Union Station. She searched a crowd of faces for Sneakers' friend. They'd talked on the telephone before she boarded the train. He planned to meet her and Frankie. Union Station was too big, too noisy, and too filled with people. She now wished she had stayed in the Maritimes. At least she would have been closer to Dorchester Penitentiary. Apple turned in the direction of a voice calling her name. A tall, well-dressed handsome man with a broad smile approached her. "I'm Smithers," and he reach out to shake her hand. "You must be Apple. I have been waiting for the train to come in searching for a pretty girl with a toddler. Sneakers telephoned before the police arrived. I'm sorry for what happened."

It was obvious to the man that Apple hadn't known he was Black. He saw an expression of doubt on her face. He pulled out a teddy bear from his knapsack. Frankie reached out and grabbed it. Apple mumbled, "Thanks."

He picked up the suitcase and guided Apple and Frankie to a subway station. "You and the child will be safe in Toronto."

Apple couldn't believe how many stone-faced people were packed into the subway. No one smiled. No one talked as the subway whizzed from station to station. She held onto a squirming Frankie for dear life. Crazy thoughts flashed through her mind about the strangers on the subway. She feared losing Frankie in a crowd while dealing with the emotional pain of the family breaking up.

Sneakers had a temper, but she'd never imagined his anger would rob Frankie of a father. It dawned on Apple that her life had changed in the flash of a knife. She was now a single parent in hiding.

Apple watched Smithers out of the corner of an eye. Could she trust him? Sneakers didn't trust easily, so he must be a good man, she figured. Smithers grabbed Apple's arm and guided her to the safety of a seat. Smithers recognized fear in her face and knew she would be an easy target in the city.

The subway stopped at Pape Station. She blindly followed Smithers for blocks to an apartment above a pizza shop. She stepped into the living room that would become more of a prison than a haven for the next several months. The apartment stank of pizza from the shop below. A large picture window provided a view of Danforth Avenue. The only other window was in the bedroom at the back of the apartment. "My girlfriend left a month ago. I only have the one bedroom. You and the child can have it. I will bunk out on the sofa."

Smithers had to be about the same age as Sneakers and she wondered how they met. There was so much she did not know about Sneakers before she met him on the streets of Charlottetown. He had been a good father...and a skilled criminal. And she could see the goodness in his heart when she gazed in his eyes.

"Sneakers and I go way back," Smithers told Apple without being asked. "We shared a cell back in juvenile days. I was not very popular being the only Black teen in a white jail cell. Sneakers always had my back. He used to come to Toronto, and we would hang out. Up here, I blend in better than in small towns."

Smithers told stories about hitchhiking across Canada with Sneakers, living rough, and getting into trouble along the way.

Apple noted Smithers had made the effort to clean the place. A garbage can had been filled with pizza boxes and beer cans. A few washed dishes dried in a rack. He had folded fresh towels on the bed. Apple wrapped Frankie in a blanket and hoped the toddler would sleep for the night.

"Sneakers told me that nun will never bother you again. But hopefully you feel safer here than back home."

But Apple never trusted Sister Henrietta and worried if the nun would honour the deal she made with Sneakers. For now, she needed a safe place to stay until the dust settled and time to figure out what to do.

"I will take you to the park tomorrow where there is a playground for Frankie to play," Smithers suggested. Apple didn't respond.

"The park is a safe place. No one will bother you," he added, trying to reassure her.

❀

Smithers pushed Frankie in a swing and bought ice cream cones trying to cheer up Apple, who was holding back tears. But his efforts only made her sadder.

It should be Sneakers pushing his baby girl and not a stranger. She questioned why it had happened. Why did she keep losing the people she loved? Was she cursed?

❀

Life in Toronto compared to the Maritimes was like being on a fast rollercoaster - a culture shock Apple was unprepared for.

There were swarms of people in Toronto, and many of the people were talking in foreign languages. It intimidated Apple. She seldom left the apartment. Smithers would come and go throughout the day and be gone most of each night.

Frankie crying for her daddy the first week rattled her nerves. She nervously ventured out to the park. Frankie stopped fussing as Apple pushed her on a swing. The daily trips to the park calmed Frankie, but homesickness shadowed Apple.

The days were becoming longer and hotter. Apple cried more often than Frankie. She wanted to go home. But there was no home to go to.

The news came weeks after she had moved to Toronto. Sister Henrietta had survived the stabbing. Sneakers was locked up and was going to plead guilty to attempted manslaughter. Apple cried a river of tears. Mourning is not reserved for the dead.

❋

Apple had been in the city for more than a month and was still afraid of getting lost.

There was just too much of the unknown outside of the safety zone of the apartment. There were days she cursed Sneakers for stabbing the old nun. He had been sentenced to life behind bars. They could have run away and would still be a family. She would have followed him to the moon if he had asked. She feared Smithers would become tired of having a houseguest and an active toddler. What if he demanded she get out? Where on earth would she go? The brown bag of money would not last forever.

"Why don't we go out for the evening? I have a friend who could babysit Frankie," Smithers asked one night.

Apple did not have anything suitable to wear to a nightclub. Frankie might fuss. Would she be betraying Sneakers?

"A woman like you needs to have fun. I know of a clothing shop a few blocks away. I will take you and Frankie. You can shop for some funky clothing at a good price. You deserve to treat yourself. I would never cross Sneakers. You're safe with me."

Apple purchased tight-fitting black dress pants, high heels, and a flaming red blouse. The fun night began with a trip to Yonge Street. Apple stepped into a world with sidewalks packed with people moving in all directions, flashing neon billboards, and traffic inching along Yonge Street. The bright city lights drowned out the night. A mesmerized Apple had never experienced the vibrations of Yonge Street on the east coast. Trickles of excitement soared through her.

She and Smithers stepped into a nightclub blaring with music and strokes of flashing lights. The taste of alcohol gave Apple false security. She craved a second and third shot of rye and ginger.

Sneakers had trusted Smithers and a girlfriend to protect Apple and Frankie. Smithers failed to tell Sneakers the girlfriend had dumped him. Temptation got the better of him.

He seduced Apple with a handsome smile and guided her to the dance floor. She and Sneakers had never gone dancing. Their date nights were hanging out in coffee shops and walking the streets of St. John.

"A foxy lady like you should go dancing more often. That Sneakers was one lucky bastard to snag a woman like you."

Apple stroked his face and twined her fingers through his hair. She allowed him to take her finger and suck on it as if were a Popsicle. A surge of burning desire shot through her body.

She nestled into his arms, feeling happy for the first time since arriving in Toronto. They staggered into the apartment at two in the morning. Smithers paid the babysitter and put her in a cab. Apple allowed Smithers to undress her. It would be one of many nights of lovemaking.

❀

Apple woke up to a note on the kitchen table months later. Smithers had paid the rent for the month. He was leaving for the west coast where the weather was warmer, and he had friends. There was no apology, no excuses for the abandonment. Apple figured Smithers pulled a disappearing act because he feared Sneakers might learn about their sexual relationship. Sneakers

was behind bars, but Smithers knew he had contacts on the outside willing to earn quick money.

She was now pregnant and figured Smithers was not prepared
to be a daddy.

Apple had no intention of sharing the baby news with
Sneakers until after the baby was born.

Smithers had not made any promises. She had willingly per-
mitted him to take her to bed without a commitment. She did
not hate him; nor did she love him.

But she did need to figure out what to do next.

CHAPTER 18

S tan and Hilda had settled in Newfoundland. Hilda wrote a letter about getting a fresh start in another province. Stan had secured employment in a place called Come by Chance.

Stan and I think about you and Frankie all the time. The people are right friendly. The rent is not bad. Our old age pension will be able to cover it when the day comes that we are no longer working. We are doing okay. You and Frankie are welcome to visit and stay if you want. It is a beautiful place: quiet, slow-paced, and people are laid back. We have made friends with the people in the community. Give Frankie kisses for us and tell her we love her. Write back soon and tell us how you are doing in the Big Smoke.

Apple could not fathom living in an isolated seaside village of Newfoundland and did not want to move back to Saint John without Stan and Hilda. She was more familiar with Charlottetown than Halifax.

Hilda had heard from Harry's sister, Thelma, that Mary-Lou had enrolled in a private school in the Maritimes after the attack on Wayne and she later moved to the west coast of Canada with a wealthy husband. Wayne had been locked up with insane people. Apple had cursed reading the letter. She wrote back: *that cow Mary-Lou probably had no remorse that our sweet Harry died in the attack.*

Wayne roamed about the institution for the insane with a hockey stick, slapping an imaginary puck. It served him right, thought Apple. Her friend Harry was dead because of Wayne.

Stan and Hilda had been given no choice but to leave their Charlottetown home. The nun had made sure Stan lost his job cleaning streets just like she said she would.

The old fear of being raped disturbed her sleep and daylight hours. The fear kept her indoors, too frightened to venture out into Toronto.

Forced to decide to stay in the city or move back to Charlottetown, she rationalized that Wayne was old news to the hockey buddies. The players were finished school, and probably busy with families and working. But still, her heart raced at the thought of being gang raped. She also questioned if she could trust that Sister Henrietta would keep her part of the bargain and leave her and Frankie alone. Thoughts of encountering the nun on the streets of Charlottetown nagged at her. Was she making the right decision?

In the end, she packed the suitcase and penned a letter to Stan and Hilda.

I do not know anyone in Toronto except Smithers, a friend of Sneakers. We have been staying at his place, but he is not around much. I do not have anyone to take care of Frankie if I were to go out and get a job. And rent is too expensive without a job. It is not that easy to make friends. Toronto is not like Charlottetown, where people talk to each other. I took the subway with Smithers one day and said hello to the person sitting next to me. She acted as if I was invisible.

I am going mad cooped up all day with Frankie. I am taking Frankie to Charlottetown while I still have money. It's the best I can do in a bad situation with no family or friends and no job to pay the rent.

I am too old for foster care. The nuns cannot touch me. I will write when I get settled in Charlottetown. Frankie sends kisses and love. She misses you so much. Hugs, Apple

With suitcase in hand, she asked the pizza shop owner to be so kind as to call a taxi to take her to Union Station.

❁

Bessy Flops took in boarders. The rooming house was sandwiched between a bootlegger and a cheap three-level apartment building in need of a coat of paint. Bessy had house rules: No overnight company. No noise after ten in the evening. No parties. Rent was collected the first day of every month, no excuses. It was impossible to get away with breaking any of the rules because Bessy Flops lived in an apartment in the back of the first floor.

Apple offered three months of rent in advance. Bessy, hungry for money, agreed with a warning: "You keep the little girl quiet at night. She's not to run around the place and disturb the other boarders."

The room had a twin-sized bed, a table and two chairs, and a dresser. Four renters on the top floor had to share kitchen facilities and a bathroom with Apple and Frankie.

Apple figured three months would be enough time to find an affordable apartment before the baby came. Apple befriended Tilly on the second floor of the boarding house.

"What do you plan to do with Frankie when it's time to go to the hospital?" Tilly inquired.

"No idea." It was enough getting through the day keeping an active child quiet without worrying about the future.

"I have a friend, Sandra, who takes care of children. I can ask if she would be willing to look after Frankie for a few days."

Good deeds were often traded between the friends. Apple thanked Tilly and paid a visit to Sandra. Her house was clean and there were toys for Frankie to play with. Apple hesitated, but what choice did she have? For a price, Sandra agreed to take care of Frankie.

Apple flipped the light switch off as soon as it was dark and crawled in bed with Frankie and would softly sing songs in Frankie's ear until the toddler drifted off to sleep.

❀

Apartments were more expensive than boarding houses. Three months of searching and Apple still couldn't find an apartment. Frustrated with searching for cheap rentals in residential neighbourhoods, she realized she would have to lower expectations and settle for a slumlord near the railroad tracks where rentals were more affordable.

Sooner or later, Apple would have to put on a brave face and contact social services for financial assistance. She was not overly familiar with the welfare system but figured it couldn't be much different than the foster system. The system controlled your life, but Apple had learned street smarts being with Sneakers. She'd outwit the system and would make it work to her advantage.

❀

"When did the doctor say you were due?" inquired Tilly during a visit.

But Apple didn't trust doctors after the encounter with Dr. Jay. "I don't have a doctor," she told Tilly. "I plan to go to the hospital, have the baby, and come home."

Tilly looked at Apple as if she were crazy. "What? You don't have regular checkups? Don't you need a doctor to let you know when the baby is due and have him deliver it?"

Apple stuffed a handful of fries in her mouth and gulped a mouthful of milk. Tilly dropped by with food from the restaurant for Apple and Frankie two or three times a week. The fries and burgers were a welcome change from soup and sandwiches made in the messy shared kitchen.

"I didn't have a doctor when I was pregnant with Frankie and I got along fine. I don't need a doctor to tell me when the baby will be born. The baby will come when it is ready to be born. A nurse can deliver it if there is no doctor around."

Tilly pitied Apple living in a boarding house, pregnant and caring for a toddler. And yet admired her for being bold and brave to go to the hospital alone and have a baby.

"I have a date tonight with this guy I've been seeing. We are going to stay at Sandra's house for the night rather than risk getting caught sneaking him into my room. Sandra has a couple of spare bedrooms. And she owes me a favour."

Apple couldn't remember the last time she had been on a date. Smithers had taken her to nightclubs in Toronto, but most evenings he went out alone, came back to the apartment late at night, and crawled into bed with her.

She longed to get dressed up, put on makeup, and go dancing with a fellow. But she might as well dream about going to the moon than dream about a fun date. She tucked Frankie into bed and sulked. Her dating days were over.

❀

The birthing pains began early one morning. Apple packed a bag with clothes for the few days Frankie would be staying with Sandra on the next street. There were two hospitals in the town: one for Catholics and one for Protestants. Apple had no plans of giving birth at the Catholic hospital with Sister Henrietta lurking about. It would be safer to have the baby in the Protestant hospital.

"I have no intention of staying for a week at the hospital," Apple told Sandra. "I plan to have the baby and return home to rest."

Wearing a fake wedding band, Apple signed her name Mrs. J. Shea, and under *Father* on the registration form, she wrote *Deceased*. Being a widow would be more acceptable than being an unwed mother. She was not going to risk losing another baby at birth because she was unmarried. She planned to take the baby to the boarding house before anyone discovered the lie at the hospital.

Two nurses and a doctor encouraged Apple as she pushed out the baby in the delivery room. The baby slid out of the womb without much effort. "It's a girl." The nurses cleaned the wailing infant. There were no expressions of congratulations from the doctor or the nurses. No one said a word. Was there something wrong with the baby?

A sombre-looking nurse gave Apple the wailing infant. Apple examined the newborn, expecting to see a deformed baby by the reaction of the medical team. The new mother peered into dark button eyes of a wailing, brown-skinned infant with a head of tightly knotted black curls.

A social worker visited Apple the next day with information about an orphanage on the mainland for Negro children. "It would be better for the baby to be adopted by one of their own," explained the social worker.

"Get the hell out of my room." Apple dressed the newborn -who she'd named Sammi-Jo - and called a cab.

She staggered in pain to the babysitter's house with the newborn bundled in a blanket the next day. Out of compassion, Sandra suggested Apple go home and rest for a few days. She would take care of Frankie at no extra cost. An exhausted Apple welcomed the offer and later collapsed on the bed with the newborn. Tilly checked in on her in the evening with restaurant food that would have been thrown out.

The boarding house did not cost much, but it was no place to raise children. Frankie cried anytime Sammi-Jo wailed for feedings. Renters complained. Apple got an eviction notice the same day she found a furnished apartment near the railroad tracks. The little family of three moved across town to a community of cheap apartments owned by a slumlord on a street bordered with towering chestnut trees.

The pink-painted apartment building stretched along the street and around a corner. The building had three floors that housed six apartment units. Apple rented a two-bedroom on the second floor of the apartment building. The bedrooms were small, but the living room, kitchen and bathroom were spacious.

❁

Apple and the children had settled into their new place and befriended single mothers living in the apartment building. They welcomed Apple into their circle of friendship without judgment. Like Apple, they were suspicious of strangers and trusted no one. She learned that other tenants in the building were aware of Sister Henrietta, and they hated and feared her as much as Apple.

Tilly was a regular visitor and Apple welcomed the company. Late one morning, Tilly banged on the door with urgency. She'd come searching for advice.

Apple ignored the rapping on the door thinking it was probably a neighbour wanting to borrow bread or something. The rent had been paid, so she ruled out the landlord. It could be Annie on the first floor or one of her kids looking for pop bottles to sell at the corner store. Frankie had been put down for a morning nap.

The overtired mother was in no mood for company. The banging might wake Frankie if she did not answer the door.

Apple opened the door balancing Sammi-Jo in one arm. "Tilly. What on earth is going on? It is not a good time for a visit. I just put Frankie down for a nap. And I am going to join her after I get Sammi-Jo settled."

Tilly pushed past Apple and plunked down on a kitchen chair. "I'm pregnant," she said as calmly as if she were talking about the weather. "He wants to marry me."

Tilly blabbed and blabbed and blabbed about Bobby. He was much older, a boozer, but he had steady employment on construction sites. He promised to slow down the drinking if they got married.

"Are babies a lot of work? You make it look so easy."

"I have years of experience taking care of kids in foster homes," Apple explained.

Tilly had been a good friend at the boarding house. Apple owed it to her to tell the truth. She wrapped Sammi-Jo in a blanket like a hotdog in a bun and handed her to Tilly.

"Sammi-Jo keeps me up most of the night. I smell like baby puke most of the time. I am lonely and tired, and I have no boyfriend or a husband to give me a break. I had to apply for welfare so I can pay the rent."

Tilly held the baby now sleeping in her arms and listened. She was eighteen years old. Her mother had more boyfriends than Tilly. Bessy Flops would put her on the street if she could not pay the rent. Getting married seemed to be a better option than begging for welfare.

"It's good that he wants to marry you and be a daddy," Apple continued. "Most guys would run like the devil was chasing him. It's not an easy road on my own, but the girls are my life."

Frankie came running into the kitchen, half asleep and crying. Apple placed Sammi-Jo in a bassinet and cuddled a sleepy Frankie.

Tilly said goodbye and walked uptown to shop for a wedding dress.

❄

Apple received an invitation to a splashy church wedding a month later but declined. Who would babysit? She didn't have a proper dress for a wedding and didn't want to attend a splashy event looking poor. And there was no cash for a present.

Sneakers had been a good thief, but Apple would not risk stealing and getting caught.

"You don't need a fancy dress for the wedding," Tilly argued. "I am not asking you to come to my wedding to get a gift. And you babysit for Annie downstairs. She can watch your girls for a few hours."

Apple agreed to go. But she couldn't get the idea of wearing a nice new dress out of her head. She bought a flouncy summer dress for the wedding using a good portion of the rent money. She left the price tag on the dress and put the receipt in her purse. "I can't watch the kids and try on the dress," she told the cashier. "I am pretty sure it will fit," she said, knowing it did.

The price tag was tucked out of sight at the wedding. The following Monday, Apple returned the dress for a refund saying it was too small and didn't fit properly.

❄

It was on a trip uptown when Apple noticed a sign in the store window. A professional photographer would be at the store the following Saturday. *Buy one photograph and get the second one free* caught her attention. She figured it was probably a scam to entice people to buy more than they planned to. The offer got her thinking. The girls deserved to have their photo taken by a professional photographer as much as anyone else.

She'd managed to score a dress worth half the rent money and had no problem returning it after Tilly's wedding. She hatched a plan to dress up the girls as if they were little princesses without having to buy the clothing.

Frankie and Sammi-Jo splashed in the tub Saturday morning. Apple scrubbed the girls clean because it was a very special day.

She tied bright yellow ribbons in Frankie's long reddish hair and tied matching yellow ribbons into clumps of Sammi-Jo's tight black curls.

"Where are we going, Mummy?" Four-year-old Frankie wanted to know.

"We're going somewhere special. I want you to be a good girl and no fussing."

Frankie helped push the stroller to the Eaton's Department Store. "Listen carefully, Frankie. We are going to get photographs taken today by the picture-man. But first Mummy is going to do some shopping."

Apple selected two satin white dresses, yellow socks, and black leather shoes. She slipped into a dressing room with the children.

"We need to hurry and get the dresses on. We will put what you are wearing in the stroller. You cannot get the clothes dirty. They go back on the rack after the photographer takes your picture. Do you understand, Frankie? We cannot keep the clothes."

Apple hurried to the lineup before an employee noticed. "Why can't we keep the dresses?" Frankie whispered in her ear. "Hush, Frankie. Be good and we will stop at the store for candy on the way home." Apple snuck into the lineup with the girls without being noticed.

Apple saw a familiar face suddenly though a little older than the last time she'd seen her. Millie was in the lineup with two toddlers. She speculated Millie no longer lived in poverty by the expensive clothing she was wearing. "Hello, Millie." Apple waited for an answer, but Millie ignored her. "Stuck-up cow," Apple muttered under her breath. She picked up Sammi-Jo and held her tightly. A happy, smiling Sammi-Jo squeezed Apple's neck melting Apple's raging anger towards Millie.

The picture-man advertised photographs for a $1.99 for an eight-by-ten. Apple knew the catch. He would try to sell a package of photos for much higher. She did not need a dozen photos of the girls. Who would she give them to? The neighbours in the apartment building would not be interested or care. She might buy a couple of wallet-sized photos to mail to Stan and Hilda living in Newfoundland. She would have the picture-man take a photo of Frankie without Sammi-Jo. Sneakers might be in prison, but he was still Frankie's daddy.

Sneakers knew about Sammi-Jo. He wrote to Apple that he'd had no idea Smithers' girlfriend had moved out. Smithers had pulled a fast one promising he and the girlfriend would take good care of his woman and child and then taking advantage of the situation. Sneakers was understanding about the pregnancy, but there was no point in rubbing it in by sending a photo of Frankie and Sammi-Jo together.

"What beautiful girls you have," the picture-man told Apple. He did not act surprised one child was Black and the other white like most people Apple encountered. She figured when it came to money, the colour of the skin did not matter to the picture-man.

Frankie and Sammi-Jo giggled at the antics of the picture-man as he snapped the camera. A sudden tinge of heartache of losing

her firstborn tarnished the moment of the joy of raising two little
girls smiling for the camera.

CHAPTER 19

Gracie was new to living in Charlottetown after drifting around the country. She had been a sixteen-year-old runaway in search of fun and adventures.

Her father had arranged for her to work at a fish plant, but it was not the life she'd dreamed about. Her plan had been to finish high school and attend university. She stole money while her parents were sleeping to avoid a life of drudgery. Early morning, she snuck out of the house with a few belongings and hitchhiked to the ferry that transported her to another life.

She hitchhiked across North America with a girlfriend for three years. A hippie lifestyle became a ticket to freedom and fun, until she began missing the smells of ocean air, salty swims and beach walks.

You could have cooked eggs on the burning hot highway pavement the day she hitchhiked back to the Island to an unforgiving father. Gracie had been banned from her home for stealing and running away. She had no choice but to settle in Charlottetown. She moved into an oversized bachelor apartment on the third floor of the building Apple lived in.

Gracie had painted the apartment an assortment of colours with images of flowers and tiny birds on the living-room window. The oversized bathroom had enough space for a dresser and floor-to-ceiling shelves she used to store clothing, bedding, and towels. The sofa converted into a bed at night and the kitchenette overlooked the street below. Towering chestnut trees reached the top of the bachelor apartment. Gracie would sit by the floor by the window and recite poetry to the chestnut trees.

She had secured employment as a waitress at a Charlottetown restaurant where she earned good tips. The teenager lived life on her own terms with the freedom of coming and going day and night without strict parents to answer to. But her independent lifestyle came to an unexpected end. An affair with an older man resulted in a pregnancy.

The father abandoned Gracie long before she gave birth to their son, Elijah Blue, in the dead of winter. The young mother purchased a long blue sheet and hung it from the ceiling in the living room to act as a divider to create a makeshift bedroom for Elijah Blue.

Gracie was heading up the stairs cradling a squirmy Elijah Blue in her arms as Apple was going down the stairs holding Sammi-Jo with Frankie in the lead.

Gracie was heading to the park with Elijah Blue to bask in the sunlight rather than staying indoors.

"Hello, sweetie. What is your name?" Gracie asked Sammi-Jo. "You must be the same age as my little boy."

Frankie answered for Sammi-Jo. "She's my little sister. Who are you?"

Apple intervened before Frankie could say more.

"I have been meaning to visit you, but my girls keep me busy."

Nineteen-year-old Gracie, lonely for a friend her age, invited Apple and the girls to visit anytime. "I am home most of the time." The encounter on the stairway was the start of a friendship.

Another rainy day reflected the misery Gracie had been challenged with for days. It was too wet to push the stroller around town. Being indoors for days with only Elijah Blue for company gnawed at her nerves like a bad toothache. The tears flowed as she wished for company, someone to talk with.

Sitting at the window, she spied Apple coming up the street with a bag of groceries. She and the girls were wearing black garbage bags that served as raincoats with holes for arms and their head. Apple rushed the girls down the street and out of the rain.

Gracie stuck her head out the door and shouted a greeting as Apple and the girls climbed the stairway to their apartment.

"Do you want to come up for a visit? I have the kettle on, and I have a box of store-bought cookies." She tried to entice Frankie up to the third-floor landing. It worked. "Please, Mommy," Frankie begged. Apple shouted back, "Give us ten minutes. The girls need to change out of soaked clothing, and I need to put the groceries away."

Annie, who lived on the bottom floor, overheard the conversation on the landing as she stepped outside to throw out a bucket of dirty water. A clean floor was almost impossible with five kids sharing a three-bedroom dwelling. Annie was giving the floors a good scrubbing while the kids were in school.

"What's all the racket up there?" Annie yelled out to Apple. Annie was skinny and stood less than five feet tall but no one in the neighbourhood dared mess with her. She cursed, smoked constantly, and would not think twice about giving a person a swift kick in the butt or a slap across the head. "Gracie invited us for a visit," Apple shot back to Annie.

Annie didn't wait for an invitation. "I'll join you soon as I finish the cleaning." A taxi driver pulled up to the apartment building. The driver rolled down the car window and shouted to Annie, "I got your smokes."

Bingo Alice was one of a few female cab drivers in the town. She and Annie were the best of friends. And it was not uncommon for Bingo Alice to park the cab at Annie's place for a few hours in the morning while the kids were at school. Bingo Alice was six feet tall with an army-style cropped haircut, and she tipped the scales at 240 pounds. Her body language was intimidating dressed in tight fitting blue jeans and a baggy T-shirt.

❀

Bingo Alice played bingo and Annie joined her most Wednesday nights. The two friends had a knack for winning. When they won, Bingo Alice, Annie, and the kids feasted, chowing down on plate-fuls of Chinese takeout.

"I am going upstairs to visit Gracie. Do you want to come?" Annie hollered. Bingo Alice accepted the invitation and parked the cab in front of the building.

Gracie got her wish for company as the kitchen filled up with Annie and Bingo Alice and Apple and the two little girls. The teapot steamed on the stove and a plateful of biscuits and jam, and the promised plate of store-bought cookies were served. The women sat around the kitchen table and Frankie sat on steps that led to a bedsitting room and nibbled cookies.

"Sammi-Jo can play with my little boy," suggested Gracie. She dumped a box of plastic toys on the floor.

❀

Bingo Alice told a story about a guy who tried to stiff her on a fare the night before. "I knew he was acting fishy just as I was pulling up to the address he gave me. This punk kid thinking he could cheat me by doing a runner when I stopped the car. I hit the gas pedal, scaring the bejesus out of him. I said, 'Look here you little dick-stick, you pay me or I will drop you off on the outskirts of town and you can hitchhike home.' I pulled out my old friend, batty, from under the passenger side to let him know I was talking business. He took one look at the bat and threw me a five-dollar bill for a two-dollar fare. I dropped him off at the end of the street. He'll think twice before trying to cheat a cabbie again."

The morning slipped away, and the apartment filled with laughter and storytelling. Frankie was getting bored and fussed to go home. Apple bribed her with a treat if she behaved. It worked. Four-year-old Frankie ignored the adults and played with Sammi-Jo and Elijah Blue.

Gracie unloaded disturbing thoughts seeking advice from the more experienced women that tackled problems head-on such as forcing a roughie to pay the taxi fare and Annie setting teachers straight at school. She admired and envied the women sharing morning tea and biscuits, wishing she, too, could be brazen and fearless.

"I had a dream last night," Gracie began. "I dreamed I was sitting on the grass. Everything was black and white. And I was crying, and I couldn't stop. I sat in a pool of tears and couldn't move. The pool of tears was getting higher and higher and soon I would drown if I didn't stop crying but I couldn't stop."

The laughter at the kitchen table came to a screeching halt like a car that hit the brakes at a fast speed. Bingo Alice lit a cigarette and inhaled and gawked at Gracie.

"I thought about the dream this morning. And I believe my soul had gone to Limbo while I was sleeping," Gracie continued knowing she had the full attention of the group. "I was crying because I was trapped in Limbo. And I didn't know how to escape. I was dying in a sea of my own tears mourning my failures, my mistakes and all the horrible stuff that ever happened to me since I drew my first breath."

Bingo Alice passed the cigarette to her girl, Annie. "What were you smoking last night before you went to bed?" Annie asked with a puzzled expression.

The question clearly caught Gracie off guard. It was not the emotional support she was expecting. Apple quickly stepped in, concerned that Gracie would start bawling and embarrass everyone. "It was just a bad dream, Gracie. We all have 'em." She spoke with experience having had human-crow nightmares since early childhood. But she would never share the nightmares with anyone and put herself at risk to be ridiculed.

"You can't let the bastards get you down. You must stand up for yourself because no one else will," Annie added. "You need to get out more without pushing a stroller. Come to bingo with us Wednesday night. My Tessy will babysit for you. She's right good with kids, but you must pay her in advance in case you gamble the babysitting money playing bingo."

The Pecker Detectors were financial workers with Social Services. They reigned over low-income earners who relied on social services. Home visits determined the amount of income social service recipients were entitled to and to ensure rules were not broken.

The Pecker Detectors would sniff like hound dogs around apartments for a man living with a welfare woman. And the women endured the demeaning search for clues of being shacked up.

Thoughts of the Pecker Detector poking around forced Gracie to decline the invitation.

"But Annie, what if a Pecker Detector recognizes me at bingo?" Gracie inquired.

Bingo Alice answered for Annie. "You worry too much about stupid things. Just give him a good blowjob and he will leave you alone."

Gracie dropped the teacup as she envisioned the thought of being forced to sexually satisfy a Pecker Detector.

Apple was quick to speak to protect a speechless Gracie. "Watch your mouth. The kids are in the next room." The children, engaged in playing, paid no attention to the adult conversation.

It dawned on Gracie that she was living the bad dream of being in Limbo and craved the freedom of being treated with respect just like any other mother. She would continue to live in Limbo being dependant on a social program that determined if she had a home or not, and food on the table.

"I will babysit Elijah Blue while you visit the library or go for a walk alone and you can babysit for me while I clean houses ," offered Apple.

Not to be outdone, Bingo Alice offered cab service for a reduced price if Gracie needed a drive. And Annie piped up that Tessy could babysit if Gracie and Apple ever had a desire to go out for an evening of fun.

The sun broke through the clouds. She would bundle up Elijah Blue and head for the park after the company had gone home.

The summer sun had toasted Sammi-Jo's skin to a rich dark brown colour. Apple teased the girls, saying Sammi-Jo was her brown sugar baby and Frankie, her ginger baby.

Frankie started grade one in the fall and Sammi-Jo cried to go to school with her big sister.

Brenda and Charlie Mac had a houseful of children a few houses down from the apartment building where Apple and the girls lived. Brenda suggested Apple send Sammi-Jo over to play with the children. "I don't mind keeping an eye on her while she's in the backyard. I will take her home if she cries," Brenda assured Apple.

Apple sat on the front doorstep chatting with Annie and Bingo Alice. School was out. Frankie dashed home. "Sammi-Jo is playing in the backyard at Brenda's house. Go fetch her and bring her home," instructed Apple.

Frankie came down the street with Sammi-Jo who was bawling and covered with soapy water.

"What on earth happened?" Annie went indoors and came back with a towel and wrapped it around Sammi-Jo.

"The kids were trying to wash the dirt off my skin, Mummy. It hurt," Sammi-Jo cried.

Annie went indoors and came back outside and offered Sammi-Jo a cookie. "Stupid kids," Annie mumbled.

Bingo Alice pressed a quarter into Sammi-Jo's hand. Frankie marched up the street, grabbed the bucket of soapy water, and dumped it on the kids. "You touch my sister again and I will beat the snot out of you."

Gracie was hoofing down the street with Elijah Blue. It was the end of a shift at a demanding café and she was tired to the bone. A cranky four-year-old Elijah Blue bawled to stay at the daycare to play with his friends. The Department of Social Services paid for daycare services if Gracie was working.

"What happened? Did Sammi-Jo get hurt? A concerned Gracie asked before heading up the stairs to her apartment.

A raging Frankie blurted out what had happened earlier to her little sister before Apple could answer.

"Sammi-Jo needs a hug," Gracie suggested to Elijah Blue. "Give her a hug."

"My sister doesn't need a hug. Those brats need a good kick in the arse," six-year-old Frankie snapped at Gracie.

Bingo Alice and Annie howled with laughter. A red-faced Gracie grabbed Elijah Blue and headed up the stairs saying it had been a long day and she was tired.

Apple cuddled Sammi-Jo long into the evening. Sammi-Jo continued to cry to go to school with Frankie. But Apple refused to allow Brenda to babysit.

CHAPTER 20

A strong winter wind battered the apartment building. Snow drifts churned through the street, erasing rows of houses. Christmas was a week away. The two sisters were anxious about Santa's big visit. "Mummy, we don't have a tree. Will there be gifts for me and Sammi-Jo if there's no tree?" Frankie's eyes were as round as saucers.

"Santa is not coming because we don't have a tree," Sammi-Jo wailed.

"Look what you've done. You made your little sister cry," Apple scolded. "It doesn't matter if we get a tree or not, Santa will still come. Get dressed. I am taking you upstairs to Gracie's place. You can stay with her while I go uptown."

The girls kicked up a fuss. They did not have the same freedom of running and playing like they had in their own place. Gracie was nice, but she could be bossy.

"We want to come with you. We don't want to stay with Gracie."

Christmas could be stressful enough without the girls fussing. Apple had purchased gifts for the girls with most of the Christmas money Stan and Hilda sent earlier in the month and hid the box of wrapped presents under her bed. Sneakers mailed money from prison probably earned on the prison black market. But the cash had been spent the same day it arrived in the mail.

The gift of money allowed her to purchase Christmas groceries, candies, and fruit to fill the Christmas stockings and gifts for herself. The gifts were usually underwear, nylons, nail polish, and a tube of lipstick. She would open the presents Christmas morning and act surprised for the girls.

The Christmas tree lots that sprang up around the town were almost sold out. There was little money in the piggybank for a tree. A cheap tree would cost ten dollars. The more expensive trees were twenty dollars. Twenty dollars would buy much-needed Christmas groceries.

"It's too cold to take the two of you with me," Apple explained. "I will bring back a treat if you behave for Gracie. I do not want to hear any complaints about fighting with Elijah Blue. Play nicely."

Apple dragged the girls up the stairs to the apartment on the third floor. She pounded on Gracie's door. "What on earth are you doing out in such nasty weather?" Apple and the girls tumbled inside the warm kitchen. "It smells yummy in here. What are you baking?"

Elijah Blue was hunched over the kitchen table decorating oven-baked gingerbread ornaments. He punched a hole in one for a string. The gingerbread ornaments would later dangle from the tree branches.

"We're making decorations for the Christmas tree. We got a tree last night. It's in the corner of the living room. It's a cheapie, but it will look stunning when we finish decorating it."

The girls peered into the room and squealed with excitement. In the corner stood a four-foot tree in a basin of water to keep it from going dry. Gracie had fastened a string around the centre of the tree and tied it to the wall to keep it from toppling over. The only store decoration was a shiny gold star on the top of the tree. Twirls of cut-out coloured tissue paper were coiled around the branches. Handcrafted angels dangled on the tree. Gracie had put discarded cardboard to good use. She used it to cut out and paint an image of Santa and two little elves. A cluster of crafted ornaments made from coloured tissue paper swayed from the ceiling. A Christmas album Gracie borrowed from the library spun on a record player. The girls were now eager to stay with Gracie and Elijah Blue.

Gracie agreed to watch the girls for Apple. Sammi-Jo and Frankie could help Elijah Blue with icing the oven-baked decorations for the tree.

Apple had no intention of begging or borrowing the money to buy a tree. Gracie had gone door-to-door and sold a couple of paintings she had worked on for weeks to people living in the west end of town who could afford such luxuries.

Apple did not paint, but she knew the tricks of cleaning. She earned money under the table cleaning the fancy homes of the west enders.

She gathered cleaning supplies and trotted across the railroad tracks to the west end. Gracie babysat while she cleaned houses. In return, Apple babysat Elijah Blue while Gracie visited the library or worked on paintings to sell. The trade-off worked well between the two friends.

Apple also did the tax returns for the people in the building and on the street for extra income. Gracie nagged her to study accounting. But school had been a nightmare for Apple. Why would she study for years to become an accountant? What was wrong with cleaning? She enjoyed it and was darn good at it. Gracie was her best friend but sometimes got pushy with unsolicited advice. "Go get a job at the library since you spend so much time there," Apple teased.

Apple had a good reputation as an honest person in the homes of the wealthy. She visited her usual customers but was told to come back next week. She needed the work now, not later. One of her customers suggested a house on the next street. A couple with two young children had moved in and were expecting a third child. Apple thanked the woman. It was getting late. She could not return home without money for a tree and disappoint the girls.

She bravely knocked on the door and waited. A pregnant woman answered. Their eyes locked in recognition. Apple had not seen Millie since the day she took the girls to the department store for a photograph, two years earlier.

"I clean for Mrs. Trainor over on the next street. I'm looking for work." Apple desperately wanted to walk away, but she swallowed her pride for the sake of making Christmas special for the girls. Millie motioned Apple to step indoors. "You can start with cleaning the dining room, and then vacuum and dust the living room. Walter likes a clean home after a long day at the office." Millie had married Walter just as she'd predicted to Gracie years earlier.

Apple noticed a seven-foot decorated Christmas tree in the corner of a room and tried to ignore it.

She must be desperate for money thought Millie as she peered into the living room at Apple vacuuming the carpet. Cleaning for a living was a life Millie had avoided by marrying Walter even though she knew his romantic attentions were focused elsewhere.

Walter co-owned several corporate rental properties with a business partner. Small-town gossip of suspicion about Walter and his business partner could ruin their company. Being gay in a small town could result in beatings or death threats. Walter needed a cover to save the business and continue the love affair with his business partner. Millie yearned to avoid the poverty and grim housing she'd grown up with. There were no wealthy men banging down her door. She heard the gossip about Walter. Not caring if it were true or not, she proposed marriage as a solution.

Millie now had a home in an upscale neighbourhood with access to disposable cash and children to focus on. Motherhood had been part of the negotiating terms before Millie said, "I do."

Millie could not deny Apple had been a good friend to her. She had been more loyal than the girls she encountered at the hockey rink while dating Walter. The girlfriends of hockey players had been cutthroat, sneaky troublemakers.

Millie had forged ahead into a high-society lifestyle and had no use for the past. But who was she to harshly judge Apple for being an unwed mother? In some ways Millie, too, was a single parent by choice—not by chance like Apple.

Millie did not attempt to engage in a conversation much to Apple's relief. "How much do I owe you?" Millie asked. "Twenty dollars for the two hours." It would be enough for a cheap Christmas tree and some sugary goodies to fill Christmas stockings.

The children were busy tearing through the kitchen in search of Christmas candies. Millie cupped a growing belly. She had no patience for their demands. "Santa is not coming to our house if you don't behave." The children stopped in their tracks. The warning had worked.

Millie chased the kids out of the room. She returned and handed Apple an envelope. Apple crammed the white envelope into her purse without opening it. She mumbled, "thanks," with no intention of ever returning.

Apple remembered the promise of a sugary treat as she crossed the railroad tracks. She ducked into a shop for a bag of penny candies. She ripped open the white envelope to pay the storeowner. Her jaw dropped. Inside the envelope were five twenty-dollar bills.

Apple figured the overpayment was an indication of regret, or pity, or both, but she and Millie would never be friends. They would never acknowledge each other if they were to meet by chance. She and Apple lived in two different worlds, separated by the railroad tracks.

Apple envisioned Sammi-Jo and Frankie going wild with excitement decorating a tree with store-bought Christmas lights. A tree with store bought blinking lights and thoughts of Santa coming to their house with presents would be cherished magical moments leading up to Christmas Day. But for Apple, cherished moments with the girls would be overshadowed by thoughts of the son she'd lost. Elmer. Where was he? Would there be toys under the tree for him? Was he hungry? Was he happy? The unanswered questions disturbed her sleep night after night.

Gracie and Apple would become best friends and their children grew up together. No one messed with Frankie, but Sammi-Jo and Elijah Blue were easy targets for teasing when Frankie wasn't around to protect them.

"Mum, I'm going downstairs to play with Sammi-Jo." Elijah Blue would run out the door before she could say a word. Gracie was an overly protective mother. She had to know where he was going and when he was coming home. It did not seem fair to Elijah Blue that Sammi-Jo and Frankie had more freedom than he did.

Elijah Blue pulled a page out of a pocket and gave it to Sammi-Jo when no one was around. She read it, giggled, and put it in a cardboard box with a collection of poems penned by Elijah Blue.

"Why do you hang around that sissy kid? I would never be caught dead with a guy that writes silly poems," rattled Frankie.

Twelve-year-old Sammi-Jo argued Elijah Blue never called her names like the kids in school. "He's nicer than most of the kids I know, and he likes to read books as much as I do."

Apple was in the kitchen listening to the girls argue. Frankie was mouthy and a wildcard like Sneakers. Sammi-Jo was the opposite of the older sister.

Apple couldn't help but wonder what had ever happened to Smithers. Had he really gone out west or had he moved to another area of Toronto? She could not be angry or hate the man for abandoning her. She was grateful to have been blessed with such a beautiful and thoughtful child. She did not tell Sammi-Jo make-believe stories about her father. Gracie told Elijah Blue crazy stories about a hero dad who died treating sick children in Africa. Apple warned Gracie, Elijah Blue, would one day learn his father never cared about him and be angry for being lied to.

"Stop teasing your sister. Elijah Blue is a nice boy. Someday you'll have a nice boyfriend, too."

Frankie snickered at the thought of being with a "nice boyfriend" like Elijah Blue. "I like girls better than silly boys like Elijah Blue."

Gracie came banging at the door. It was time for Elijah Blue to come home. He had homework before bedtime. "Frankie says she'll babysit, and we can go to the Legion for a beer. I'll buy the first round. I got paid cash for a cleaning job. Elijah Blue can come down after supper and do his homework. We can trust Frankie to take good care of the kids." Apple waited for an answer. Sammi-Jo interrupted Gracie before she could turn down the invitation.

"I will behave for Frankie. Elijah Blue can help me with my homework." Sammi-Jo flashed a girlish smile at Gracie. It worked. Gracie accepted the invitation.

"I will go with you as long as we are home before ten."

The two friends hoofed up the street to the Legion for a beer. It was after midnight when they arrived home from an evening of fun.

CHAPTER 21

Nanny came down with a stomach flu. Dr. Brooks told her to stay in bed for the rest of the week. He could not afford to have the entire household get sick. The dark days of depression had returned for Mrs. Brooks; medication and sleep would keep her imprisoned in her bedroom for days.

The maid and the cook suggested fourteen-year-old Joseph go outside with a soccer ball till dinner was ready.

The nursery had been redecorated throughout the years as he aged. Now Joseph was surrounded by a collection of sports memorabilia, a walnut desk with a brown leather chair, a matching leather sofa, a floor-to-ceiling bookcase, an antique grandfather clock, a rock collection displayed in an oak cabinet, and an entertainment centre.

Joseph kicked the soccer ball around the backyard. With one powerful kick, the ball rolled across the lawn near the window of his father's study. Joseph picked up the ball and noticed the lights were on in the study. He pressed his face against the window. Floor-length curtains had been left opened.

He became bored with kicking a soccer ball and ignored the suggestion to stay outdoors.

No one was around when he entered the back door of the mansion. Joseph was curious why the lights were on with Father at work and discovered the door of the study was opened. Father always locked the double doors to the study. What did Father do in the study behind closed doors that was so important? Why couldn't people enter without permission? Joseph did the unthinkable and entered the study.

A glass paperweight the size of a grapefruit caught his attention. He picked it up for a closer look. Spools of golden thread were etched in the glass of the paperweight. His father's initials had been engraved inside on a tiny silver plaque.

A sudden noise outside the office door spooked Joseph. He stiffened with fear. Was it Father? Did Father returned home early to check on his mother? The delicate glass paperweight slipped through his hands, crashed to the floor, and cracked. Joseph panicked. He darted out of the room to hide in his bedroom.

Why did Nanny have to be sick? She would not have allowed him to enter the study. Nanny was paid to care for him and to keep him out of mischief. Mother had important charitable duties that absorbed her time when she was not ill. It was Nanny who let him down not Mother.

The maid knocked on his bedroom door. Joseph refused to answer. She thought he was feeling unwell; perhaps he'd caught the flu from the nanny. She would let Dr. Brooks know.

It was late when Carlos drove Dr. Brooks home. He took long strides to the study carrying a briefcase. The doctor noticed the double doors to his office were open.

Could he have forgotten to lock the doors in his haste to leave for the hospital?

The study was the one room in the mansion that he could escape to without any interruptions. It was his private space. No one would dare enter without his permission.

Dr. Brooks searched the room for any signs of intruders and noticed the cracked paperweight that had been a Christmas gift from Mrs. Brooks. The maid was summoned but she had no answers.

"Master Joseph was outdoors kicking a soccer ball. I heard him go to his room. I knocked on the bedroom door, but he did not answer. I didn't want to disturb him in case he was resting."

Joseph had cried himself to sleep waiting for Dr. Brooks to return. He did not hear Father entering the bedroom. Dr. Brooks shook Joseph awake. "Were you in my study?" he demanded.

"No, Father. I saw the maid cleaning the study. I heard a crash like something broke. I came upstairs to study for a test. And I guess I fell asleep waiting for you to come home."

Dr. Brooks dragged a screaming Joseph across the floor and into the bathroom. He turned on a cold-water tap and pushed Joseph's head under flowing water. Joseph gagged on mouthfuls of water. He feared Father was going to drown him. "It wasn't me, Father. I swear it was the maid. Please stop, Father." Dr. Brooks turned off the water tap. Snot and tears streamed down Joseph's reddened face.

"You are a liar. I gave you a home and the best of everything. You have cost me a fortune. And this is how I am repaid, with lies and deceit, you ungrateful brat."

A red-faced Joseph coughed up a mouthful of water and cried out in desperation for mercy. "I am sorry, Father. I didn't mean to drop it." Dr. Brooks slapped Joseph across the side of the head. Joseph slumped to the floor. Dr. Brooks slammed the bathroom door shut behind him.

❅

Rosa stepped into the bedroom one last time. She had spent endless hours caring for Joseph in the room six days a week. She had sacrificed her youth to care for a pampered child.

She studied the room with a king-sized bed, a walk-in closet filled with expensive clothing, and sports equipment. There was a small refrigerator stocked with drinks and snacks, a colour television, and a collection of games and books filled shelves.

Her siblings would never know the luxuries Joseph took for granted, but her younger siblings were more fortunate than Joseph with all his riches.

Dr. and Mrs. Brooks gave Rosa a three-week notice after fourteen years of service. She had been told Joseph was getting too old for a nanny. They were sending him to a military boarding school in Switzerland because he required stricter discipline now that he was in his teens.

Rosa declined an offer of a letter of reference. She had been nothing more than a servant to the couple. "I would rather return to Mexico than waste my life raising children for rich families," she confided in Carlos.

Joseph had blamed Rosa for being shipped to a boarding school. He refused to say goodbye to her before leaving for the airport with his parents. "I loved and cared for him as if he were my little brother," she confided in Carlos. Tears welled in her eyes as she spoke. "He's treated me horribly for the last two weeks, shouting at me, demanding I get his books or his soccer ball, and being rude, saying he hates me, and it was my fault that he was being shipped to a boarding school." Carlos wrapped his arms around Rosa as she wept on his shoulder.

She confided in her cousin, Maria, that Joseph was no longer a cute little boy Mrs. Brooks could dress up and show off to high-society friends. And Mrs. Brooks was becoming more mentally unstable for longer periods of time. Dr. Brooks did not have the time or energy to deal with the demands of a teenager hungry for acceptance and love.

Rosa's family would celebrate her return with a celebration of food, music, and dancing. She would be meeting for the first time a nephew born while she was living in the States. Rosa would be considered a wealthy woman with the savings she'd acquired.

She whispered in the quietness of the bedroom. "Goodbye my sweet Joseph. Stay safe."

Carlos put the suitcases filled mostly with gifts for the family in the trunk of the car and opened the car door for her. Rosa was finally going home.

CHAPTER 22

The streetlamp outside the apartment building lit the October evening. The days were becoming shorter, and in a couple of months the street would be snow-covered and icy. A gang of neighbourhood kids were enjoying the freedom of playing in the streets before being called home.

Elijah Blue and Sammi-Jo raced up the street while Frankie lingered behind with friends. "Let the babies go home," fourteen-year-old Frankie bellowed. "Let's go see who is boozing at the blue house."

The blue house was a bootlegger establishment near the end of the street. It had a well-worn path around the side of the house to the back door. Frankie and the gang sneaked along the edge of the pathway. They could hear guitar music and singing, but the blinds were pulled down. Raisin, one of the teens, easily recognized the singer; it was her father. Raisin slapped the window with the palm of her hand in anger. Her mother and two younger siblings were at home in need of warm clothing before winter settled in. Her old man was drinking the family allowance and singing for booze at the bootleggers. The gang of teenagers scattered out of fear of being caught. Frankie grabbed Raisin by the hand. They ran down the street and ducked into an alleyway.

"You can come to my house, Raisin. My mom cooks a load of food for supper," offered Frankie. Raisin and her family had

moved to the street a year earlier. She and Frankie became best
friends. Raisin was a smartass like Frankie. Like Frankie, she
would beat the piss out of the snotty girls in the schoolyard. Both
teens had no tolerance for silly boys that teased the girls, snap-
ping their bra straps. Raisin was a mouthpiece and had a strong
vocabulary of curse words.

Frankie confided in Raisin and told heroic stories of her
father in prison who'd sold his soul to protect his family. Raisin
listened with admiration. One night, she risked kissing Frankie
and waited for a response. Frankie smiled.

"Naw, I better go home. Mom will be wondering where I am."
The two teens kissed in the darkness and parted ways. Frankie
watched Raisin walking down the street to her house.

Talking about Raisin's father got Frankie thinking about visiting Sneakers in prison. She had vague memories of him. What
did he look like? Would he know her? Would he like her? Why
had they never visited him in prison? The questions swirled in
her head.

Her mom read his letters from prison only a couple of prov-
inces away, but he might as well have been living in China. Apple
refused to take her to see Sneakers no mattered how much she
begged. "It is no place to bring a child," she told Frankie without explaining why. But the truth was Sneakers would not have
his daughter see him locked up and wearing a prison uniform.
Sneakers wrote to Apple it would be better for Frankie to remember him riding on his shoulders, laughing, playing with her, and
smothering her in kisses. Not a middle-aged man hardened with
years behind bars unable to be the father he once was.

Frankie spotted Gracie sitting on the landing as she climbed
up the steps to the second-floor apartment. She considered Elijah
Blue's mother weird. She heard Elijah Blue telling Sammi-Jo his
mother was gifted with a third eye. She could see things and hear

things that other people could not. And she read tealeaves, predicting the future. What could anyone see in a cup with dribbles of tealeaves? It did not stop Gracie from staring into cups.

Gracie offered to read Apple's tealeaves. She refused, saying it was best not to know the future and to allow it to happen.

Gracie was wrapped in a blanket crying and babbling. Frankie did not believe Gracie could predict the future but perhaps the tealeaves had predicted trouble. "Nonsense, crying about such foolish stuff," Frankie murmured to herself.

"Why are you late? The streetlamp has been on for the last half hour," Apple lectured. "You know I worry. Why do you make me worry?"

Sammi-Jo took a plate of warm food from the oven and served Frankie supper. She would wash Frankie's dirty dishes later and neatly stack them in the cupboard.

"You are a goody-goody two shoes," joked Frankie. "The good sister."

Sammi-Jo tugged a handful of Frankie's reddish hair. She adored her big sister.

The two girls had different personalities. Apple figured it was because they had different daddies. Sammi-Jo was shy and quiet. She did not like roughness or fighting. She tagged along with Apple to help with cleaning jobs on the weekend. Frankie did not have a motherly bone in her body. Sammi-Jo loved children and enjoyed babysitting. The sisters were close despite the personality differences. Apple bought bunk beds at a second-hand furniture store so the girls could each have their own bed instead of being cramped in one. She checked on the girls at night only to discover they were cuddled up sleeping in one of the twin beds.

Frankie told her mother about seeing Gracie sitting in the dark bawling. "I figured the tealeaves gave her bad news," chuckled Frankie.

Sammi-Jo stopped washing dishes. "What if it's bad news about Elijah Blue?" "Mom, you should go see if he's okay. Please, Mom," Sammi-Jo pleaded.

It was dark and cold and late in the evening. Apple did not want to leave the comfort of the kitchen but grabbed a jacket. She could hear Gracie sobbing as soon as she opened the door.

"What is the matter? What are you doing bawling outside in the cold?" Apple plunked down on the steps next to her friend. Gracie shook with sobs and tears dripped down her face.

Apple became concerned for her friend knowing social services would be quick to knock on the door if Gracie were going bonkers and not able to care for Elijah Blue.

"I did not want Elijah Blue to know I was crying. We had an argument and I told him to go to bed," sobbed Gracie. "We argued after supper about his father. He wants to know his name. And talks about calling his father and going to visit him, going to ballgames, and working on old cars. The stuff he hears the other kids talk about in school. I told him his dad did not live on the Island, but it is a lie."

Apple did not pry for information. She asked Gracie years ago about the missing dad and was told he didn't exist. But fathers do exist. They live with their families, or housed in prison, or they disappear without a trace, but they still exist somewhere on the planet.

"His father lives in a rich neighbourhood on the outskirts of town and is married with a family. The bastard warned me he would report me to child protection if I ever contacted him or his family. He said I was uneducated, foolish, and too wild to be a responsible parent. He would crush Elijah Blue without mercy to protect himself and his family. I know he would."

Apple had no answers. She'd told her daughters the truth about their fathers. It was not an option for everyone, she knew.

Apple had lived with rejection for years in foster homes. Apple understood the desire for Gracie to protect Elijah Blue.

Apple wrapped her arms around Gracie and sat in the dark with her until the tears dried. Fathers were not supposed to be locked behind bars or drinking the family allowance while children needed winter footwear. Good fathers did not leave a note saying *Goodbye, I am heading west.* Good fathers did not abandon their child or threaten to falsely report their mothers.

Sammi-Jo was waiting for Apple at the textbook-covered kitchen table.

"Elijah Blue is fine, Sammi-Jo. Finish your homework and go to bed," Apple commanded before Sammi-Jo could ask any more questions.

Gracie stepped into the apartment and stumbled about in the darkness. She sat out on the sofa and gazed into the darkness while Elijah Blue dreamed about a father he had never met.

❊

A year later, a *For Sale* sign was stabbed in the ground in front of the apartment building.

It was the only home thirteen-year-old Elijah Blue had ever lived in. Most of the tenants had lived in the building even longer. This was their home.

What would happen if the building sold? Would they have to move and pay higher rent? The apartment building was more than just apartment rentals. It was the home of a fellowship of neighbours who laughed, gossiped, argued, and genuinely cared for each other. The *For Sale* sign threatened the very fabric of their sheltered life.

The landlord gave tours of the apartment building to potential buyers. The tenants remained silent and fearful as strangers invaded their personal space, looking at this and that, and asking questions.

"The thought of me and the girls moving makes me sick with worry," Apple confided in her neighbour Annie. "What is going to happen if the new landlord hikes up the rent or puts us out? Christ-bejeezus, I can hardly afford this place."

Annie pulled a long drag on a cigarette before speaking. "Why bother getting so worked up about something that hasn't happened? Who knows, the next landlord could be better than the one we have now. Do you remember last winter when the furnace broke down? We went without heat for almost a week before it got fixed. Him, a big businessman with apartment buildings all over town, and he's mean as cat shit." Annie's lecture brought no comfort to Apple. She fretted the day away worrying about what changes tomorrow might bring.

The tours by prospective buyers became less frequent. The talk of the building sale simmered down until one evening *Sold* was slashed across the sign.

The new landlord and his snooty daughter entered the apartments without knocking. They made life miserable for the tenants. No one protested out of fear of being evicted. Apple got a bolt lock for the door so the new landlord could not walk in on her. Annie and the family moved back to Newfoundland, and they took Bingo Alice with them. Gracie got an eviction notice.

Elijah Blue kicked up a fuss. He did not want to move and leave friends and the only home he had ever known.

"It's just across town, Sammi-Jo. Elijah Blue will come back to visit. His mother and I will still be best friends," Apple assured a sulky Sammi-Jo.

"We're starting a new life on a new street. We'll each have our own bedroom in the new place. There is a big backyard we can enjoy. I can finally grow flowers and vegetables. One day, you will be leaving home for university. And you will be old enough to do as you please. You can move out and go anywhere you want. But for now, you are moving across town with me." The conversation ended with a defeated Elijah Blue stomping out of the apartment.

Elijah Blue moped about the new apartment. He did not know anyone on the street. His mother began meeting new friends. She enrolled him in art classes and introduced him to the sons and daughters of her new artistic friends. They invited Elijah Blue to their pizza parties and backyard bonfires. The visits to the old neighbourhood eventually phased out.

CHAPTER 23

An early morning fog swallowed the seaside town as the clanging of church bells beckoned the faithful to Mass. Sister Henrietta scurried through the streets towards the church. Her black-heeled shoes smacking the cracked sidewalk shattered the silence. Her black robe dusted the sidewalk leading to the house of God.

A startled paperboy noticed a tall black figure walking in a sea of white mist and feared it was a ghost wandering the streets of Charlottetown. As it got closer and closer, he realized the eerie phantom was only a nun. The boy swore and released the fear building up inside of him.

The Catholic Church had been a second home to Sister Henrietta since childhood. Her family had tramped down a mud-caked road to attend Sunday Mass. Her father carried a toddler and a baby nestled in the arms of her mother. A string of children staggered behind their parents through a narrow pathway barely passable in winter to a country church.

Sister Henrietta had been groomed at an early age to become a bride of Christ and entered the convent on her sixteenth birthday. Obedience to God and the Catholic faith protected her soul from the agony of purgatory and the eternal fires of hell.

She prayed for her deceased sister, Marion, in the front pew of the church. Sister Henrietta begged God to have mercy on

Marion's wicked soul. As she prayed, her memory drifted back to the day she'd arrived home from school to find Marion gone. No goodbyes. Her parents told the children Marion had gone to the States in search of employment.

It was years before Sister Henrietta learned Marion had been pregnant and sent to stay with relatives in the countryside. They'd agreed to board Marion for the price of a milking cow. Marion's father hitched a team of horses and tethered the cow to the back of the wagon for the twenty-five-mile journey through the back roads of the Island. Marion had been warned to stay out of sight under a bed of straw in the back of the wagon.

"Get out from there," ordered Marion's father when they arrived at the farm. "You're not to make any trouble or the family will put you out in the cold." Marion climbed down from the wagon with a burlap bag of clothing.

"Untie the cow," he ordered. She did as she was told. He whipped the horse and headed for home without saying goodbye or looking back at Marion. It was the last time she saw her father.

Marion stood in the yard, not knowing what to do. The door of a farmhouse opened. An aged couple took the cow and ushered Marion into the house. Her cousin led her up the stairs to the bedroom where she was told to stay.

"I am not going to wait on you like a maid," her cousin told Marion in an annoyed tone. "You come downstairs after dark to get something to eat."

She gave Marion strict instructions not to look out the bedroom window during the day and to keep the curtains closed. She was warned not make a sound if anyone came to the house. No one must know she was there.

Marion craved outdoor sunlight and fresh air but did not dare leave the room during the day for fear the cousins would tell her to leave. And where would she go?

She stumbled about in the farmyard to empty the chamber pot in an outdoor toilet by the light of the moon and stars. She savoured the freedom as she stood under the night sky.

A scream ripped through the farmhouse early one morning announcing the baby was coming. She cried out in agony as the little life inside of her struggled to leave the womb. It would be hours before the baby entered the world with only the assistance of the cousin. Marion had no choice but to give the baby up for adoption.

The cousin had arranged for the parish priest to come late at night for the baby. Marion wrapped her three-day-old infant in a blanket for the long drive to an orphanage.

The pain of her breasts, hardened with milk, became unbearable. She moaned and curled up in a ball in the bed. The relatives had done their duty and kept their part of the bargain. It was time for Marion to move on. It was arranged for the parish priest to drive Marion to a train station. The young woman boarded a train for Boston in search of a new life.

Marion wrote sporadic letters to her mother which is how Sister Henrietta learned what had happened to her. But Marion never returned to the Island.

❀

Sister Henrietta pushed these memories aside as she hustled through the streets to the home for unwed mothers that also served as a charity centre for people. The office had a desk, two stiff wooden chairs, and a filing cabinet in a corner of the room. Religious artwork depicting a suffering Jesus graced the wall behind the desk. A crucifix hung over the entrance of the door. The office had been painted a dull brownish colour. The window shades were pulled down. A single dim lightbulb in the centre of the ceiling was the only source of light.

From behind her desk, Sister Henrietta studied the pregnant woman clutching a tearstained handkerchief across from her. "What's your name? How far along are you?" Sister Henrietta demanded.

The young woman stuttered, trying to find the words to explain the unwanted pregnancy.

Sister Henrietta repeated the questions in an irate tone. She was expecting an important visitor later in the morning and did not have time for drama.

"Mary McNeil. I am five months and showing. I lost my job and couldn't pay the rent at the boarding house. I have no money and no place to go."

The gloomy office atmosphere matched the dismal circumstances of the unwed mothers staying at the home. Mary McNeil shared one of the many confessions Sister Henrietta was privy to in the cheerless office.

Mary had been reared to be polite and passive which made her an easy target for unwanted attention. An uncle had been in town selling turnips and cabbages door-to-door and visited Mary at the boarding house. She invited him to her room for a family chat. He'd grabbed Mary and raped her.

Mary said her parents called her a liar through fits of gut-wrenching sobs. The uncle was a devoted Catholic, a good-living man, the family rebutted. A wife and adult children of the uncle were mortified Mary would fabricate such a lie.

"I don't want the baby," Mary confessed. "I don't want to see it."

Good, thought Sister Henrietta. The girl at least had some common sense. "You put yourself in a vulnerable position," Sister Henrietta lectured. "God gave men uncontrollable instincts to be capable of reproducing. You should never have been alone with your uncle or with any man, for that matter."

Mary argued her parents taught her to respect older people. "It would have been rude not to invite him inside for a visit. My parents would have been angry if I'd asked him to leave."

The nun frowned at Mary for being disrespectful and talking back.

"Don't blame your parents for the situation you're in. It was their duty to teach you to be polite and respectful and to act decently," Sister Henrietta scolded. "It's you who have sinned by becoming pregnant before marriage. The suffering of childbirth will redeem you from your mortal sin."

Mary McNeil had an angelic face framed with golden hair, a flawless complexion, and deep blue eyes. Her beauty triggered memories of Marion.

Marion had also been cursed with beauty that attracted men and had disgraced the family. It was bad enough Marion became pregnant and shamed the family but the father of the bastard had been a Protestant from the mainland working on a neighbouring farm. The young man had visited the night before Marion disappeared. Sister Henrietta had been a frightened twelve-year-old crouched under the kitchen table. Her father was at the door shouting at the Protestant to leave. Their father threatened to take the gun down that hung on a wall in the farmhouse. Marion cried and begged him not to hurt the unwelcome visitor. The Protestant vanished in the darkness of the night.

Sister Henrietta inherited the shame and disgrace Marion had inflicted on her parents.

The nun exited the office and returned with the housemother, a woman in her late forties, who stayed at the home for unwed mothers. Her duties included accompanying the pregnant women to a nearby hospital to be certain there were no relatives or boyfriends sneaking around, interfering with adoption procedures.

Mary McNeil could stay at the home for unwed mothers. Sister Henrietta warned Mary never to leave the home without permission and no visitors were allowed. She was never to use the front door leaving or entering the building.

A knock on the office door alerted Sister Henrietta of an appointment with Mr. Eldon, Deputy Minister of Social Services.

Mr. Eldon was troubled by the reports from the minutes of meetings of Family Services saying the church was requiring large donations for international adoptions. He voiced concern to Sister Henrietta.

"You cannot accept money from the people who adopt babies, Sister Henrietta. If it comes out in the papers that two thousand dollars came back to you, the media will have a field day. Your name will be plastered in every paper in the country that the church is profiting from the sales of babies born to unwed mothers. That could lead to an investigation of human trafficking. It has the potential to create scandal."

The nun had no intentions of allowing Mr. Eldon take charge of what she considered charitable work.

"Take your concerns to the Board of Directors or to my good friend, the premier of the province. He is on the advisory board that recommended me for the Order of Canada." Sister Henrietta explained the donations covered extensive, time-consuming work involved in the American adoptions. And she was protecting infants from growing up in the shadow of the sins of fallen women. "Illegitimate babies are being raised by honourable, wealthy Catholic families. I'm doing God's work. Do you have any idea the operational costs of the home for unwed mothers? The women searching for food and shelter are a disgrace to their parents and the community. Where would they go if the home closed? Do you have any idea the number of people who show up at my back door begging for money to buy coal or for food to put on the table? Where do you think the money comes from? I have never done anything outside of the law."

Their conversation became heated. Mr. Eldon stormed out of the office. He recognized Mrs. Sellers sitting on a bench outside of the office with two school-aged children as he was leaving.

"Good afternoon, Mrs. Sellers. How is the family? Is there no school today?"

Mrs. Sellers, a heavyset woman with missing front teeth was dressed in worn-out but clean clothing. Mr. Eldon noticed the boys were barefoot. The fall weather was much too chilly to be without socks and shoes.

"We are doing just fine. The boys cannot go to school until I can get some shoes for their feet." Mr. Eldon nodded. The poor woman figured Sister Henrietta would have pity on the shoeless children. He glanced back at Mrs. Sellers with sympathy as he opened the back door that led to an alleyway.

Mrs. Sellers knocked on the office door. She and the boys stepped inside the dreary office without waiting for an invitation to enter. Mrs. Sellers dropped down on the chair that Mr. Eldon had sat in moments earlier. The boys stood behind their mother.

"How are you, Sister?" She didn't wait for an answer. "I am right sorry for barging in on you, but it's an emergency. Peter is working on the boat way up in the Great Lakes. He has no way to send me money and he is not going to be home till near Christmas. My boys can't go to school because they have no shoes. Their old pair is tattered and way too small for their big feet. I am expecting a little one in January. It would be awfully nice to take the baby home from the hospital in store-bought sleepers and a new blanket."

Mrs. Sellers had arrived unannounced last month asking for money to buy coal. Next month, it would be something else. The story was always the same—her husband Peter was working on a boat in the Great Lakes and the family would be in dire need of coal or food. Today it was money for shoes and baby clothing.

"Let them wear the old shoes till winter sets in. Then they can wear boots to school. The church is not responsible for dressing your children. That is your husband's job."

Nine-year-old Hayden stuck his tongue out at the nun. He hated her for being mean to his mother.

Hayden did his part feeding the family. He and a bunch of kids would go down to the wharf to snatch potatoes and turnips that spilled on the loading dock. The workers on the dock would purposely throw potatoes, carrots, and turnips out of the bins being loaded on ships. The kids would grab what they could and head home.

Sister Henrietta snapped at Mrs. Sellers. "Is this what you teach your children? To stick their tongue out at a nun."

Mrs. Sellers stood up and chastised Hayden with a smack on the side of the head. "Show some respect," she said and winked at Hayden.

"I don't want to see you back here." Sister Henrietta thrust a twenty-dollar bill into the waiting hand of Mrs. Sellers.

"God bless you, Sister Henrietta. Say thank you to the kind nun."

Hayden and Henry would rather fight crocodiles but were forced to mumble, "Thanks."

Mrs. Sellers and the boys walked uptown to buy new shoes. "You did good boys. I will treat you to a milkshake, but you'll have to share it." She warned Hayden not to be so bold the next time and jokingly threatened to give him to the nuns. "That's not a nice thing to say, Ma," Hayden replied with a tone of anger.

Mrs. Sellers cupped her belly as if protecting the little life nestled in the warmth of the womb. "Don't fret, Hayden. It's not you she wants to get her hands on."

✷

Sister Henrietta yelped as a quick stabbing pain punctured her stomach, a reminder of the stabbing she almost didn't survived. She had been hospitalized for weeks. God had protected her as she seesawed between life and death on the operating table.

Her attacker had been sentenced to life in prison. Sister Henrietta received a Christmas card with a cartoon drawing of a hangman every year. There was no return address or name inside the card. She knew without a doubt it had to be a warning from Frank – who the others called Sneakers – to keep the oath to stay away from Gladys and his daughter. It was his way of reminding her he had connections to the criminal world outside of prison.

Sister Henrietta snickered every time she saw Gladys around town with the two girls. She had the patience to wait for the opportunity for revenge, to pay back Gladys for the pain she'd suffered even if it took years.

CHAPTER 24

Sister Henrietta was on her deathbed. No one thought she would ever die. It seemed the nun had been born old. Not many people could recall her ever being young. The towns people gossiped that if anyone could cheat the Spirit of Death it would be Sister Henrietta.

Apple got wind of the news and waited until Sammi-Jo and Frankie had gone to school. Apple searched her closet for a proper black skirt that dropped below the knees and a faded black blouse.

The mourning outfit was snug, but it had to do; it was the only suitable attire she owned to wear to visit the dying nun.

She stopped to pluck a handful of flowers growing in front of a house on the way to the convent, a twenty-minute walk.

She approached the massive doors to the convent and with a speeding heart rate and false courage, Apple rang the door-bell and waited. For a fleeting moment, she considered turning around and heading for home before someone answered the bell. She stood straighter and held her ground when a stern-looking matron answered. Before she could change her mind, the words tumbled out.

"I'm here to visit the good Sister Henrietta," she told the matron who answered the door. "I heard she was feeling poorly and brought her some flowers."

It was not uncommon for Sister Henrietta to have visitors, but most of the visitors had been older than the woman standing on the doorstep.

"My name is Catherine Anne Tweedy. My uncle, Judge Tweedy, was a good friend to Sister Henrietta. She visited my family many times." Apple lowered her head and pretended to sob.

"Come on in. Your uncle was a good man, God rest his soul."

Apple faked a smile and thanked the matron, then followed her through the convent and up a flight of stairs to the infirmary.

"I will put the flowers in a vase while you visit. You can sign the guestbook on a table near the door if she is sleeping."

Apple stepped into the room. The smell of medicine gagged her. A bag of bones was laid out in a bed like a corpse in a coffin.

She jabbed the nun in the stomach with a finger. A startled Sister Henrietta opened her eyes and noticed Apple standing at the side of the bed. Apple snatched the bell before Sister Henrietta could ring for a nurse.

"Confess who bought my baby boy and save your wicked soul," Apple demanded. "You had no right to take my baby and give him away. Where is Elmer? Who took him?"

Apple knew she had little time to get information before the matron returned. She softened her voice. "Please. I need to know what happened to my baby boy. I beg of you."

The skeleton under the bedcovers gawked at Apple and hissed, "I'll take the names to my grave."

Apple grabbed a pillow. She could snuff out the life of the feeble nun without a struggle. The nun shrank in fear under the bedcovers.

Apple lifted the pillow and brushed the nun's face with it. "Tell me where my baby is."

In a raspy, strained voice, the nun replied that she would rather suffocate than tell. Apple threw the pillow across the room in a flurry of anger. She would end up in prison and her daughters would go into the foster care system if the anger raging through her won.

Apple spat on the deathbed and stomped out of the room more determined than ever to find her stolen baby.

CHAPTER 25

I t was 1999 and the dawning of a new century. Twenty-nine-year-old Elijah Blue had crossed the tracks of poverty years earlier and never looked back. A law degree earned him the privileges he didn't have as a child.

He grabbed the receiver on the second ring and answered in a sharp tone, "Elijah O'Brien speaking."

His top-floor office in the downtown building had an eagle's-eye view of the coastal town he grew up in. A burning red sunset was lazily sinking into the waiting sea. It would be another late evening at the office.

"Elijah Blue, my gawd, it's good hearing your voice after all these years," echoed a voice through the telephone receiver.

No one had called him "Elijah Blue" since he was a boy. He remembered the voice but not the name. She blurted it before he had a chance to ask. "It's Apple. I used to babysit you, remember, in the old neighbourhood?"

The name "Apple" was from a former life. He had gone to university and studied law and become a criminal lawyer with a reputation for winning. He never stepped back in time to the days growing up on the east side of the tracks. He had buried his memories of the old neighbourhood when he became a lawyer.

A stack of files needed his attention, and he was due in court in the morning. It was a high-profile case he had been working on for months. He had no time for idle reminiscing.

But Apple was not looking to reminisce. "I need a good lawyer, and I read in the papers that you are one. That's why I'm calling. Years ago, Sister Henrietta took my first baby at birth, my boy, before I had Frankie. You remember Frankie? But Elijah Blue, I never signed any adoption papers. She stole him."

Elijah had heard the stories of Sister Henrietta. He recalled the days of playing road hockey with friends. The kids would disappear into an alleyway if a sleek black Cadillac motored down the street. Sister Henrietta was the town boogeyman on the prowl in search of children to snatch. The memories were disturbing, and he didn't have time to reminisce.

"I work in criminal law. I suggest you contact a family law firm."

Did Apple thank him for the tip? No. She apologized for taking up his "precious time" and slammed the phone down.

He placed his receiver on the hook and tried to return to the task she had interrupted. But he could not focus. His memory drifted back to his boyhood days. Apple had been his mother's best friend. She'd babysat him and allowed him to get away with things his mother would have lectured him about. Apple was never strict like his mother. She never corrected his grammar or punished him for saying the occasional swear word. His mother would be ashamed by the way he treated an old friend.

❄

He didn't recognize the visitor waiting for him outside the office the next day. But she recognized Elijah. "Well, if it's not the big-shot lawyer. You don't remember me, do you?"

A lanky woman with a boyish hairstyle blocked him from entering the doorway to his office building. Perhaps she was a friend or relative of one of the drug dealers from a former court case. He threatened to contact the police if she did not leave the premises.

"You, ungrateful little snot. My mother babysat you and wiped your shitty arse. You repay her by acting like you're too important to treat her with decency and respect."

There was no mistaking Frankie even if he hadn't seen her since he was a teenager. He ushered Frankie inside the building and guided her into his office. She was still bold and mouthy.

He recalled the time a gang of boys from the west end had roamed their neighbourhood searching for trouble. She threw rocks at the troublemakers. She told Elijah to run home. She was probably still a fighter.

"Your mother is chasing old ghosts. I am a criminal lawyer for the Crown. I have little knowledge and no experience of family law." He hoped the explanation would satisfy Frankie.

"A criminal lawyer is what we need not some fluffy family lawyer. You and I know that old battle axe was selling babies. The entire town knew. There needs to be a criminal investigation. Just because Sister Henrietta is dead and dancing with the Devil doesn't mean she shouldn't be held accountable for what she did to my mother and countless other women."

Elijah knew it was useless trying to explain how the law worked. It was not as cut and dry as Frankie thought. It would be a complicated challenge. The home for unwed mothers had shut down years ago; unwed mothers were now raising their children without shame.

"You need to come visit Mom and talk with her. You can explain why you are not willing to represent her. You owe her that much."

He glanced at his calendar. "Okay, Frankie. Bring her in about four tomorrow and I will talk to her."

But the answer didn't satisfy Frankie. "No, I won't. You'll have to go see her."

It was not the answer he was expecting. He picked up a pen and notepad with reluctance. "Where does she live? I'll drop by, but I will not make any promises."

He rocked back in his brown leather chair waiting for the address. Frankie eyed the office with its massive mahogany desk in the centre of the room. One side of the wall was lined with bookshelves. In a corner were filing cabinets. There was still plenty of space in the room despite a leather sofa, plush velvet chairs, and a stack of papers on a long, narrow table. Framed documents of university credentials and a law degree decorated the wall behind the desk.

Frankie smirked. "You know where we live. Do I need to draw a map? Perhaps you've forgotten the old address? Come by tomorrow evening after my shift at the hospital, about six. Try not to be late."

He knew from experience there was no point in arguing with Frankie. The sooner he met with Apple, the quicker he could put the intrusion behind him.

Frankie walked out of the office without saying thank you or goodbye.

She had mentioned she worked at the hospital. Apple had cleaned apartment buildings for landlords as well as the homes of wealthy people when he was a boy. He figured Frankie probably worked as a cleaner at the hospital. Even if she earned a decent wage, she could probably use more work. There was a need for a custodian in his office building. If he could not help Apple at least he could offer Frankie a cleaning job.

❋

Elijah had been a young teen when he and Gracie moved from the old neighbourhood.

Gracie had been devastated when they were evicted and had bouts of depression for weeks in the new place. She missed the old neighbourhood, the daily interactions with Annie and Apple, and she missed good friends that she could count on.

The visits to the old neighbourhood fizzled out with time. His mother, never one to muck in misery, took a leap of faith and enrolled in college. It opened the door to new friendships, and it sparked a desire for new adventures and opportunities for dating without needing to hire a babysitter. She could come and go as she pleased with no worries about Elijah Blue being home alone. He had his own collection of friends and interests.

His mother had studied photography at a community college, working nights waitressing to pay for the classes, camera equipment, and tuition. She had years of experience documenting him growing up through a camera lens. It was what she enjoyed and what she was good at. Photography created a new purpose in her life.

❋

The impoverished days on Chestnut Street were long behind them. But as he stepped out of the car and onto the curb in front of the old apartment building, the past greeted him with long-forgotten memories. There were too many old ghosts coming from all directions. He recalled Bingo Alice and Annie sitting on the doorstep of the apartment building, talking, drinking and smoking.

Bingo Alice had been one of a few female cabbies in town.

Elijah heard stories that Bingo Alice had kept a knife under the seat of the cab to scare late-night drunks who tried to stiff her.

He once asked his mother what the word *dyke* meant. She asked why he was asking. He had overheard a neighbour call Bingo Alice a dyke. His mother told him it was not a nice word and to never to repeat it or Bingo Alice would box his ears.

Annie had moved the family to Newfoundland after being evicted by the new landlords. She and his mother had exchanged letters for the first year or two. His mother had talked about going to Newfoundland to visit Annie, but it never happened. He realized long ago his mother was a dreamer and a talker.

He wanted to get in his car and drive away but there was no turning back. When he was a kid, he thought he lived in the best neighbourhood in the whole world, surrounded by friends and with a paper route for pocket money. He'd never noticed the poverty, shabbiness, and roughness of cheap rentals that landlords neglected. His mother, too, had treasured the neighbourhood.

She would often tell the snowsuit story. He had been a winter baby, and his mother did not have money to buy him a snowsuit. Money was scarce and there were no second-hand baby stores. One night Annie won big at bingo and covered most of the cost of a snowsuit from Eaton's, collecting money from the other people in the building for the rest.

His mother took the snowsuit out of a box in the closet the day he started university. She stroked the plushy blue fur with a faraway look in her eyes. The fact he had received a scholarship for university proved the Eaton's snowsuit had indeed been a good omen, according to his mother.

He climbed the stairway to the second-floor apartment now without looking up at the flight of steep stairs that led to the tree-house apartment. If he did, it might unleash memories buried deep in the past that he was not prepared to deal with.

"You cut your long hair" were the first words out of Apple's mouth as Elijah stepped into the kitchen. "I've never known you not to have long red hair. You and Gracie looked like twins from the back."

Elijah stood in the kitchen not knowing what to say or how to stop Apple from talking about his mother.

"Look at you, in a suit and tie. I am not surprised you have done well, not at all. Your mother groomed you for success from the time you were born, always bragging about how smart you were. She must have been right proud of you when you got that big law degree."

Elijah changed the subject and lied about how good it was to see her and the girls after so many years.

Apple had aged. Streaks of white hair had appeared. She still had a roly-poly body, with more pounds now. Her personality had not changed. She was still a talker and a schemer. It seemed to be a survival skill with single parents.

"I'm still on this side of the sod. I'm not ready to be put down anytime soon. My girls have done well. Frankie's an OR nurse at the hospital."

Elijah glanced at Frankie with surprise. Apple did not miss it. She had witnessed that look on the faces of people surprised to learn that a child of a welfare parent could become a registered nurse in an operating room.

"My Frankie is smart as anyone over on the west side. She could be a doctor if she wanted to. But unlike some people, my girls have never forgotten where they live and who raised them."

A flash of guilt stabbed Elijah and he flushed with embarrassment. He had to admit, he was surprised Frankie had made it through high school, let alone university. She had been suspended more than once for fighting in the schoolyard—and not with the girls. School had been a hateful experience for a lot of east side kids.

"And my Sammi-Jo is working in a daycare."

"Elmer is my oldest. Every year we celebrate his birthday. The girls make cards for him. I have a box of the cards in the closet to give him."

Elijah had been having trouble getting his head around the news of her son since she'd called his office. Apple and her daughters had been a big part of his growing-up years. He had sleepovers at their house. They shared childhood secrets vowing to never tell a living soul or else the Bad Man would steal them. Never had the sisters mentioned an older brother let alone yearly birthday celebrations. He would overhear conversations while pretending to be sleeping. He was often privy to stories never meant for his ears, but never did he hear Apple talk to his mom about a missing baby boy. Did Gracie know? Did Annie or Bingo Alice know? There were very few secrets in the apartment building and on the street.

"The nuns took my baby. I never signed papers giving anyone the rights to adopt my baby boy and I never wanted my baby to go to strangers. My foster parents, Hilda and Stan, were going to raise my baby. Elmer is thirty-three years old now and I have no idea if he is still living. For all I know, he could be homeless, living on the streets, or dead. I need a good lawyer who can find out what happened to him. Who took him? Where is he now? I never signed adoption papers."

Frankie and Sammi-Jo bowed their heads with sorrowful expressions as if in mourning.

"That old nun who snatched my baby died. But she should still be held accountable for what she did. Not just to me. She tried to take you from your mother, too. Your mother was always looking over her shoulder, raising you. We all looked over our shoulders with that baby thief stalking the town."

Elijah was well versed in the story of how the old nun tried to abduct him at birth. His mother had given birth at the Catholic hospital. A nurse in the delivery room refused to give him to his mother. It was the doctor who'd rescued him from the nurse and placed him in his mother's arms.

The old nun came like a thief in the night searching for him. A younger nun hid with him in a closet until the old nun had left the hospital. A week later his mom bundled him in the Eaton's snowsuit and took him home in a cab. The treehouse had been his mother's haven, and she believed the treehouse had spiritual protectors that could stop evil, like Sister Henrietta, from entering.

"I can pay for your services if that's what you are worried about. Frankie's girlfriend, Raisin, is a teacher. They both make big money. Frankie and Raisin bought a house not far from here. We will all chip in and pay the legal bill."

He explained she had been a minor, and not legally recognized as an adult. Child welfare had had the legal rights to intervene. He would be denied access to the sealed adoption records. Human trafficking would be impossible to prove. It was a sad ending, but one Apple would have to accept.

"Save your money, because another lawyer will tell you the same. You were a minor in care."

"I should have hammered the snot out you when you were a kid," thirty-one-year-old Frankie spat. "How dare you speak down to my mother in that legal jargon. This is not a courtroom. What about the right to be treated like a human being? My mother was underage and in foster care, but that did not give the nun the right to take a baby at birth without permission. She never even got to see him."

Sammi-Jo got up from the table and stepped across the kitchen floor. "Get out. Get in your fucking car and leave the street. You don't belong here anymore." Apple and Frankie looked at each other in disbelief. It was the first time they'd heard Sammi-Jo curse.

Sammi-Jo stood at the open door waiting to slam it behind the fancy-pants lawyer.

But Elijah could not allow Sammi-Jo to think he had become self-important.

He took a notepad out of a briefcase. "I'll need details about the birth of the baby," he said with a hint of shame in his voice.

CHAPTER 26

Mother telephoned the Brazil office. "Your father had a heart attack and died peacefully in his sleep. Please come home, Joseph."

Thirty-three-year-old Joseph stood in his New York office standing at the window deep in thought, a few days later.

His thoughts were interrupted by the buzzing of an intercom. Why couldn't the secretary follow a few simple instructions? He'd told her no interruptions and to cancel appointments for the week.

The buzzing of the intercom again caused him to jump. "Damn it. What?" It was a moment before the secretary replied in a nervous tone of voice. "I am sorry, Mr. Brooks, but your mother insists on speaking with you."

It was only midmorning. He was surprised she was out of bed and functioning. "Put her through," he demanded and picked up the telephone receiver.

"Darling Joseph, I just spoke with Father Regan. He has arranged for the bishop to say the funeral Mass for your father. The Knights of Columbus will stand guard at the wake and at the funeral. You need to be here to go over the details with us."

Joseph had never denied a request from Mother. She would parade him around like a show poodle and brag to friends of his achievements. She used to host luncheons at the house and have him recite Bible verses or play the piano for the guests. And then later she would reward him with an expensive gift. When he didn't comply, there was trouble.

Once she hosted a dinner party for a group of friends. Mother laid out an outfit that a page in a royal wedding would wear. He was a hockey star, not a little kid, he told her. Mother would not listen. Nanny took him downstairs to play the piano. He acted rude and embarrassed Mother. Nanny quickly escorted him out of the room. Father taped his mouth shut and forced him to stand in a corner for most of the evening. Never again did he embarrass Mother.

"Of course, Mother, I'll be there," he assured her. "We can start planning the funeral and a reception following the burial."

Joseph had just returned from a business trip to Brazil. It had been a long and exhausting flight. But the trip had been successful for the property development company he owned. Good fortune had smiled on Joseph. He resided in a penthouse condominium in the heart of Manhattan. He wined and dined with the wealthy and high-profile politicians. And he could boast of being in a long-time relationship with Rachel, the daughter of a popular senator.

❁

A warm southern breeze swept across the neighbourhood with a hint of summer in the air. Elijah parked the car and walked towards the law office. He spotted Sammi-Jo escorting daycare children to a nearby park. It stirred up an old boyhood crush.

The morning routine of office paperwork was interrupted with thoughts of Sammi-Jo. He could not get her out of his mind. He'd never thought of her as a person of mixed race when they were kids. No one in the apartment building pointed out the dark colour of her skin or the tightly coiled black curls. But the schoolkids teased her, calling her Oreo just as they called him Bastard Boy.

Sammi-Jo was no longer just pretty; now she was strikingly beautiful. Elijah wondered why she'd never married and whether she was dating. He decided to walk to the coffee shop next to the park where Sammi-Jo and the daycare children were playing.

He exited the coffee shop with a bag of doughnuts. Sammi-Jo and the children were still in the park. With a sheepish smile, he approached Sammi-Jo with an offer of a doughnut. She laughed and accepted. Their eyes locked. She blushed. He blurted out an invitation to dinner. She replied. "What time will you be picking me up?" He squeezed her hand like an excited child.

His mother greeted Joseph with a hug, and he planted a quick kiss on her cheekbone. He always told her that work took him out of the country for weeks at a time. The truth was, he stayed away purposely. Too many memories were stashed in the walls of the mansion he'd grown up in. He was the happiest playing hockey and rugby with teammates. Carlos drove him to the early morning practices and his games. Mother did not like sports. If Father attended a game, he would leave early for home or for the hospital. It had been his dream for Joseph to become a doctor and continue in his footsteps, but Joseph craved freedom and distanced himself.

His mother handed him a newspaper, showing the lengthy article that had been published about the passing of his father, Dr. Arthur Brooks. It listed his achievements in the medical world and the charitable organizations he supported. A flood of condolences continued to arrive.

"I had the maid clean your old bedroom," his mother said. "I will have Carlos drive you to the city after we meet with the bishop and Father Regan."

His mother was the master of organizing and had a household staff to take care of details. The long drive to the city would have been a welcomed escape. There would be an endless stream of relatives, hospital colleagues, friends, and even strangers eager to be part of the spotlight at a high-profile funeral. Mother had hired a photographer to capture the funeral procession. She would be dressed entirely in black with a veil covering her face. It would be his duty to escort the grieving widow. The family doctor had been on call in case Mother required immediate medical attention. She had been plagued with headaches and depression for years and feared the curse of crippling pain would interfere with the funeral.

Mother would need rest after the funeral. It would be his duty to take care of the estate and to make certain there were provisions for Mother to maintain a wealthy lifestyle. He would arrange a meeting with the family lawyer for a reading of the will after the funeral.

❊

Sammi-Jo announced she had a date with Elijah Friday evening. They were going for dinner and a movie. Frankie kept her mouth shut. On the third date, she broke the silence. "He's a momma's boy. She comes with the deal. His mother can be a right bossy cow. And I bet she still believes in fairies." Frankie chuckled. "She told him the fairies gifted her with a baby. She found him in a basket with a note from the little people. The poor kid believed it. She was always filling his head with nonsense. Instead of telling him the truth that his daddy took off when she got pregnant."

It was not until he was a teenager that Elijah learned his absent daddy lived in one of the richest neighbourhoods in Charlottetown with a wife and children and they did not want anything to do with him. He was a dirty little family secret.

"We talked for hours one night," Sammi-Jo said to Frankie. "We learned that we had a lot in common. Elijah is a sweet, caring person. He's going to help us find Elmer."

❄

Apple watched Gracie walking up the street. She could spot Gracie in a crowd, with long red hair down to her bum, an ankle-length skirt, purple blouse, and dangling red feathered earrings. Apple used to joke Gracie looked like a lost hippie. In many ways Apple had been right. Gracie was a wandering soul in search of meaning in life. Other people pegged her as a dreamer.

Gracie hadn't recognized Apple's voice when she'd telephoned earlier in the week with an invitation to visit. She had not seen or heard from Apple in years. And now she was almost begging a reluctant Gracie to visit.

Gracie agreed to stop by the apartment. It would be the first time in almost ten years she'd visited the old neighbourhood.

"You haven't changed," Apple cried out and rushed to the bottom of the landing. The two friends embraced. "You don't look a day older than the last time I saw you, and you haven't gained a pound over the years; still thin as a zipper."

Gracie blushed with guilt for not maintaining the friendship and wanted desperately to say sorry, but the words would not come out. "It's so good to see you, Apple. You look great too. The years have been kind to you."

Gracie looked up the street with a faraway gaze in her eyes, remembering. This had been such a good place to raise Elijah Blue.

She had been blessed with caring neighbours. She now lived alone in a lower-middle-class neighbourhood where people minded their own business and seldom socialized with each other.

Apple pumped the questions to Gracie. "Are you still living in the same place? Is there a man in your life? Did you ever get to travel to all those places you used to talk about?"

Gracie was still in the same apartment, hanging out in the coffee shops, reciting poetry with artists. There was no man in her life. "I visited Ireland twice. I would move there if I could. I am working as a photographer, mostly freelancing but it pays the bills. And I am writing a novel about the unethical adoptions of babies born to unwed mothers."

It didn't surprise Apple that Gracie would attempt to write a novel. She never knew anyone like Gracie who could get overly excited about books and visiting the library. If Gracie wasn't reading a book, she would be writing in journals or telling wild stories about magical creatures. Apple recalled Gracie daydreaming about becoming a journalist and reporting news from the four corners of the earth.

"If I am in the novel and it becomes a movie, I want Raquel Welch to play me," Apple jokingly responded.

"I am going expose the sins of the church and Sister Henrietta," Graice murmured with conviction.

The teapot sizzled on the stove burner. A plate of biscuits and jam and assorted cookies on a plate graced the table.

"On a more serious note, Gracie. In your novel, tell readers I gave my baby to the nuns to adopt rather than the nuns took him."

"Why?"

"Because I want to tell my own story when I am ready to."

The two friends sat in silence. Apple was unsure of how to approach the subject of hiring Elijah Blue. In the distance, dogs barked, kids played, and people on the street shouted greetings to each other. Music flowed out of a blue house at the end of the street. Gracie broke the silence.

"What about life for you, Apple?" Gracie asked, sipping tea.

"Life's good. I don't bother with men anymore," Apple told a surprised Gracie. "I wasted too much time waiting for someone to come rescue me. I have a good-paying job cleaning a bunch of government buildings at night. My Sammi-Jo is still living at home and dating your Elijah Blue. But I suppose you know that." Apple burst out laughing. "Who knows, perhaps we'll be in-laws someday and babysit grandkids. Now that would be a hoot. I could be Granny and you could be Nanny."

Gracie frowned. She would have known if Elijah Blue was in a relationship. She was his mother; he would have told her. Apple was teasing her, and she did not like it.

"Sorry, Gracie, I forgot you never liked being teased."

Apple explained why she'd invited Gracie over. She had contacted Elijah Blue for his services. She needed Gracie's help. "You know as much as I do about the Baby Train operation. I want to find out who adopted my Elmer. That hag of a nun is dead, but there are still people alive who can be held accountable. We know who they are. Everyone in town knows who they are." Apple grabbed Gracie by the hand. "Remember when Sister Henrietta died, and everyone hailed her as a saint? We contacted your friend, that former nun and she blew the whistle on Sister Henrietta. The papers across the country picked it up and reported how Sister Henrietta got paid thousands of dollars for babies born to unwed mothers and called them donations. She didn't get your baby, but she got mine."

Only a week ago, Gracie had burst into uncontrollable tears, triggered by a mother holding a newborn wrapped in a blue receiving blanket. She would get weepy when photographing babies. She suffered from post-traumatic stress for years because of Sister Henrietta. It had made her an overly protective mother to the point of suffocating Elijah Blue.

"Sammi-Jo and Frankie said they would chip in to pay legal expenses. Your Elijah Blue is right smart. He can charge the people with child trafficking. We all know Sister Henrietta never worked alone. There are still people alive who worked with her. We could provide a list of names ourselves. We can start with Father Bart. He is old and I heard he is sickly, so we need to act fast before he croaks. Dr. Jay and Judge Tweedy are dead, but we all know they were part of the Baby Train. Dr. Jay must have kept some records that Elijah can get access to. And that cruel caseworker at the home for unwed mothers must know where the babies were being shipped to. She is probably still around."

The past always had a way of digging its way out of the dirt Gracie buried it in. It came back to haunt her time and time again. She excused herself to use the bathroom. She turned on the tap so Apple would not hear the sobbing. The memories of Sister Henrietta were still raw after all these years. Gracie sat in Apple's bathroom unable to breathe as she fought another panic attack. Apple had been robbed of raising Elmer, but Gracie, too, had been robbed of a normal life. Gracie slapped cold water on her face and waited for the attack to end.

"You don't owe Elijah Blue a penny for his services. I'll threaten to move in with him if he so much as charges you a penny."

Apple bear hugged Gracie. "Gawd, I missed you. I knew you would help find my Elmer."

Gracie embraced Apple and tried not to cry. Why had she stayed away from the old neighbourhood all these years chasing dreams? Why didn't she keep in touch with Apple? Had she become too big feeling, living in a middle-class neighbourhood? Staying away did not erase the past. She was still the same person hating and hurting over being used and abandoned by Elijah Blue's father.

❀

Joseph escorted Mother down the aisle of St. Patrick's Cathedral. The pews were filled with parishioners joined in mourning Dr. Arthur Brooks. The bishop delivered a homily worthy of a saint. Mother quietly sobbed. Joseph held her hand.

The photographer aimed the camera at the double row of Knights of Columbus at the entrance to the church. Pews had been designated for the Catholic Daughters of America, who were dressed in designer attire. The row of political allies, hospital colleagues, and close friends did not escape the camera lens. A choir of angelic voices sang out. More than a dozen priests were on the altar.

A beautiful young woman with jet black hair wearing a sleek black dress approached Joseph at the reception following the funeral. He slid an arm around her slender waist and softly kissed her lips. "Rachel, my love, you could have sat with us. Mother adores you." He apologized for being neglectful as the funeral arrangements had kept him occupied. "I will be staying with Mother until I can get Father's affairs in order." He promised a vacation to any global destination she fancied.

"I love you, Joseph," she whispered in his ear. Mother caught a glimpse of Rachel holding hands with Joseph and suddenly became ill with a pounding headache. It was time for Joseph to escort her home – without Rachel.

"Is there anything you need? Should I send for Dr. Shulman?" Joseph asked as the car cruised along the highway.

"Please, promise you will never leave me. Not until I am feeling well. Promise me, Joseph."

At home, Mother slowly ascended the staircase to the sanctu-
ary of her bedroom with assistance from Joseph.

"I'll have Dr. Shulman come by the house. You need to take
your pain medication and rest. I will have the maid bring a light
supper to you. Try to eat. You must get your strength back." But
Joseph was more concerned about being trapped in the home
with an aging, sickly parent. The quicker she got better, the
quicker he could leave.

❀

An appointment had been scheduled with their lawyer for the
reading of the will. Joseph travelled to the law office alone. Mother
had no interest in legal affairs. His father had been responsible
for such complicated matters. Days passed since the funeral and
Mother was still feeling unwell. Dr. Shulman had prescribed
medication to help her rest. Joseph resented being the dedicated
son. He longed to hold Rachel in his arms and feel the warmth
of her body next to his.

The estate and a Florida residence had been willed to Mother,
along with a small fraction of money. Father had willed the bulk
of his fortune to support a mistress and a daughter. The will dis-
closed his father's double life.

Dr. Brooks willed Joseph a small amount of money compared
to his hidden daughter Hannah's inheritance.

Had he been shipped to a boarding school in Europe so
Father could indulge in an affair without the responsibility of a
teenager? It would have been easier to be a daddy to a cute little
girl than be a responsible father to a troubled teenager. But had
he been a troubled teenager? It had been a label Father slapped
on him, an excuse to send him away to boarding school.

Joseph had been chasing freedom for years. He had earned a fortune without riding on the coattails of his father. With a swipe of a pen, he signed his share of the money over to his mother. She would need it more than he would.

The last will and testament had one final shock for Joseph. The lawyer handed Joseph a sealed envelope and a key to Father's study. The hearing of the will ended with the lawyer suggesting Joseph open the envelope in private.

❀

"Let's compile a contact list for Elijah Blue," Gracie suggested. "It will be a starting point. He respects confidentiality with clients, so you need to give him the list."

The ringing of the telephone interrupted their conversation. Sammi-Jo had called with news she had plans for supper. And would not be home until later in the evening.

"I have plans for supper, too. Elijah Blue invited me to his place. We're probably having steak, something we couldn't afford when he was a kid. He's making up for it now. I don't care for red meat, but I don't have the heart to tell him."

Apple didn't tell Gracie she knew of the invitation and her Sammi-Jo would be there, too. She and Elijah Blue planned to announce their commitment to each other. Poor Gracie did not know Elijah Blue as well as she thought. Apple approved of the relationship between Sammi-Jo and Elijah Blue, but would Gracie?

The day dragged on until the list was completed and Catherine O'Grady, a former nun, was at the top. The names of a well-known doctor, a social worker who worked at the home for unwed mothers, an Island lawyer, a retired judge, and a retired politician were also on the list.

"I need to go for a walk and get some air." Apple put down the
pen. "All this talk is giving me flashbacks. My head is started to
ache. Let's go to the square like we used to when the kids were
small." They locked arms and journeyed down memory lane as
they strolled down the street like they had done years earlier. "Do
you remember Dory who lived downstairs from us, and the time
she had a bad toothache? She cried all night, she did. I gave her
the little whisky I had stashed in the apartment." Gracie mumbled that she remembered. "Welfare told Dory they would pay to
have it pulled. But they wouldn't pay for a filling."

The two friends crossed the street and strolled towards the
square. Welfare had such stupid rules. Dory cried more about losing her smile than she did about the pain. Word got out Dory had
an appointment to get the tooth pulled. The neighbourhood ral-
lied together and started a Save the Tooth campaign. The neighbours collected what they could and the bootlegger at the end of
the street put in the rest.

Gracie became lonesome for the past. "Where is Dory now? I
lost touch with everyone from the old neighbourhood. She had
such a pretty smile. I'm glad she got to keep it."

They plunked down on a park bench. Gracie waited for an
answer. "Dory had a breakdown. Welfare took the kids. She just
could not cope. Not used to being on her own." Gracie shivered
in the warm sun. Welfare had no soul, no conscience. The poor
woman had been used to being cared for by a husband and without any warning, she was on her own with a pack of kids.

"Did she get the kids back?" Gracie had feared child protection
while raising Elijah Blue.

"Yes, she did. She married the first fellow who asked and
moved to the mainland. He was a mail-order groom."

Dory placed an advertisement in the local newspaper which
had been a popular method of finding romance. She was brutally

honest. *A pretty widow in late twenties searching for a hardworking man to love and care for. Must like children.* She screened the replies. A fisherman from Nova Scotia wrote he was in his forties with no children and owned a home. He needed a wife who could cook and clean and would not give him any trouble. "It was her ticket off welfare, and she grabbed it. Dory was always a clever one." Gracie nodded in agreement with Apple.

Apple saw a pack of crows eating from a dumpster. Crows still terrified her. "Ignore them," Gracie demanded. She had witnessed Apple being traumatized by flocks of crows.

Apple screamed and chased the crows. "Get out of here. Leave me alone. Stay out of my life."

The crows took off in flight. Apple screamed louder at the crows. "I fucking hate you."

Gracie watched in horror. But there was no stopping a hysterical Apple from screaming on the street.

"I want my baby back. I want to know what he looks like, to touch his face. He needs to know I loved him from the time he was kicking in my belly." She gave way to uncontrolled and unrestrained sobs releasing the anger and the guilt buried deep in the marrow of her bones. "It's my fault they took him. I'm to blame. I didn't protect him from Sister Henrietta. It's my fault," she repeated. "My fault."

It was not the first time she'd yelled and cursed at flocks of crows as if they were enemies. Her fear of crows and screaming used to scare the girls when they were younger. The sisters would run down the street scaring the crows away from their mother as they grew older.

"Pull it together Apple. Or you will end up in the crazy house watching Wayne chasing imaginary hockey pucks. Stop blaming yourself for losing Elmer. None of it was your fault. You were too young to outsmart Sister Henrietta. She was an evil cow; you were only a teenager."

She guided a distraught Apple up the street to the park. They sat under a tree until Apple had calmed down. "Nana abandoned me. No relative claimed me, so I was sentenced to a life in foster homes. It kills me that Elmer might think I abandoned him and wants nothing to do with me."

Two little boys were playing on a jungle bar. Apple watched the athletic youngster with sadness. Teardrops dripped down her face. "When I used to see a little boy with black or red hair, I wondered if he was my Elmer. And now when I see an athletic little boy with black hair and dark eyes, I wonder if it could be my grandson. All these years, and I am still wondering, Gracie. For years, I could hear my baby crying at night." Apple sniffled. "He was crying for me, his real mother. I was not there to comfort him. I know he's a man now, but I still think about him as a little baby."

How many nights had Gracie woken up confused and frightened? She would check Elijah Blue in a panicked state of mind. Nightmares still plagued her of Elijah Blue being snatched.

"My Elijah Blue will find Elmer. There have got to be adoption records."

It was time to head home and get ready for the barbecue. Elijah Blue had hinted about having big news to share. Perhaps he planned to start his own law firm. Or perhaps he had news of a promotion.

The two friends locked arms and walked down the street. "Are you okay now?" Apple nodded and mumbled. "The old nun is dead. She'll never hurt me again."

❊

Why was he late? She had booked an early morning photography shoot and wanted to be in bed before ten. Photography was her bread and butter. The more work, the higher the income. Her rent had increased to the point she was considering searching for a lower rental. The red convertible finally pulled up to the curb. "You're late."

"I told you I'd be picking you up at six. You got the time wrong," said Elijah.

They drove across town in silence to his two-bedroom condo. One of the bedrooms had been converted into office space. A balcony had an ocean view of sailboats in the distance.

The condo became a status symbol for the young lawyer. Gone were the days of dorm living, Kraft Dinner, and hamburgers throughout his university years.

University had been his first taste of freedom from Gracie stalking his every move, and the freedom from public school teachers with their pet pupils. Freedom from being tormented by privileged students.

Elijah Blue parked in the underground parkway. Gracie often hinted the condo was big enough for two people. Elijah Blue ignored the comment. It was a starter home. He planned to build a house in the country in a few years. Gracie spied the champagne bottle in the back seat. "Are we celebrating a promotion?" She followed him to the elevator bursting with pride. Her Elijah Blue had done her proud.

"No, Mum. I did not get a promotion. I have someone special I want you to meet. We have not been dating for long, but I care deeply for her."

Gracie got a sinking feeling in the pit of her stomach. What if Apple had not been teasing her? No, it could not be Sammi-Jo. Elijah Blue would not have kept such news from her.

But Gracie and Elijah Blue were greeted by an attractive young woman barbecuing on the balcony. "Mum, you remember Sammi-Jo from the old neighbourhood."

The blood drained from Gracie's face. Apple had not been joking.

Gracie pouted that Apple knew about the relationship before she did and frowned as he greeted Sammi-Jo with a kiss on the lips. She'd never dreamed Sammi-Jo and Elijah Blue would become intimate as adults.

Her son would be a good prospect for any woman. And he had been in a serious relationship with the daughter of a rich family. Elijah Blue had refused to divulge the details of their breakup. He could have any woman. Why Sammi-Jo?

"Hello, Gracie. You look gorgeous," Sammi-Jo said and hugged Gracie. But Gracie stood as stiff as a post and mumbled a greeting. Elijah Blue noticed the smile fading from Sammi-Jo's face. He glared at Gracie then cracked open the champagne. He toasted the love of his life and their future together.

Gracie did not congratulate the couple and she declined an offer of a glass of champagne. They ate in awkward silence. Sammi-Jo fidgeted with nervousness and Elijah Blue winked at her.

"I made dessert. Bread pudding with caramel sauce. Elijah says it's your favourite."

"No thank you, Sammi-Jo. I have an early morning photography shoot. Elijah Blue, would you please take me home?"

A frown crossed Sammi-Jo's face. It was obvious Elijah's mother was not enjoying the evening. She wondered why. Elijah was probably all she had. Did she fear losing her son to another woman? That the focus would be on her and not Gracie? She would ask her mother for advice. Gracie and her mom had been best friends. Her mother would have an answer.

❀

"Why were you impolite to Sammi-Jo?" Elijah Blue demanded on the ride back to Gracie's apartment. "Why can't you be happy for us?" The car sped through the familiar streets to the apartment. Gracie remained silent. She had learned to pick fights carefully with Elijah Blue. "Sammi-Jo and I have a lot in common. She is beautiful and loving. You better get used to the idea of us as a couple." Gracie had enough lecturing. She turned the tables by creating doubt in his mind.

"What about your ex? She was perfect too: educated, beautiful, and charming. What makes you so certain it will work with Sammi-Jo if it didn't work with her?"

He had been blinded by his ex-fiancée's beauty and stylishness. But he'd asked for the engagement ring back because of the callous remarks about his mother and his upbringing. He had done well in life, she'd told him, despite being raised in poverty and having an uneducated old hippie for a mother.

Gracie had no clue. His mother would never fit into his ex's privileged world. And neither would he. But he remained silent. The truth would only hurt her.

CHAPTER 27

Joseph marched through the house in search of his mother. The maid said she had gone out. He opened the locked door with the key the lawyer provided. He instructed the maid not to disturb him, even if Mother returned.

He could now look through his father's personal affairs without fear of being caught and punished. Joseph had never re-entered the study since the day he cracked the glass ornament.

Joseph slit the seal with an envelope opener. His hands shook. Inside the envelope were adoption papers—no letter of apology or explanation about the mistress and daughter.

The truth of his identity cut like a knife. He remembered a nun from Canada who visited every year. Mother would have him play the grand piano for her. The nun and Father would enter the study before she departed. And then one year the visits stopped. She had played a role in the adoption; he was certain of it.

Joseph searched the office with madness. He ripped files from the cabinets. Tore books off the shelves. For his reward, he discovered photos of a laughing little girl with his father and a young woman. His father's double life spilled out of a folder of photos of Father and the much younger woman skiing, sailing, and dining on a beach.

He discovered a safe in the back of the desk. The maid banged at the door. Joseph yelled that he was not to be disturbed. But it was not the maid. It was Mother.

He ignored her pleas to let her in. The key to the safe had been taped on the bottom of a desk drawer. "Not very clever, Father," Joseph mumbled. The key fit perfectly.

His body went numb with shock. The safe was stuffed with receipts for thousands of dollars to Sister Henrietta. A ledger with payments had been folded in sections. On his birth date was a $25,000 donation to Sister Henrietta for adoption services. There were entries for donations of thousands of dollars to Father Regan, the parish priest who'd tried to groom him for priesthood when he was an altar boy.

The truth hit him as if he had been struck by a bolt of lightning. He had been a purchased item and his entire life had been a lie. The adoption papers gave no indication of his heritage. The crucifix that hung over the doorway protecting the study watched Joseph curse in a fit of uncontrolled rage.

Mother banged again on the door. She clearly knew the truth. The business side of Joseph kicked in. He photocopied the receipts, the ledgers, and photos of the mistress and the daughter. It would be evidence he would need to blackmail Father Regan and Sister Henrietta. Father Regan had been one of the dozen priests on the altar at the funeral Mass. He planned to visit him and get answers to the deceit he had been part of. Sister Henrietta had not visited since he was a youngster. But he knew she lived in Canada. And Mother would know where.

Joseph banged on her bedroom door, but he did not wait for an invitation to enter before pushing through the door. She had been waiting for him. He flung the photocopies of receipts and the adoption papers at her. She flinched. "You never told me I was adopted. No—I was not adopted. I was bought. Well, I hope you got your money's worth. Did you? Was I worth the twenty-five thousand dollars you paid for me? Was I, Mother?"

Mother collected the documents and tossed the papers in a waste basket. Joseph had been a handful since he was a teen. She blamed the nanny. The nanny had been too easygoing and allowed him to get away with bad behaviour instead of correcting him.

"We gave you a good home, a good education, and a lifestyle fit for a prince. You should be grateful we rescued you from a life of poverty and disgrace."

Joseph glared as if seeing her flawed character for the first time. Mother was acting as if she were the victim, not him.

"Your biological mother didn't want you. She was glad to get rid of you. You would have ended up in the streets or part of a gang if it were not for me. I wanted you. But you loved that Mexican nanny more than you loved me. And I am the one who saved you."

Mother would whisper poison in his ear that Nanny was being paid money to care for him and she was only nice to him because she feared being fired. He later came to realize it had been a lie. Mother had been jealous. Now she was jealous of Rachel. It was not until he was an adult that he realized Nanny had loved him. She sang him to sleep at night and chased the monsters away from under the bed. She listened to his stories about school friends. When he was a little boy, he wished Nanny could be his mother and blew out the birthday candles. In later years, he came to regret not saying goodbye to her before leaving for boarding school. But he had been a hurt and angry young teenager. His anger had been misdirected.

"Did you know Father had a mistress and a daughter?" He demanded. "Were you aware he had a second family—or perhaps it was a first family, and we were second?"

She didn't appear surprised. He could have easily been discussing the weather by the reaction on her face.

"High-calibre professionals often have a mistress. A mistress never has the same status as a wife. What he did was his business. I had legal claim to his name, money, and status and that's all that mattered to me. It's how the real-world works, Joseph."

Joseph passed his mother a copy of the will and suggested she read it carefully. Mother had the status, but the mistress would be getting the bulk of Father's fortune. He questioned if there would be enough money for the upkeep of the estate, continuing wages for staff, and the personal expenses Mother had become accustomed to.

Joseph demanded answers. Where was the mistress? How old was the daughter? Did they attend the funeral?

"They're living abroad. He attended a medical conference in France. She was a barmaid serving drinks at the resort. Your father always had a weakness for young floozies. I knew it when I married him. I wouldn't know if they were at the funeral. I've never met her. She became pregnant to trap your father. I would not give him a divorce, so we agreed to live separate lives. The arrangement worked perfectly for both of us."

The secret life of his father had been an arrangement. The vacations to Europe as a couple had been a sham. They'd shipped him off as a convenience to live out their lie. But why reveal the adoption now? Why didn't they explain it to him when he was a boy? It would not have mattered if he were adopted. Could he trust Mother to be truthful?

"We raised you. You are our son and belonged to us. There was no need to explain the adoption arrangement. Why are you being ungrateful, as if we did something wrong? Your father had no right to share the information with you through a lawyer. I refused to give him a divorce and now he is trying to get even with me from the grave by having you turn against me."

Joseph realized he had been a pawn in a love triangle.

It would be easy to forget about the adoption papers if he wanted to. And life would go on as it had before the visit to the lawyer. Father's mission would have failed. Mother adored the attention of having a successful son, another status symbol.

"What about my biological mother? Who is she? Where is she now?"

His mother could not answer. She'd had no connection with Sister Henrietta for years. "Sister Henrietta became greedy, demanding more money. Your father ended the friendship and the visits stopped."

Joseph remained silent. His mother continued. "Your father cared for you, Joseph. He gave you a name to be proud of. You are part of the family legacy. No one needs to know. What would Rachel's family think if they learned the truth? I will give you and Rachel my blessing if you remain quiet."

"I'm really not different from you, Mother," he said. "We are not blood related, but we are cut from the same cloth. We will continue with the role-playing. But I am going to search for my biological mother before she shows up on my doorstep and embarrasses me. I will not have what I worked for flushed down the drain."

Joseph drove his car with madness to the privacy of the penthouse to map out a plan to protect his reputation from a scandal that could end a future with a politically elite family.

❉

The rain showers contributed to Joseph's dark mood as he parked the car in front of the Clergy House. He followed a servant down a hallway to Father Regan's residence filled with religious master-pieces, chandeliers, and murals painted on high ceilings. Father Regan lived in a luxury familiar to Joseph.

Father Regan had been waiting. He welcomed Joseph with a smile and a handshake. But his smile faded when Joseph demanded answers. What had been his role in the adoption? What did he know about Sister Henrietta? How could he contact her? Did Father Regan know the biological parents? Why had Joseph's father gifted Father Regan thousands of dollars in dona-tions? He would not leave until he had answers.

"I've been studying the paper trail of you and Sister Henrietta. Human trafficking is illegal, you know."

Father Regan scanned the contents of the folder Joseph thrust at him. He and Sister Henrietta had been careful with the adoption procedures. The cheques did not specify the purpose of the donations…but this could lead to public suspicion and accusations.

"Your family name will be ruined with such accusations. What about your mother? The gossip would destroy her social standing. Your mother is a fragile person. A scandal could have dire con-sequences for her mental health." Father Regan sat back in his leather recliner with a triumphant sneer. Joseph had as much to lose as he did.

"Sister Henrietta and I saved you from living in the shadow of your birth mother's sin. Sister Henrietta, God rest her soul, was a saint, providing unwed mothers with food and shelter and finding good Christian homes for their little bastards."

Joseph ignored the threat. It was Father's signature on the cheques. Mother was too mentally unwell to be incriminated. Joseph was an innocent pawn in a human-trafficking scheme orchestrated by religious clergy.

It was as if Father Regan and Joseph were in a high-stakes card game. The priest was trying to bluff him into remaining silent. But Joseph had the winning hand.

"Mother and I will still have the luxuries we are accustomed to, whereas you will be trading your treasures for a prison cell. I suggest you find out how I can contact my biological parents. Or you will be hearing confessions from a jail cell."

Father Regan had been forced into a corner. He wiped droplets of perspiration from his forehead. Sister Henrietta never provided personal information about the biological parents. His job had been to find wealthy Catholics willing to adopt.

"I will give you a week to find out the name of my biological mother." Father Regan remained seated; his face marked by fear. Joseph stood up. "You disgust me," he spat and stormed out of the office.

An envelope addressed to Sammi-Jo came in the mail with no return address. Apple tossed it on the kitchen table. Apple wished the letter would contain good news. Sammi-Jo could use cheering up. She had come home in tears the night of the barbecue and been miserable all week. Sammi-Jo could not understand what she had done to upset Gracie. How could she stay in a relationship with Elijah if his mother did not approve? She entertained thoughts of ending the relationship.

"Don't allow Gracie to steal your happiness. It is not you she has a problem with. Her entire world has been Elijah Blue. She hardly let him out of her sight when he was a kid. He is all she ever had. Knowing Gracie, she probably has a wife picked out for him. Some high-society woman she figured would be a good catch for her precious son. And then you came along, and her scheming sailed out the door," reasoned Apple.

Sammi-Jo slumped on the sofa. She knew Gracie had been an overly protective mother, but Elijah was no longer a child in need of protection, especially from her. A relationship with Elijah would never work if Gracie thought she was not good enough.

"That cow always thought she was better than the people on the street," said Frankie. "Consider it a lucky escape." The words, meant to comfort, only brought more emotional pain.

Sammi-Jo spied the envelope on the table. "It is probably a chain letter that's circulating around the neighbourhood, just what I need," she mumbled. Her eyes widened and she let out a girly squeal. Inside was a photograph of her and Elijah Blue clowning around as youngsters. An enclosed note read: *Dear Sammi-Jo, Sweet memories of yesterday. Welcome to our family. Hugs, Gracie.*

❊

Catherine O'Grady arrived at the law office at the appointed time. "Elijah Blue, you are a success story. Your mother must be very proud. I am."

Catherine had been a good friend to his mother and the reason he had not been sold at birth. Sister O'Grady used to visit the treehouse with bags of good used clothing her nephews outgrew when he was a lad.

She was no longer a nun. She'd denounced the Catholic faith and joined a radically changing world. She was now just 'Catherine,' an aging woman with a daughter and a granddaughter living in the United States.

Elijah Blue got right to the point about the purpose of why he requested to meet with her.

"I am going to tell you a story, Elijah Blue. A distraught young fellow full of anger accused Sister Henrietta of selling his sister's baby. The receptionist told the brother to sit in the waiting room. She later motioned him inside her office. Sister Henrietta told him, 'I've heard you've been accusing me of selling babies. I have been expecting you. The police are on their way.' Sister Henrietta was highly respected by politicians and clergy who deemed her a saint for finding good homes for children born to unwed mothers. A judge who signed the adoption papers of babies born to unwed mothers found the young man guilty of defamation of character and sentenced him to five months of jail time."

"The judge and the doctors involved with the Baby Train are deceased. You cannot jail a dead man," Catherine said, hoping he would give up the idea of pursuing the case.

The young lawyer slapped his desk in anger and frustration. The former nun was his only hope of acquiring information about human trafficking through threatening the people involved. She had been associated with Sister Henrietta when she was a nun and would be privy to names of people involved with the adoptions of babies born to unwed mothers. He was not about to let her walk away.

"What about the young mothers who had their babies taken and adopted to strangers?" he shouted. She flinched. "I'm told you saved me from boarding the Baby Train the night Sister Henrietta searched the maternity ward. You hid with me in a broom closet. Mum refused to sign the adoption papers. But other unwed mothers who were deemed unfit by the nun lost their children without signing adoption papers. Sister Henrietta could have claimed my mother was wild and unsuitable to care for an infant. She didn't need her signature. Why did you protect me from Sister Henrietta? Who are you protecting now?"

Elijah planned to expose the truth about the Baby Train scandal with the assistance of Catherine regardless if she was unwilling to support him.

"The nuns took my infant daughter. I never got to hold her. Seeing Sister Henrietta on the maternity ward that night knowing what she was going to do triggered memories of my baby crying moments before she disappeared out of the delivery room. I wanted to spare Gracie the trauma I have suffered. My daughter and I reunited. She lives in the States. We visit each other. She is now married with children. I risk being denied crossing the border if I tell you what you want to know. I have protected you since infancy. I am still protecting you, Elijah Blue. But I cannot protect you if you proceed with chasing old men and ghosts with stories about child trafficking. You will discover the church is more powerful than the law, just as I have. I don't know who adopted Apple's infant. My daughter found me with the support of her adoptive parents. They were good people and provided my daughter with a good life. She became suicidal and suffered from depression in her teen years. She has never suffered from depression since we connected. My daughter suspected she had been adopted. It caused stress and anxiety not knowing who she was and where she came from. When I first met her, I saw the face of the man who raped me. But she was my daughter. I created her. I loved her first and I loved her the most. My daughter found me. There is hope for Apple."

She stood to leave, but the meeting was not over.

"I've contacted the county court clerk where the adoption occurred. I secured the name of an Island judge involved with the finalization of the adoption. I need you as a witness willing to testify you have knowledge of the unethical and illegal adoption practices. The names on the affidavit were involved with the Baby Train movement. The affidavit is nothing more than a paper threat; it will never go to court, but it might force the judge to provide the names of the couple that adopted Apple's baby. With family to protect, the retired judge will not want his name dragged through the mud. Apple would be satisfied with finding her son. It is no different from you wanting to find your daughter."

Elijah slid an affidavit across his desk. She scanned the document that implicated high profile names.

Catherine closed her eyes as if in prayer and choked back tears. The infant she'd rescued from boarding the Baby Train had become a streetwise lawyer using emotional blackmail to get what he wanted. She could walk out the door without signing, leave the Island, and never look back. Her American daughter would welcome her. If she signed, she risked serious consequences. Elijah waited with eyes that could have pierced the soul of any hardened criminal.

She signed the document, walked out of the office and out of his life. A lifelong friendship with the lawyer and Gracie was over.

❀

Joseph acted as if he were walking on eggshells or waiting for an explosion to happen. Rachel attempted to comfort him. But it was not grief that consumed his thoughts. It seemed as if he were in a race with time. What if his biological mother discovered his financial worth? What if she blackmailed him?

Father Regan entered the tower office with a sealed envelope addressed to Joseph. He waited in the seated area while a personal assistant entered Joseph's office. He had to be certain the envelope had been received. "Mr. Brooks instructed me to show you out," said the personal assistant and walked Father Regan to the elevator.

Father Regan walked out of the tower building and out of the lives of the Brooks family. The Baby Train had come to a final stop.

The envelope contained information about Joseph's biological mother. The colour drained out of his face. Not only had she been unwed, but she had also been a troubled foster child. The father of her child was unknown. The document noted the name of the mother, and the name of the town and Canadian province she lived in. She had never married, and she'd raised two daughters on social assistance. The news shocked Joseph. He never questioned how Father Regan collected the report but figured the priest paid a handsome price for the information. Prison could be a cruel place, especially for a priest convicted of trafficking babies.

If Rachel found out, it could destroy their relationship.

It dawned on Joseph how blessed he was to have been raised by adoptive parents rather than being born and raised in an impoverished family. Joseph contacted his lawyer for legal advice and was told he had no legal obligations to the biological mother, and she was not entitled to any of his wealth.

CHAPTER 28

Elijah signed for the registered letter personally addressed to him. There was no indication of the sender. But enclosed was a baptismal certificate of Joseph Brooks. A name and a telephone number were scrawled on the back of the certificate. Elijah smiled. He was one step closer to reuniting Apple with her son.

The office phone rang as Joseph stuffed papers into a briefcase in preparation for a business meeting.

Joseph listened as Elijah explained the purpose of the telephone call. His biological mother had a lawyer. She had been looking for him. Why? How did she find him? Thoughts of being blackmailed by a cunning woman consumed his energy and thoughts.

Joseph cancelled his meetings for the rest of the week and had his assistant book accommodations and a round-trip flight to Prince Edward Island.

The conversation had been cordial, but Elijah was uneasy. Joseph explained he'd only learned of the adoption after the recent death of his father. Now, he was planning a trip to the Island to take care of complicated issues with the biological mother. He agreed to meet with Elijah later in the week. Elijah did not share this with Apple or Sammi-Jo. Elijah instructed the assistant to research Joseph and his company and the family name. He would learn as much as he could before the meeting.

"Prince Edward Island," exclaimed Rachel. "I've never been there. But it's been on my wish list to go since I was a young girl and read the Anne of Green Gables books."

It was a business trip, Joseph argued. She would be bored on her own while he attended meetings. He promised Rachel a future fun vacation to Prince Edward Island together.

No need to tell Mother about the trip. It would be too risky for her or anyone to know. He would meet with the lawyer, return home, propose marriage, and get on with a perfect life. Rachel must never learn his true lineage.

❀

A legal assistant entered Elijah's office with a file. By lunchtime, Elijah learned Joseph had been raised in a million-dollar mansion, attended private schools, and owned global companies.

Elijah had realized at an early age his mother couldn't afford luxuries. There were kids at school who bragged about trips to Disney World during the March school breaks. He desperately wanted to go to the magical land of year-round sunshine. He flinched recalling the sadness he'd inflicted on his mother, blaming her for being too poor to go on vacations like the other kids.

As an adult, he came to realize poverty had been the opinion of people who measured success by financial worth. His mother had never allowed the word *poor* to be used in their home.

For a moment, he wondered if he had been adopted by an American family like Joseph what his life might have been like. In his experience growing up in a single-parent home, the mis-use of power came from the privileged. How many times had his mother and Apple cringed with fear and uncertainty of welfare workers sniffing around the apartment building? People would lock their doors when they saw a person wearing a business suit walking on the street he lived on. Mothers cried out for babies whisked away at birth and trembled with fear at the power and privilege of the church and people like Joseph's adoptive parents. Elijah decided to meet with Joseph before contacting Apple.

❋

Joseph had a bird's-eye view of his birth province as the flight zipped across Prince Edward Island. The beauty of patchwork swaths of land caught his attention. He might have considered developing seashore condominiums that wealthy vacationers would appreciate if he did not have an unwanted connection to the place. The sooner he finished the business of silencing his biological mother, the quicker he could return home to Rachel.

He stepped out of the cab wearing a well-tailored suit and tie and handcrafted designer footwear and entered the law office with confidence. Elijah was waiting.

"I will get right to the point. I have a letter from my lawyer informing your client she is not to contact me. If she violates the order, I will be forced to take further legal action. She has no legal rights of entitlement to my money or my properties. The original birth certificate says the father is unknown. I do not need or want to know who fathered me. Why would I upset his life with an announcement that I am his son? The man is entitled to his privacy, and so am I."

Joseph waited for a response. Elijah thought carefully before replying. This was not the happy ending Apple had waited years for. It was obvious Joseph judged Apple by his own privileged, selfish standards.

"My client is not interested in financial support." He responded to the attack of Apple's character. "She wants to meet the infant son who was stolen from her. She never signed adoption papers.

It was not her decision to give you up for adoption. You were adopted without her consent because she was a foster child under eighteen. My client has never given up hope of reuniting with her firstborn."

Joseph listened without interrupting Elijah. He had no interest in the drama of a distraught woman but would wait till the lawyer finished before he responded with one final warning not to be contacted by the biological mother.

Elijah continued: "People financially profited from your adoption. Many unwed mothers suffered emotionally because of the Baby Train."

"The Baby Train," Joseph said, "transported me down the tracks from a life of poverty and misery to great wealth and power, and I am grateful."

Elijah glared at the well-dressed man sitting across the desk. His heartlessness stirred up memories of Elijah's own ruthless father. He became anxious to get Joseph out of his office and back on a flight to the States.

"I will meet with your client, but only to warn her not to bother me or attempt to contact my family," he told Elijah.

Elijah listened and took control of the situation to protect Apple. He had no choice but to present Apple with a copy of the letter now on his desk. But he would not allow Joseph to meet Apple and break her heart with rejection and cruelty.

"I'm her lawyer," Elijah retorted. "I will hand-deliver the letter from your attorney to my client. And I will explain she is not to contact you, or you will take legal action."

Apple would be devastated to lose her son all over again. But it would be better, Elijah figured, if he were the person to deliver the news and not Joseph.

"I have no interest in a relationship with her or any of her family," Joseph continued. "The woman is a stranger. She gave birth to me, but she did not raise me. I have a family and a reputation to protect. I am not responsible for her pregnancy, and I am innocent of any wrongdoing. I have been blessed with a reputable family who provided every opportunity to become the success I am. Surely you understand."

"I am staying at the Hyatt Regency in the penthouse suite," Joseph continued. "I will visit her if I have not heard from you by Wednesday. I do not have the luxury of time as I have urgent personal business in the States."

The meeting ended with an impersonal handshake.

Apple answered the phone and Elijah spoke immediately: "I have been in contact with the son you've been searching for."

Apple was silent. Elijah took a deep breath. "His name is Joseph, and he lives in the state of New York, where he was raised." He arranged to meet Apple later in the day with more information.

Elijah walked slowly up the stairway to the second-floor landing. But, he reasoned, it would be better for Apple to hear it from him than Joseph.

Apple and her daughters were waiting in the kitchen. On the table was the stack of birthday cards waiting to finally be opened by the missing son. Apple greeted Elijah with a bear hug and tears. He had found her Elmer.

There was no way to sugar coat what he had come to tell her. He could see the shock on her face as he explained how the meeting had gone.

"What do you mean he doesn't want to meet me? Why? I need to see him. I need to see his face. I need to tell him I loved him, and I never forgot about him. See, look at the cards we've been waiting to give him." Apple picked up a handful of cards tucked in envelopes on the table. "There must be a mistake. He must think I got rid of him and never loved him. I need to see him to explain they took him from me without my permission."

Frankie glared at Elijah as it were his fault that Joseph did not want anything to do with the family. Sammi-Jo comforted a distraught Apple.

Frankie grabbed the envelope Elijah passed to Apple. She read it in disbelief. "The little shithead thinks we want his precious money," she snapped at Elijah. She passed the letter to Sammi-Jo. Elijah wished he had never heard of Joseph. It would have been better for Apple if Joseph had remained missing.

"Joseph is a wealthy businessman. He's judging Apple by his own character," Elijah Blue explained.

Apple searched in a drawer for a letter from Jackie, her friend from the Halifax home for unwed mothers. Apple had mailed a letter to Jackie years earlier, not expecting a reply. Jackie responded and throughout the years they'd written each other. Apple read one of her letters through fits of sobs. Jackie wrote she had married a good man, kind and loving, and they'd raised a family. The daughter she surrendered at birth had telephoned her. The adoptive parents were wealthy and kind, but Jackie's daughter still wanted to have a relationship with her biological mother. If Jackie's wealthy daughter could talk with Joseph, he might change his mind and want to meet her.

"What does he look like? Did he even ask about me? He must have asked something about me."

Elijah wished there were a hint of good news he could share about Joseph. At least he could provide the details he had learned earlier in the week.

"Joseph is tall, athletic, with reddish hair and dark eyes. He attended private schools, including a private school in Europe. Joseph only learned about his adoption after the recent death of his father. His mother is a senior and not in good health. He will have a lawyer serve a legal notice if you attempt to contact him."

Apple could not find comfort in Elijah's words. Frankie sneered with disgust. She would find a way to get even with the half-sibling that had snubbed the family.

"I could have never provided Joseph with the advantages he grew up with. But I would have loved and cherished him. I raised two daughters and they've done okay in life. Just because my girls never owned a pony, attended private schools, or wore trendy clothing, it does not make me a bad mother. There was always plenty of food on the table and a clean home to live in. Joseph would have been my precious baby boy, my little prince."

Being stabbed would have been less painful than being rejected by her flesh and blood.

Elijah witnessed Apple losing her precious son for a second time. He lowered his head in sadness for Apple and the girls and rediscovered gratitude for his childhood: a rich, caring life surrounded by good people. Elijah embraced Apple and mumbled, "Sorry." He drove home, parked the car, and in the privacy of the condo broke down in tears.

Joseph took advantage of having a golfing day on Prince Edward Island and toured the coastline in a rented car. The shoreline had development potential. But he would not entertain the thought of developing shoreline condos and risk meeting with Island relatives.

A surprise greeted him at the hotel suite near the end of the day. The fragrance of her perfume lingering in the air caught him off-guard. "Rachel, what on earth are you doing here?"

❄

Frankie and Raisin waited in a car outside of the Hyatt Regency on a mission of revenge. "Wait in the car," Frankie commanded. "I am willing to bet a paycheque he's staying here. Where else would the wealthy roost? I'll knock on every door until I find him."

She recognized him when he opened the penthouse door. There could be no mistaking his identity. They were both ginger, just like their mother. She spotted a woman in designer clothing. "The name is Frankie. If you do not want your lady friend to know we're siblings, I suggest you follow me." Joseph explained in haste to Rachel he had an unexpected business meeting. The company had sent a driver. He grabbed a briefcase and followed Frankie.

"Get in the car," she bellowed. "We're going for a drive." The car sped down the street with Joseph trapped in the back seat.

"I will have you charged with kidnapping."

Frankie shouted at him to shut up before he had a chance to speak another word. "You better listen to my woman," Raisin warned.

The car motored along a stretch of highway to the outskirts of the town before parking in front of brick buildings with bars on the windows and staff dressed in white uniforms walking about.

"Get out of the car," Frankie demanded. "We're going for a walk. There is someone I want you to meet. If you do not get out, we can take you back to the Regency Hotel and I can meet your girlfriend. Do not threaten me with legal bullshit. You have more to lose than I have. My father died a hero in prison. Jail doesn't scare me."

There were people resting in chairs in the shade. Nurses in starched white uniforms were walking with a group of people. A middle-aged man wearing a hockey jersey with the number nine was chasing an imaginary puck. A group of older people shouted,

"Go, number nine, go!" The middle-aged man ran in all directions, shouting, "He shoots, he scores!" The group cheered him on.

"Hey, number nine. Come over here," Frankie yelled to him. The middle-aged hockey player chasing an imaginary puck dashed towards Frankie and Joseph. "Did you come to watch me play?" he asked Joseph, his face beaming with eagerness, waiting for a reply. There was something familiar about the man pretending to play hockey, thought Joseph. What was it?

An orderly recognized Frankie from the hospital and approached her and Joseph. "Come on, let's get you back to the hockey game." Number nine ignored the orderly. And he stepped closer to Joseph.

"Thank you for coming," number nine repeated with an ear-to-ear smile. Joseph gazed at the middle-aged man with confusion. Number nine gawked at Joseph. Their black eyes locked. A shocked Joseph saw a mirror image of his face. Frankie watched the interaction with amusement. Wayne might be brain damaged, but she could swear he had an idea Joseph was family, like the relatives who visited on weekends. He grabbed Joseph's hand and shook it. It was as if Joseph had been touched by the living dead, and he quickly pulled away his hand.

"It's time to get back to the game," said the orderly again. Number nine glanced back at Joseph and waved as the orderly led him away. A confused Joseph watched in horror, realizing the point of the visit was somehow connected to number nine. He studied the wrathful grimace on Frankie's face, and the truth struck him like a bolt of lightning.

"That's your daddy," Frankie sneered. "Number nine. My mother – our mother – thought the big hockey star loved her. But he assaulted her, got her pregnant, and then dumped her. She was only fifteen, but she still loved you. She had plans to have her foster parents adopt you so she could be a part of your life and watch you grow up."

Only the name of the biological mother was on the document he received. The father's name had been omitted, unknown. The lying little bitch had to be bluffing. Frankie saw the doubt in his face.

"Your daddy was a mean little shit that tormented and teased Harry, a man with the mind of a nine-year-old. Harry was protecting my pregnant mother from being attacked by your daddy on the street. Harry almost killed the big hockey star in a street fight that left your daddy a brain-damaged teenager. It's ironic, really; Wayne, a popular hockey star all the girls chased in high school, changed places with the brain-damaged man he tormented."

Joseph watched horrified as the middle-aged man continued playing an imaginary hockey game.

"They took you at birth and sold you to a rich American couple. Every year, we celebrated your birthday with a cake and a card. Our mother prayed you were safe and being cared for. She had no idea if you were alive or dead, or if you were homeless or sick. All along, you were living the life of a king while she cleaned apartment buildings to take care of my younger sister and me. We do not want a penny of your filthy money. Do not even think about having a bigshot lawyer contact my mother now that you know who your real daddy is. Or I will make certain the world knows."

Frankie marched back to the car where Raisin was waiting.

"Let the piss-ant walk," Frankie laughed. "We are going to pay a visit to his lady friend." Raisin grabbed the briefcase and threw it out the car window.

Joseph stood and watched Frankie driving away. Number nine had been escorted inside. His first impulse was to call the

police and report Frankie, but he remembered her warning. So
instead, he asked the receptionist to call him a cab.

❄

Frankie and Raisin drove back to the Regency and rapped on the
door of the penthouse suite. Rachel answered.

Frankie walked in without waiting for an invitation and
dumped a bag of birthday cards on a table. She shared with Rachel
the story about her mother being raped by a hockey star who now
chased imaginary pucks after a street fight that left him brain
damaged. "I introduced Joseph to his daddy this morning. I left
him there to find his own way back."

Rachel read a few of the cards addressed to Elmer as Frankie
explained Joseph had been taken at birth and adopted without
the consent of her mother.

"Mom named the baby Elmer after her father. She grew up
in the foster care system because her parents were killed in a
hit-and-run. Mom got pregnant while in foster care. The nuns
took her baby at birth. She never even saw him. It tormented her
every day, not knowing if her son was safe, happy, or loved. Mom
baked a birthday cake every year and we would make cards and
sing 'Happy Birthday' to a ghost child. And now the bastard does
not want to meet her."

Rachel fumbled in a handbag for a tissue and wiped the tears
welling in her eyes. This was not the man she loved and respected.
"He might visit your mother and be nice to her if I ask him."

She and Joseph had been blessed with opportunities and
luxuries. The political popularity that won her father a Senator's
seat came from the support of marginalized citizens. She had
been privy to dinner table conversations about the underpriv-
ileged and their needs. She grew up hearing the story of her

grandfather's migration to the United States at the age of nineteen with little money and a big dream. He had never forgotten the poverty he managed to escape as he built a new life in a new country. She admired her grandfather for his values and caring for people trapped in poverty.

"No, it would only cause more grief for my mother if he were to visit. Do you have a picture of Joseph I could give her? A photograph would end the curiosity of what he looks like."

Rachel reached into a purse. "I will not need these anymore." She handed photos of Joseph to Frankie. "I'm sorry. Your mother did not deserve to be treated so badly. She must be a very brave and confident person to raise a family on her own. I wish her well. You have no need to be concerned about any legal action from Joseph. You have my word he'll not bother your family."

Frankie quietly shut the door without saying a word. She and Raisin drove to an isolated beach outside of the town. They strolled arm-in-arm along the edge of the water as Raisin comforted a distraught Frankie. There would be no more phantom birthday celebrations. The ghost child was dead.

A fuming Joseph arrived at the Regency in a taxi. He ducked into a lobby bathroom and splashed cold water on his face before heading to the penthouse suite. He planned to leave the Island as soon as possible. The living nightmare would soon be over.

He stepped into the penthouse with a fake smile and greeted Rachel with a hug. In anger, she pulled away and started packing. "I had a visitor – your half-sister. And she left you a stack of birthday cards." She pointed to the pile of greeting cards on a table.

"That little bitch," he cursed. "I promise no one will know the circumstances of my birth. I've warned the family not to contact me."

Rachel grabbed the packed suitcases. She had been fooled by his ambition and intelligence. "Do you think I'm leaving because of that? Don't you dare judge me by your standards. You're not the man I thought you were. He would have never treated his biological mother as shamefully as you have."

Joseph tried to speak but was voiceless. This was not the reaction he'd expected.

"Only a monster would threaten to take legal action against a defenseless woman searching for her baby taken at birth. I am warning you to keep lawyers away from Frankie and her family. Never contact me or my family."

Rachel slammed the door behind her. Joseph poured a stiff drink and then another. He read a handful of the birthday cards. With anger, he pitched the cards across the room. He would return home on the first flight and get on with his life.

❋

Apple showed Gracie the photos of Joseph. "He's so handsome, and a ginger like me and Frankie. But he has Wayne's facial features and eyes. I know it did not turn out the way I thought it would. But at least I no longer worry about him. I know he's alive and doing well."

Apple gazed out the kitchen window deep in thought as she sipped a mug of tea. "He's still my son," she told Gracie "I will tell anyone who asks, I have three children."

CHAPTER 29

Elijah cleaned out the office. His law career was over. The court-room had been a stage to release his anger at being rejected by his father. In the courtroom, he spared no mercy, earning a reputation as a tough, uncompromising lawyer. For too many years, the bitterness had gushed through him. No matter how many cases he won, it never erased the emotional pain of being abandoned by a ruthless, uncaring father.

"My mother refused to answer any questions about my biological father," he explained to Sammi-Jo over dinner one night. "I was curious about him. Did I look like him? Did he like cars and collecting stuff like I did? I wanted to know why he never visited." Elijah Blue choked up with emotion, recalling getting his mother to arrange a meeting with his father.

"Mum begged me to abandon the idea. But I would not listen. I cursed at her. I accused her of being selfish that she did not want to share me with my dad. And it was her fault he had stayed away. I was fifteen, angry and confused. He agreed to meet with me. He took me for a drive around town and threatened to call the police if I ever contacted him or anyone in his family."

The cruelty had cut him to the bone. He was just a kid, helpless to fight back. In a courtroom, he could fight and win legal battles. The battles he wished he had fought with the man who fathered him, who abandoned him before birth as if he had no value. "I never knew till years later that mom had threatened to sue for child support if he didn't comply with her request to meet me," he told Sammi-Jo with a faraway look in eyes brimming with tears. "He only agreed to meet with me to protect his 'real' family and avoid a legal battle.

"Mother hated him and didn't trust him taking me. But she did it because I bullied her into making the arrangements. She knew it would all end in tears. I stayed in my room for days and bawled my eyes out. She was so angry at the way he treated me and got revenge by contacting a lawyer and went after him for child support and won."

The candle of hatred had been snuffed out reconnecting with Sammi-Jo. He no longer had the desire or the energy to fight old hurts. The father who'd threatened him in his teen years was now a feeble old man. Elijah had been walking down the street and hardly recognized him. Elijah took long strides, stepped by the aged man, and snickered. He was young, strong, and healthy with a promising career while the sickly old senior hobbled.

He now mourned the lost years wasted on the anger and hatred he'd fed on like a hungry pig at a trough. It had ruined relationships and friendships. Good fortune had smiled on him. He had it all: the condo, a flashy car, and a law career. And yet, it did not bring happiness.

Elijah sold the condo and bought a house in the old neighbourhood. It was as if he had been on a long and tiresome journey that circled back to his childhood home.

❄

"I'd rather teach in a classroom," he told Sammi-Jo as they settled into their new home, unpacking boxes that littered the rooms.

"I know from being a student what makes a good teacher and most importantly what makes a bad teacher. I want to give students a chance to learn in a safe environment with zero tolerance to bullying. I want to make a difference in the classroom. There will be less need for criminal lawyers if I can reach high-risk students falling through the cracks. And I will have the summers off to spend more time with our own little family."

He winked at Sammi-Jo. "We can plan a wedding and decorate a baby room." He lovingly rubbed her growing belly.

The unpacking was interrupted with someone knocking at the door. "I will answer it," Elijah Blue volunteered.

"Welcome back to the neighbourhood!" said Apple.

"We knew you'd be busy getting settled in so, we cooked supper," added Gracie. The two women marched through the house in search of the kitchen.

❀

Elijah Blue sipped hot coffee while Sammi-Jo took a shower early one Monday morning. He flipped through the newspaper. The words tumbled off the page. Old hurts resurfaced with the death notice of his absent father, the one he'd longed for as a child growing up in a single parent home. The notice included the names of a wife, adult children, grandchildren, and siblings. His name had been omitted, which was no surprise, but it still hurt. His father had denied him in death as he had in life. Elijah Blue put the newspaper down.

"He was still my father," he told Sammi-Jo.

She understood. Her own father had disappeared without a trace, and she had no idea if he was alive or dead. "My mom told me that my father was a kind man, handsome and charming. I'm grateful he gave me life, and that's how I deal with the emotional pain of never knowing him." She hugged and comforted the grieving little boy inside of Elijah Blue, wanting his daddy.

"You're not only beautiful but you are wise." As they clung to each other for comfort, Elijah vowed to be a devoted father to the growing baby inside of Sammi-Jo's belly.

❁

Sammi-Jo and Elijah were getting married by a Justice of the Peace instead of in church. The entire neighbourhood had been invited to drop by their new home after the ceremony.

Apple and Gracie were busy with planning the celebration. There was an endless to-do list. A new family had moved into the neighbourhood. Music would spill out of the blue house at the end of the street. "They have eight kids and the oldest is a guy called Scotty," says Apple. "I heard he's a good musician, really knows his stuff."

Gracie added Scotty and his family to the invitation list. Inviting neighbours to stop by for food and music was the proper thing to do. It would be a good way to reintroduce Elijah Blue to the neighbourhood – a place that Gracie decided to move back to so she could be closer to her grandbaby. Apple and Gracie agreed it had been a good neighbourhood to raise their own children in. And it would be a good neighbourhood for Elijah Blue and Sammi-Jo to raise a family.

"Sammi-Jo says if it's a boy, they're going to name him Elmer. You don't mind the baby being named after my father, do you?"

Gracie answered Apple with a hug. "I hope it's a boy, too. Elmer is a good, strong name."

❋

The banging on the door around midnight woke Gracie out of a deep sleep. It had been a busy three months with photography assignments and decorating and painting the new place. The banging continued, getting louder. She fumbled in the darkness for a housecoat.

"Open the door, Gracie. Get dressed," Apple demanded from the other side of the door. "Frankie and Raisin are outside in the car waiting."

A panicked Gracie opened the door with a frantic expression. Had there been an accident? Was Sammi-Jo, okay? Did anything happen to her? She was not letting Apple answer before asking the next question.

"Elijah Blue took Sammi-Jo to the hospital. The baby is coming."

Gracie dressed in record time and jumped in the back seat of the car. She and Apple held hands as the car sped towards the Protestant hospital.

Raisin slammed on the brakes and the car stopped at the hospital entrance. Frankie planted a passionate kiss on Raisin's lips. "We're going to be aunties!" Frankie said to Raisin with a gush of excitement.

Gracie and Apple raced through the hospital to the maternity ward. Out of breath they inquired about Sammi-Jo. "Did she have the baby? Is she okay? Where is Elijah Blue?"

"Sammi-Jo is doing fine. Her husband is in the delivery room with her. We will let you know as soon as she delivers," replied a nurse.

Frankie gave a frantic Apple a quick hug, then grabbed Raisin by the hand and they headed towards the exit.

"I need to be in the OR early morning, so Raisin and I are heading home. Don't worry, Mom, I will check in with Sammi-Jo before my shift starts. If you need us, telephone, and we'll come back to the hospital." Raisin nodded in agreement.

The clock on the wall ticked the minutes into hours with no baby news. Something had to be wrong, thought a frantic Apple. A childhood memory of her foster mother Agnes resurfaced. Agnes going into labour. Agnes screaming. And then—silence. The husband had left the house to get an undertaker to remove Agnes's body. Apple had tiptoed into the bedroom and discovered the dead bodies of Agnes and an infant. Frightened, she'd fled the room and hid under the bed. Later in the day, the nun came to fetch her.

Frankie marched through the door and into the waiting room just as Apple reached a breaking point. "Lord Mercy, you're finally here. Go into the delivery room and see if your sister is okay. If you don't, I will."

Frankie entered the delivery room and returned minutes later to the waiting room with comforting news the wait would soon be over.

"I'm not a religious woman, but I've been praying hard."

Gracie grinned at Apple. "Me, too." The two soon-to-be grandmothers embraced.

Elijah Blue finally came out of the delivery room with an infant bundled in a blue receiving blanket cradled in his arms. "Say hello to Elmer Sammy O'Brien." The grandmothers peered at the infant wrapped in a blanket. "The nurse is going to take the baby to the nursery room," he explained. "You can come back later during visiting hours this afternoon."

Tears streamed down Apple's face like a river escaping a dam. "Let me hold him, please. I need to hold him." Elijah Blue glanced at the nurse, seeking approval. Gracie intervened before the nurse could speak. "Give Apple the baby, now." Elijah Blue recognized a tone of voice that was not to be argued with. He gently placed the newborn in her arms. Apple studied the rounded face as if she were trying to memorize it. In a few short moments, she drowned in the sorrow of never holding her firstborn and basked in the immense joy of holding her first grandchild. She studied the baby's creamy complexion and head full of brownish curls. The nurse was becoming impatient.

"We will have thousands of days and nights to cuddle the baby. Let's go shopping for the biggest teddy bear Sears sells and come back during visiting hours."

Apple ignored Gracie and cuddled the baby as if she were in a trance. Frankie burst into the room just as the nurse stepped towards Apple to take the baby to the nursery. Gracie stepped in between the nurse and Apple.

"Frankie will take the baby to the nursery," said Gracie in a commanding tone of voice. "I swear to you no one will take our grandbaby, Apple. Pass him to Frankie, please."

Frankie reached out for the infant. "It's okay, Mom. Let me have the baby. And you go home with Gracie and get some rest. Elijah Blue is going to stay with Sammi-Jo until she gets settled in a room."

Apple came out of the trance she had been in and surrendered the infant to Frankie. Elijah Blue and the nurse trailed behind Frankie.

"Let's go home, Apple." Gracie guided Apple towards the exit. The friends exited the hospital and locked arms. Gracie broke the silence, suggesting she could paint animal characters on the baby's bedroom walls.

"Frankie and Raisin bought a rocking chair and a cradle. We can take turns rocking the baby to sleep while Sammi-Jo is resting. I am going to give their house a good cleaning before Sammi-Jo and the baby come home."

They continued walking and talking and sharing their joy of becoming doting grandparents.

"We can plan a baby shower now that we know it's a boy," proclaimed Apple. "But we will wait for a few weeks."

A young woman pushing a baby stroller across the street caught their attention interrupting the baby talk. Apple waved to the mother. "She has a little girl. They live not far from here. Our Elmer will have a little friend in the neighbourhood." The woman waved back. "We have a boy!" shouted Apple to the young mother. "Sammi-Jo had a baby boy."

The young mother shouted, "Congratulations" from across the street.

"Elijah Blue and Sammi-Jo bought a fancy baby buggy that converts to a stroller. We can take turns strolling the baby around town." Images of pushing their grandson in a stroller occupied their thoughts as they continued home. "I am going to start reading books to our grandbaby and telling stories about his daddy when he was a little boy."

"Me, too," Apple piped up. "I have my own stories to tell about Sammi-Jo and Frankie when they were little girls."

The two grandmothers disturbed a flock of crows feasting on tossed garbage as they turned a corner. The crows screeched at the intrusion. A startled Gracie held her breath waiting for Apple to react.

Apple was occupied with thoughts of baby snuggles and rocking the grandbaby and ignored the cawing crows fighting over discarded fries.

Gracie surmised the miracle of a new life ended an old nightmare for Apple. Baby Elmer had broken the evil spell of tormenting crows pecking at bedroom windows.

The two long-time friends strolled along Chestnut Street anxious to share the baby news with friends and neighbours.

Tormenting shadows from the past had been erased and replaced with a beautiful life unfolding on Chestnut Street as Apple and Graice embraced a blissful future as doting grandparents.

As the two friends strolled home, their bones hummed with the sounds of love for their first grandchild.

ACKNOWLEDGEMENTS

Acorn Press Canada: I am thankful to Terrilee Bulger for providing publishing opportunities for Maritime writers. Blessings for publishing my novels. Grateful for the support!

I truly appreciate the professional services of the **Acorn Press Canada team**. It's been a wonderful experience working with all of you.

Penelope Jackson: Thank you for your interest in the voices of the unwed mothers in my novel. I appreciate your editing skills and constructive feedback.

Thank you to **Patsy Bernard**, a proud Mi'kmaq grandmother, for her guidance in writing the land acknowledgement. *Wela'lin.*

The Baby Train was written on Epekwitk also known as Prince Edward Island, located in Mi'kma'ki, the ancestral and unceded territory of the Mi'kmaq People. The Epekwitnewaq Mi'kmaq have occupied this Island since time immemorial. We honour the "Treaties of Peace and Friendship" which recognized Mi'kmaq rights and established an ongoing relationship between nations. We are all treaty People.

Joshua Shepard: My son, you have done me proud. We, sort of, grew up together in Charlottetown. I was a young, unmarried mother and you were my sweet baby boy. No one could have loved you more than me, your biological parent. **Erica**, daughter-in-law, thank you for caring, your love and support and for spreading the word about the novels.

Damian Shepard: My dear grandson you are a blessing in my life. Someday, the stories you tell your future children will begin with, "My grandmother told stories." **Linda**, mother of my grandson, I am grateful for our years of friendship and your support of my novels.

Reg Phelan: Thank you, husband, for listening to the endless chatter about the characters in my novel, for being my rock and a fierce supporter of my writing.

Roseanne Shepard: Much love to my sister, Roseanne. Her journey with cancer has taught me to live my best life, and to appreciate the simpler everyday joys. Roseanne has truly inspired me with her positive attitude and emotional strength co-existing with a life-threatening disease.

Oscar: My faithful canine companion that kept me company while I wrote *The Baby Train*. Oscar would sense when I became overtired. He would nudge me with his nose and gaze at me with eyes that read, 'You need a break. It's time to close the laptop and take me for a walk.'

Julia Dubnoff: MA Columbia University; PhD Tufts University, for believing in me, encouraging me to write, and for providing feedback on two drafts in preparation for submitting the manuscript to Acorn Press Canada. The doors of the universe opened wide for us to meet by chance at a Prince Edward Island kitchen party.

Norah Pendergast: An artist, a writer, and a public-school teacher has researched and published articles about the unethical adoption practices of babies born to unwed mothers on Prince Edward Island. I appreciate her skillset and time, reading and providing feedback on the drafts. Her support and positive energy inspired me to continue writing on the days I was emotionally exhausted.

Blessings to **Julie Pellissier-Lush**, a Mi'Kmaq Knowledge Keeper, for the support of the novel, and for reading the manuscript and offering feedback. *Wela'lin & Kesalul*

Colleen MacQuarrie: A psychology professor at the University of Prince Edward Island for using my first novel, *Ashes of My Dreams*, as required reading in an Adult Development course. It is an honour to speak with the psychology students and sign copies of my novel. Grateful for the longtime friendship and our great conversations.

Linda Wigmore wrote the play *The Shame of the Meek*, based on interviews, and researched by Norah Pendergast. The play became a stage drama production about the experiences of Prince Edward Island unwed mothers between the sixties and eighties who were unwilling to give up their infants but lost their newborns to forced adoptions.

Rock Barra Co-op: A private artist's retreat for the contemplation and practice of the creative and healing arts on the northeast corner of Prince Edward Island. Rock Barra Co-op generously offered a writer in residence weekend at Rock Barra, where I edited *The Baby Train* manuscript surrounded by ocean views, sand dunes, and guided by spiritual energies that surrounded the retreat.

Margie Carmichael: A talented Prince Edward Island singer/songwriter. Thank you for the engaging conversations about *The Baby Train*, for reading the manuscript and offering feedback before submitting to Acorn Press Canada. And most importantly for the long-time friendship, the visits, the cups of tea, laughs, and the stories we have shared throughout the years.

Louise Knockwood: A proud and strong-minded Mi'Kmaq woman, my son's godmother, and my chosen sister. Thank you for reading the manuscript and providing feedback before submitting to Acorn Press Canada. Blessings for the long-time friendship we've shared. *Kesalul, Louise.*

Scott Parsons: Singer/songwriter, and an educator of the history of Black Islanders through songs and stories. Scott, an award-winning Island musician released a song called "*Stella's Dream*" inspired by my first novel, *Ashes of My Dreams*. Grateful to Scott for promoting my novel at his performances. You are the best, Scott, and I value our friendship.

Sara Phelan of Evalu8-Evolve Business Coaching for taking the time to travel to PEI from Nova Scotia providing marketing tips and personal coaching before the book launch and sharing success stories inspiring me to believe in my dreams of becoming an established, successful writer.

Kinley Dowling: Singer, songwriter, and an award-winning Prince Edward Island musician. Thank you for taking the time to read the manuscript, providing feedback and support. You are a strong voice/advocate for women, inspirational, and one of Canada's most multi-talented musicians.

A Special thanks to: Mi'kmaq Elder Judy Clark, Irene MacIsaac, Story Thorburn Sheidow & Matt Sheidow, Charlotte MacAulay, Teresa Doyle, Darryl MacMaster, Nancy Peters-Doyle, Patricia Strickland, Reggie Pomerleau, Blair Carmen Holloway, Carin Makuz, Eliza Knockwood and Marie Knockwood, Charlotte Morris, Elizabeth Statts, Rev. Catherine Ann and Katie Statts for their gifts of wisdom, support, and respect.

Much gratitude to the empowering and inspiring women I admire and respect and who have influenced me throughout my life: Rita MacNeil, Lucy Maud Montgomery, Martha MacIsaac, Sheila McCarthy, Rosa Parks, Viola Desmond, Ruby Bridges, Susan Boyle, Shania Twain, Pamela Anderson, Anne Frank, Tina Turner, Dolly Parton, Harriet Tubman, Keisha Shepard, and Oprah Winfrey.

Grateful to the ancestors and spirit guides for their spiritual guidance and protection since birth. Maria Campbell, a Métis Elder, the author of *Halfbreed* (1973), told me our ancestors use us to tell their stories. While writing *Ashes of My Dreams* and *The Baby Train*, I believe I was channeling with unwed mothers wanting their stories to be told. The ancestors were using me just as Maria had said.

Blessings to the people for buying and reading the novels. Every time the novels are read, it frees the voices of unwed mothers silenced out of public shame, judgment, and discrimination. It's an honour when readers turn the pages of my novels. Thank you.

Blessings to the women who approached me in person and on social media and shared with me their personal birthing stories as unwed mothers. Thank you for trusting me with your stories.

And please know that I care.

ASHES OF
MY DREAMS

The *Baby Train* is a sequel to *Ashes of My Dreams*, which is a painfully honest portrait of life as a single mother on Prince Edward Island. *Ashes of My Dreams* exposes a widely known but unspoken truth and shameful secret, which went on to affect a generation of young women and their lost children.